BY JANET EVANOVICH

THE STEPHANIE PLUM NOVELS

One for the Money • *Two for the Dough* • *Three to Get Deadly*
Four to Score • *High Five* • *Hot Six* • *Seven Up* • *Hard Eight*
To the Nines • *Ten Big Ones* • *Eleven on Top* • *Twelve Sharp*
Lean Mean Thirteen • *Fearless Fourteen* • *Finger Lickin' Fifteen*
Sizzling Sixteen • *Smokin' Seventeen* • *Explosive Eighteen*
Notorious Nineteen • *Takedown Twenty* • *Top Secret Twenty-One*
Tricky Twenty-Two • *Turbo Twenty-Three*

THE FOX AND O'HARE NOVELS WITH LEE GOLDBERG

The Heist • *The Chase* • *The Job* • *The Scam* • *The Pursuit*

KNIGHT AND MOON

Curious Minds (with Phoef Sutton)

THE LIZZY AND DIESEL NOVELS

Wicked Appetite • *Wicked Business*
Wicked Charms (with Phoef Sutton)

THE BETWEEN THE NUMBERS STORIES

Visions of Sugar Plums • *Plum Lovin'* • *Plum Lucky* • *Plum Spooky*

THE ALEXANDRA BARNABY NOVELS

Metro Girl • *Motor Mouth* • *Troublemaker* (graphic novel)

NONFICTION

How I Write

TURBO TWENTY-THREE

TURBO TWENTY-THREE

A STEPHANIE PLUM NOVEL

Janet Evanovich

BANTAM BOOKS NEW YORK

Copyright © 2016 by Evanovich, Inc.

Published in the United States by Bantam Books, an imprint of Random House, a division of Penguin Random House LLC, New York.

BANTAM BOOKS and the HOUSE colophon are registered trademarks of Penguin Random House LLC.

Hardback ISBN 978-0-345-54300-4
International edition ISBN 978-0-345-54303-5
Ebook ISBN 978-0-345-54302-8

Printed in the United States of America on acid-free paper

randomhousebooks.com

2 4 6 8 9 7 5 3 1

First Edition

TURBO TWENTY-THREE

ONE

LARRY VIRGIL IS a lanky, grease-stained guy in his forties. He lives alone in the back room of his auto body shop on Baker Street in north Trenton, and he hasn't cut his hair in at least ten years. For all I know that was also the last time he washed it. He has a reputation for drinking too much and abusing women. And he has a hot dog with testicles tattooed on his forehead. I suppose it might be a penis, but it's not a very good tattoo, and I prefer to think it's a hot dog.

None of this would be any of my business, but a couple months ago Trenton's finest caught Virgil hijacking an eighteen-wheeler filled with cases of premium bourbon. Virgil was arrested and subsequently bonded out by my bail bondsman cousin and employer, Vincent Plum. Virgil failed to appear for his court appearance a week ago, and Vinnie isn't happy. If Virgil isn't brought back into the system in a timely fashion, Vinnie will lose his bond money.

My name is Stephanie Plum. I'm a college graduate with virtually no marketable skills, so for the past several years I've been tracking down Vinnie's skips. What I lack in expertise I make up for with desperation and tenacity, because I only get paid when I catch someone.

It was ten o'clock at night in mid-September, and cool enough for me to need a sweatshirt over my T-shirt. I was currently pulling surveillance on Virgil's three-bay garage, hoping to catch him entering or exiting. I was with my wheelman, Lula. We'd been sitting across from the garage for over two hours, and my eyes were crossing out of boredom.

"This isn't going anywhere," I said to Lula. "He isn't answering his phone, and there aren't any lights on in the building."

Lula is a former 'ho who Vinnie hired as a file clerk a while back. When files went digital he didn't have the guts to fire her, so now Lula shows up every day for work and pretty much does whatever she wants. Mostly she hangs with me. She's shorter than I am. She packs a lot more bodacious voluptuousness into her clothes than I do. Her hair is currently pink. Her skin is always brown. Her attitude is *"Say what?"*

I'm pale in comparison to Lula. I have shoulder-length mostly unmanageable curly brown hair that's usually pulled into a ponytail, and I've been told I look a little like Julia Roberts when she played a hooker in *Pretty Woman*. I think this is mostly a compliment, right?

"My personal opinion is that this loser skipped town," Lula said. "It's not like he got family here. And we're not lookin' at someone with a active social life. Only time this man goes out is to hijack a truck, and he got a crimp put in that activity."

Lights flashed at the cross street, and an eighteen-wheeler chugged toward us and parked in front of the lot attached to the garage. The lot was enclosed by a six-foot-high chain-link fence topped with razor wire. A man swung down from the cab of the truck and walked to the gate. He fiddled with the lock and the gate swung open.

"It's *him*," Lula said, sticking her hand into her big bedazzled purse and rooting around in it looking for her gun. "It's that punk-ass Larry Virgil. I told you he'd be back. I got a gun in here somewhere. Hold on while I get my gun."

"We don't need guns," I said. "He's not known for being armed. All we have to do is wait for him to get inside, and then we'll sneak in and slap the cuffs on him."

"I got it," Lula said. "I got my gun. Let's go!"

"Not yet," I said.

Too late. Lula was out from behind the wheel of her Firebird, running across the road, waving her gun and yelling, *"Bond enforcement!"*

Virgil went deer in the headlights for a moment, and in the next moment he bolted for the corner with Lula in pursuit. Even in the dark of night I could see that Lula was running flat-out in her spike-heeled Via Spigas.

"Stop or I'll shoot you dead," Lula yelled to Virgil.

I was running behind Lula, trying to close in on her. "Don't you dare shoot him," I shouted at her. *"No shooting!"*

Virgil crossed the street and ran back toward the garage.

He reached Lula's red Firebird, wrenched the door open, jumped in, and took off.

"He got my Firebird!" Lula shrieked. "He got my baby! And my purse is in there too. I personally bedazzled that purse. It was one of a kind. And it got all my makeup in there."

"Guess you left the key in the ignition," I said, gasping for air, coming alongside Lula.

"And you told me not to shoot him," Lula said. "This is all your fault. If I put some holes in him this would never have happened."

"I'll call it in to the police," I said.

"I'm not waiting for no police," Lula said. "I'm going after that punk ass."

"You won't catch him on foot."

"I'm not going on foot. I'm taking his truck."

"Do you know how to drive a truck?"

"Sure I know how to drive a truck," Lula said. "What's to know?"

She got a foot onto the first step to the cab but couldn't get any lift.

"This here stupid thing is too high," Lula said. "Get your hand under my ass and give me a shove up."

"Not for all the tea in China," I said.

"Then go around and *pull* me in."

I climbed into the cab from the passenger side, crawled over, and gave Lula a hand up.

"This is a bad idea," I said. "You don't have a clue where

he's headed. He's disappeared, and on top of that he probably stole this truck."

"I know where he's going," Lula said. "He's going to the chop shop on Stark. He's gonna sell my Firebird off for pieces. That's what these creeps do. They got no respect for people's personal vehicles."

I took my cellphone out of my pocket. "I'm calling it in."

Lula stared at the dash. "There's a awful lot of doohickeys here."

"I thought you said you knew how to drive one of these."

"I'm just sayin' this here's a fancy rig. It got a cup holder and everything." She looked down at the floor. "It got a lot of pedals down there. What the heck is that big one?"

"That's the clutch."

"Yeah, it's all coming back to me. I used to drive my Uncle Jimmy's dump truck before I got established as a 'ho."

She planted a Via Spiga on the clutch pedal and shifted. "Here goes nothing."

The truck lurched forward and ground through a gear.

"That didn't sound good," I said.

"No problem," Lula said. "It don't matter if we lose a gear or two on account of this baby got a lot of them."

We slowly drove down the street.

"This here's a piece of cake," Lula said.

She turned a corner and took out a trash receptacle.

"Uh, you might have cut that corner a little tight," I said.

"Yeah, but did you see how smooth this beauty rolled over that garbage can? It's like driving a tank."

"There's a red light at the cross street," I said. "You know how to stop, right?"

"I step on the brake."

"Yeah, but will the big trailer behind us stop at the same time?"

Lula looked down at the floor. "I guess it's all hooked together being that I only see one brake pedal."

"The light! The road!" I yelled.

Lula sailed through the intersection.

"You just ran the light!" I said.

"Oops," Lula said. "My bad. Good thing there weren't any cars there."

I caught flashing strobes in my side mirror. "I think we have a cop behind us," I said. "You should pull over."

"No way," Lula said. "It'll waste my time, and I gotta get to the chop shop before they start on my Firebird. I'll outmaneuver the guy behind me."

"You're driving a truck! You can't even turn a corner, much less outmaneuver someone."

"Boy, you're getting cranky. Anyways, this could be a good thing. What we got here is a police escort. He'll come in handy when we get to Stark Street and confront Larry Virgil. This is our lucky day."

The cop car zipped past us and came to a stop just before the next intersection, blocking our way. Two patrolmen got out, guns drawn.

"Hit the brakes," I said to Lula. *"Hit the brakes!"*

Lula stomped on the brake pedal, and the rig slowed down

but didn't stop. The patrolmen jumped out of the way, and Lula punted the patrol car halfway down the block before bringing the semi to a stop.

"It don't exactly stop on a dime," Lula said.

One of the cops approached. I rolled the window down and grimaced. It was Eddie Gazarra. We went to school together, and now he was married to my cousin Shirley the Whiner.

"Hey, Eddie," I said. "How's it going?"

"Oh crap," Eddie said.

Lula leaned over and looked past me to Eddie. "We gotta get going. That moron Larry Virgil stole my car, and I gotta get to Stark Street before my baby's nothing but spare parts. So I'd appreciate it if you could get your patrol car out of my way."

Eddie and I looked down the street at what was left of the patrol car. It wasn't going anywhere any time soon.

"Sorry about your car," I said. "Lula didn't totally have the hang of driving this thing."

Eddie's partner, Jimmy, was standing alongside him. Our paths had crossed on a couple occasions, but I didn't actually know Jimmy. He was hands on hips looking like he thought this was funny but was trying not to laugh out loud.

"You're supposed to ask to see her license and registration," Jimmy said.

"My license is in my purse, which is in my car, which has been stolen," Lula said. "And what you're doing here is impeding the progress of justice."

"You know this truck was hijacked, right?" Eddie asked me.

"Not exactly," I said. "Lula and I were staking out Virgil's garage, and he pulled up in this truck. One thing led to another and here we are."

"Are we going to arrest them?" Jimmy asked, still grinning.

"No, we aren't going to arrest them," Eddie said. "Her grandmother would make my life a living hell."

"What do you want to do about the car?" Jimmy asked Eddie.

"Get a tow truck out here. And report the Firebird to dispatch."

"It's red," Lula told the partner. "And it's got a one-of-a-kind bedazzled purse in it."

I swung down out of the cab. "If it's okay with you I'll call for a ride."

"You calling Morelli?" Eddie asked.

Joe Morelli is a Trenton plainclothes cop working crimes against persons. He's also my boyfriend.

"No," I said to Eddie. "I'll grab a ride on one of Ranger's patrol cars. And I can get him to check with the chop shop to make sure they don't take Lula's car apart."

Ranger is a former Special Forces operative now turned businessman and security expert. He's six feet of perfectly toned muscle. He's my age, but he's years beyond me in life experience and street smarts. His coloring and heritage are Latino. He's single and intends to stay that way. He owns Rangeman, an exclusive security firm housed in a stealth building in downtown Trenton.

"Sounds like a plan," Eddie said. He hitched a thumb in Lula's direction. "You're taking her with you?"

"I guess."

"She's going to have to come in and file an accident report tomorrow. I imagine by then you'll have come up with an explanation."

"Yeah. I owe you."

"Good," Eddie said, "because I need a babysitter next Saturday."

I squelched a grimace. Eddie's kids were monsters. "I'll be there," I told him.

I made a short call to Ranger and joined Lula and Eddie at the side of the truck.

"This is a freezer truck," Lula said. "What do you suppose Larry Virgil was gonna do with it? You think he has a big-ass freezer in his garage? How was he gonna store all the frozen stuff until he could turn it around?"

"Maybe it's empty," I said. "Maybe he already off-loaded the cargo somewhere."

"This was reported stolen by Bogart Ice Cream," Eddie said. "The compressor is running, so it's probably still full of ice cream." He walked to the back door. "No security seal. It's just padlocked."

"I could shoot the padlock off, and then we could see what we got in here," Lula said.

Eddie cut his eyes to Lula.

"That would be if I had a gun," Lula said, thinking twice about her offer since she didn't have a permit to carry concealed.

"Hey, Jimmy," Eddie yelled. "Look in the cab and see if you can find the key to the padlock on the back door."

Jimmy climbed into the cab and swung down with the key. Eddie took the key, opened the door to the freezer truck, and a body fell out. We all jumped back.

"What the hell?" Jimmy said.

It was a chocolate-covered man, sprinkled with chopped pecans, totally frozen. Hard to tell if it was a real corpse or a solid chocolate novelty item.

We all looked down at it.

"That better not be a dead person," Lula said. "On account of you know how I feel about dead people. I'm not in favor of them."

"Could just be a big Popsicle," Jimmy said, toeing the chocolate guy.

"I don't think so," Lula said. "It don't got no stick up its hoo-hoo."

"Call it in," Eddie said to Jimmy. "And tell them to get CSI out here before he melts."

"Maybe we should put him back in the freezer truck," I said to Eddie.

"Yeah," Eddie said. "I guess we could do that."

No one made a move to pick up the chocolate guy.

"Or we could leave him here," I said.

"That got my vote," Lula said. "I'm not touching him, in case he got the dead cooties."

"Keep your eye on him," Eddie said to me. "I'm going to see if I can get the trunk open on the squad car so I can get some crime scene tape and rubber gloves."

Lula looked into the trailer. "They had him jammed up

next to the back door," she said. "The rest of the truck is filled with cartons of Bogart ice cream. Somebody's gonna be real disappointed in the morning if they don't get their ice cream delivery. Personally I'm a Mo Morris ice cream person as opposed to a Bogart ice cream person. Not that I'd turn my nose up at a carton of this here ice cream if it accidentally fell out of the truck."

"That would be tampering with evidence," Jimmy said.

"Just sayin'."

Eddie returned with some yellow tape and a box of disposable gloves.

"I'd be willing to help, but those gloves are the wrong size for me," Lula said.

"They're one-size-fits-all," Eddie said.

"Nuh-uh," Lula said. "They wouldn't look good on me, and they'd ruin my nail varnish."

A shiny black Porsche Cayenne drove up and eased to a stop, and Ranger got out. He was dressed in Rangeman black fatigues. He's the boss, but he still works alongside his men if the threat level is high or if they're shorthanded. He walked over to me and looked down at the chocolate man.

"Nice touch with the chopped nuts," Ranger said. "Who is he?"

"Don't know," Eddie said. "I don't want to go through his pockets and ruin the chocolate."

Eddie and Ranger pulled on rubber gloves, crammed the stiff back into the truck, and closed the door on him.

I got into the front of the Porsche with Ranger, and Lula

got into the back. We drove to Stark Street in silence. Ranger parked in front of the chop shop. A black Rangeman Ford Explorer idled in the driveway. Lula's red Firebird was parked next to the Explorer. A Rangeman guy who looked like the Hulk with the exception of being green got out of the Explorer and walked over to us.

"The Firebird was just dropped off," he said to Ranger, handing him the car keys. "It seems to be undamaged. There's a purse in the backseat."

"Any sign of Larry Virgil?" Ranger asked.

"No. I guess he left the car here and took off."

Ranger handed the keys over to Lula.

"I got my baby back," Lula said, taking the keys, exiting the Porsche. "Anything I can ever do for you just let me know," she said to Ranger. She looked the Hulk over. "You too, big, black, and badass. Anything you need you just ask Lula."

TWO

RANGER DROVE AWAY, leaving his man grinning at Lula.

"She'll take him apart and won't put him back together again," Ranger said. "Is your car at the office?"

"No. Lula picked me up at home."

"Babe," Ranger said.

"Babe" covers a lot of ground for Ranger, depending upon inflection. Tonight it was said softly with an undertone of desire, as if he might take me home and stay awhile. It gave me an instant rush, and heat curled through a bunch of internal organs. I did my best to squash the heat and ignore the rush, but in the process of ignoring the rush I inadvertently gave up a sigh.

"What?" Ranger asked.

"Morelli."

Morelli and I have had an on-again, off-again relationship

15

since I was five years old. Lately when we're *off* again Ranger swoops in. At first glance it might appear that I'm lacking in moral character by bouncing around between men like this, but it's only *two* men. I mean it's not like I'm dating a football team. And let's be honest about this. These guys are both twelve on a scale of one to ten. And I might only be an eight on a good day. So how lucky am I? A couple weeks ago, in a moment of euphoria, Morelli and I agreed to being engaged to be engaged. It was a good moment, but I think it's a little like planning on winning the lottery or contemplating losing five pounds. I mean, what are the chances of it actually happening?

"Unfortunate," Ranger said, "but the night wasn't a complete loss. I got to see a dead guy dressed up like a Bogart Bar. What were you doing with the freezer truck?"

"Lula and I were staking out Larry Virgil, and he drove up in the semi. One thing led to another. Blah, blah, blah. And Lula crashed the truck into Eddie Gazarra's squad car."

"And the deceased?"

"We opened the door to look inside, and the guy fell out."

"As it turns out," Ranger said, "I've been hired by Harry Bogart. He wants increased security in his factory. For years he's been engaged in an ice cream war with Mo Morris. In the past it's been confined to competitive pricing, ripping off recipes, ads that pushed the boundaries of slander, and occasionally a shouting match at a family function."

"They're related?"

"Cousins."

"And I guess they don't like each other."

"Not even a little. Lately bad things have been happening to Harry Bogart. Salmonella in the double chocolate. A bomb hoax that shut down production for an entire day. One of the freezers was down for the night, and literally a ton of ice cream melted. Bogart is sure it's Mo Morris out to ruin him, but he can't prove anything."

"So he's hired you."

"His factory is old-school. No security cameras. No instant alerts when equipment goes down. Locks that can be opened with a nail file. I guess he's never needed more. It's not like he's doing nuclear research."

"You're fixing all that."

"Yes, but it takes time. It's a big job. He needs new wiring. He has to approve the system design. I'd like to give him a couple men on foot patrol until we get everything up and running, but he refuses. He says ice cream is happiness and comfort, and his customers would turn to birthday cake and mac and cheese if they thought his ice cream was under siege."

"He sounds like a nice man."

"He's ruthless and miserly. So far I haven't seen evidence of nice."

"He makes good ice cream."

Ranger nodded. "So I've been told."

"Do you think the dead guy could be Harry Bogart?"

"No. Wrong body type. Bogart is a big man."

"Eats a lot of ice cream?"

"Eats a lot of everything." Ranger turned into my parking lot. "I need someone to go inside the two ice cream factories and look around. Do you have time to moonlight for me?"

"What would I do?"

"I'd put you on the line to start. Most of the line workers are women, so you would blend in. All you'd have to do is keep your ears open and look around. I'm told everyone gets to take a pint of ice cream home with them at the end of the shift in Mo Morris's plant."

"Hard to pass that up."

Ranger stopped in front of my apartment building's back door. I made a move to get out of the car, and he pulled me to him and kissed me. The kiss was light and lingering, sending a clear message of checked passion. He released me and relaxed back into his seat.

"I'll make the arrangements for you to start work at Bogart's plant first and be back in touch," Ranger said.

It took me a couple beats to get myself together. "Okay then," I said. "Be careful driving home."

"Babe," Ranger said.

. . .

Morelli was on my couch watching television when I walked in. His big mostly golden retriever, Bob, was on the couch with him. There was a takeout pizza box on the coffee table.

Morelli looked up at me and grinned. "Have a good night?"

"Eddie Gazarra called you, didn't he?"

"Cupcake, everyone called me, including your mother and the Trenton *Times*."

"News travels fast."

"Not every day someone gets dipped in chocolate and sprinkled with nuts. Usually people in Trenton just get stabbed and shot."

I squeezed between Morelli and Bob, flipped the lid up on the pizza box, and took a slice. "I thought you might have gotten the call on this one."

"I just came off a double shift, so I was low in the rotation. Butch Zajak pulled it."

"I can't stop thinking about the dead man."

"Yeah, me too. Eddie said he was dressed up like a Bogart Bar. I don't suppose you have any."

"No, but the freezer truck was filled with cartons of them. It was like the man in the truck was part of the Bogart Bar run."

"All this talk about Bogart Bars is making me feel romantic," Morelli said.

Here's the deal with Morelli. *Everything* makes him feel romantic.

He wrapped an arm around me and nibbled at my neck. "I'm thinking after the pizza what I need is dessert. Like a Bogart Bar."

"I don't have good feelings about Bogart Bars right now."

"Okay, how about a hot fudge sundae?"

"I guess that would be okay."

"Do you have ice cream? Chocolate sauce?" Morelli asked.

"No."

"Some of that whipped cream in a can?"

"No."

"No problem. I can use my imagination."

I was warming to the idea.

"And then you know what comes next," Morelli said.

"What?"

"I get to be the sundae."

Damn! I knew there'd be a catch.

THREE

MORELLI IS ALWAYS up at the crack of dawn on a workday. When he's in his own house he usually has breakfast at home. When he's in my apartment he more often than not grabs coffee and a breakfast sandwich on the road. I'm not exactly a domestic goddess. I keep the apartment clean and I manage to have the basic necessities on hand, like peanut butter, olives, and Froot Loops for me, and green food nuggets for my hamster, Rex. Rex lives in an aquarium on my kitchen counter. He's the perfect roommate. He sleeps in a soup can, and he never complains.

The apartment was quiet when I opened my eyes. No warm body next to me. I live on the second floor of a tired three-story apartment building on the edge of Trenton. My windows face the parking lot at the back of the building, and the sound of car doors slamming and people talking drifted

21

up to my bedroom. The day had started without me. Just as well. Memories of the night before were mixed. Some were good and some were awful.

An hour later I parked my ten-year-old Jeep Cherokee at the curb in front of the bail bonds office on Hamilton Avenue. I'd gotten the car on the cheap at Big Boomer's Car Lot. It had survived a flood somewhere in the Midwest and was perfect if you didn't count the electrical system and the slight scent of mold coming from the backseat.

Connie Rosolli, the office manager and guard dog, was at her desk. Connie is a couple years older than me. My ancestry is half Italian and half Hungarian, and hers is full-on Italian. Her Uncle Lou is mob and a good guy to know if you want someone whacked. Her hair is teased, her upper lip is waxed, her bottom drawer has a loaded Glock in it. She was wearing a scoop neck sweater that showed a lot of cleavage and a short black skirt that also showed a lot of stuff that was pretty much hidden under her desk. Her nail polish was a glossy mahogany that perfectly matched Lula's skin tone.

The usual box of morning donuts was open on Connie's desk. I chose a Boston Kreme and went to the coffee machine at the back of the room.

"Where is everyone?" I asked Connie.

"Lula called in to say she had to file a report at the police station this morning. Vinnie took Lucille to the airport. She's visiting her sister in Atlanta."

Lucille is Vinnie's wife. Vinnie owns the bail bonds office; Lucille's father, Harry the Hammer, owns Vinnie. Vinnie is a decent bail bondsman but a fungus in every other way. He has a body like a ferret's and a face to match. He keeps his hair slicked back. His pants are tight. It's rumored he's had an amorous adventure with a duck, and once in a while he fancies a good whipping from the local gypsy dominatrix, Madam Z.

"Sounds like you and Lula had a fun night," Connie said.

"It defies description. You had to be there. Have you heard anything about the dead man? Have they identified him?"

"Nothing on the dead man, but the factory is shut down. They're going to have to scour it out and disinfect everything. Was the guy really covered in chocolate and sprinkled with nuts?"

"Yeah," I said. "It'll be a long time before I don't get the creeps when I see a Bogart Bar. And that really bothers me, because Bogart Bars were a favorite part of my childhood. I feel like someone's trampled on my memories."

"I know what you mean," Connie said. "I loved Bogart Bars when I was a kid, and this messes with my mind. It would have been better if the dead guy had been coated in liverwurst."

I had an instant mental picture of someone coated in liverwurst and flash frozen. I gave an inadvertent shiver and gagged.

"Two new files came in late last night," Connie said, taking the folders off her desk and handing them over to me. "Assault with a deadly weapon and Simon Diggery."

Simon Diggery was a professional grave robber. He lived in a dilapidated double-wide south of town.

"What did Simon do now?"

"He got caught digging up Myra Kranshaw. He said he was looking for worms to go fishing and didn't realize Myra was down there."

"What did he get off her?"

"Her diamond engagement ring and a pearl necklace."

"And I assume he didn't show up for his court appearance."

"I called him and he said his truck was on the bum so he couldn't get to the courthouse, but he'd be happy to say 'Howdy do' to the judge if he could get a ride."

I shoved the files into my messenger bag, finished my donut, topped off my coffee, and Lula hustled in.

"Are there donuts left?" she asked. "Because I need a donut. They didn't have nothin' to eat at that police station. How is it that they ask you to come in first thing, and they don't even have a donut for you? And you know they got them somewhere in that building. No cop worth anything starts his day without a donut."

"How'd it go?" I asked.

"It went okay. I didn't get arrested or anything. I think I might get charged with careless truck driving or something, but the cop who was taking down the information kept getting confused, so I don't know what's gonna come of it all. After a while he stopped writing things down, and his eyes got that far-off look."

"Imagine that," Connie said.

"I was being excellent about explaining it all to him, but he wasn't getting the picture," Lula said. "And he kept asking me dumb questions, like when was the last time I drove a tractor trailer and did I have a license." Lula took a chocolate glazed out of the box and wolfed it down. "I'm starved," she said. "I could use a bucket of chicken. Is it lunchtime yet?"

I checked my watch. "It's nine-thirty."

"Hunh," Lula said. "Seems later than that."

"I need to escort Simon Diggery to the courthouse," I said. "Are you on board?"

"Say what? No way. Last time I was almost killed by his snake. You remember we were in his piece-of-doodie double-wide, and his snake jumped out of the closet at me."

"That was a mop. It fell out when you opened the door, and you freaked."

"Well, it could have been his snake."

"I'll buy you a breakfast sandwich."

"Done and done," Lula said. "Let's go get Diggery. Only we gotta go in your car because I'm not putting him and his smelliness in my Firebird."

I hiked my messenger bag onto my shoulder, Lula helped herself to a second donut, and we left the bonds office. I stopped at Cluck-in-a-Bucket and took a call from Ranger while Lula ran in and ordered her food.

"Bogart's plant is shut down for a system-wide cleanup," Ranger said. "It's scheduled to go back on line tomorrow morning. Show up at the plant at eight o'clock tomorrow and they'll find a job for you."

"Any information on the dead man?"

"Arnold Zigler. He was in charge of human resources at Bogart Ice Cream. Lived alone. Last seen late Friday afternoon."

"Do you think he could have accidentally fallen into the chocolate mixer?"

"It would have to be after he was shot in the head and frozen solid."

"Any suspects?"

"I haven't got any information on that. I'm on my way to the plant now. I'll know more after I talk to Bogart."

I disconnected with Ranger, and Lula hustled over with a breakfast sandwich, a bucket of chicken, a side of biscuits with gravy, and a giant soda. I watched her buckle up and dig in to the chicken.

"Aren't you worried about the calories in all that food?"

"It's not as much as you might think on account of I got a diet soda. And I was careful to balance out my meal with something from different major food groups. I got fried protein, tasty carbohydrates, and gravy."

"Gravy isn't a food group."

"Say what?"

• • •

A half hour later I was on a gravel road that wound through a couple hundred acres of Trenton that had as yet been unmapped by GPS. People who lived here were for the most part off the grid because there was no way they could or would pay an electric bill. Small, ramshackle houses were interspersed with rusted-out mobile homes set on cinder blocks. Broken-down cars and refrigerators littered front yards. Feral cats roamed in packs.

Simon Diggery lived toward the end of the road. He was one of the more affluent inhabitants, having taken possession of a lopsided double-wide. Friends and relatives came and went in the double-wide. Simon and his pet boa constrictor were constant.

I pulled off the road a short distance from Diggery's Place and parked on the hard-packed dirt shoulder. Lula and I got out of the SUV, and I put my stun gun in my back pocket and tucked my handcuffs into the waistband of my jeans. I didn't expect to use either. Sometimes I had to run Diggery down, and sometimes he hid, but in the end he never resisted arrest.

"I'm waiting here," Lula said. "He's got a nest of snakes under that rust bucket mobile home, and he got the big boa inside with him. No way am I going near that moldy old thing."

I didn't especially want to go near it either. I walked a little closer and yelled for Diggery. "Simon! Are you in there?"

Nothing. I took a couple more steps and saw that the snakes had come out to sun themselves. They were draped over the steps and sprawled on the patchy grass and dirt that constituted Diggery's front yard. I stamped my feet and threw some stones at them and they slithered back under the double-wide.

"It's okay now," I said to Lula.

"No way," Lula said. "You just pissed them off. They're lurkin'. They're waiting to jump out at you and fang you."

"Hey!" I yelled at the trailer. "Anybody home?"

"Guess he's not home," Lula said. "Might as well leave."

"He's always home during the day," I said. "He only goes out at night to rob graves and steal food."

"I'm not leaving until you open the door," I shouted at Diggery. "I know you're in there."

The door to the double-wide opened, and Diggery looked out. "What do you want? You're disturbing the peace."

Diggery was a rangy guy with shaggy gray hair and weathered skin. He was wearing a stained wifebeater T-shirt and baggy work pants, and he had a cigarette dangling from his bottom lip.

"You need to come with me to reschedule your court date," I said.

"This here isn't a good time," Diggery said. "I'm in the middle of something."

"You can finish it when I bring you back. This won't take long. Court's in session."

"That's a big whopper fib," Diggery said. "They're gonna lock me up and take their sweet-ass time to let me out."

"Yeah, but if you stay over lunchtime they give you a burger from McDonald's," Lula said. "Fries and everything."

"Last time they forgot the fries," Diggery said. "I think they might be getting cheap and left them off on purpose."

Diggery was standing in his open door. I caught movement at his feet and realized his boa was making its way out of the double-wide and down the makeshift steps. The snake was about ten feet long and probably weighed in at about fifty pounds.

"Holy crap, holy cow, holy get me out of here," Lula said. "That snake is coming to get us."

I figured the snake's top speed was one mile an hour. I didn't think we were at risk of being run down by it. Still, I didn't want to get too close.

Diggery looked down and saw the snake clear the steps. "Ethel!" Diggery said. "What the Harry Hill are you doing? You know you're not allowed out of the house."

Ethel wasn't paying attention to Diggery. Ethel was heading for the patch of woods behind the double-wide.

"You gotta help me get Ethel," Diggery said, hustling after the boa. "Once she gets into the woods it's impossible to get her back. She'll go up a tree and sit there until she gets hungry, and it's not good to let Ethel get too hungry. She's a sweet girl ordinarily, but she mostly don't care what or who she eats if you let her get too hungry."

"Is she hungry now?" I asked him.

"Naw. She ate a big old groundhog yesterday."

"That's horrible."

"Well, it wasn't as good as a Virginia baked ham, but Ethel seemed to like it. I found it on the side of the road all swelled up."

Diggery had Ethel by the tail end and was trying to pull her toward the trailer, but he couldn't get a good grip.

"Get in front of her and shoo her back to me," Diggery said.

Yeah, right. I don't think so. "How about if you get in front of her and maybe she'll curl up on you," I said.

Diggery trotted around and stood in front of Ethel. "Come on, Ethel. I got a candy bar for you in the kitchen."

Ethel stopped all forward motion and thought about it.

"What kind of candy bar?" Lula asked.

"I got a Snickers," Diggery said.

"That's a good candy bar," Lula said. "I wouldn't mind having a Snickers. I got a piece of Cluck-in-a-Bucket fried chicken left over in the car. I'd trade you that piece of chicken for the Snickers."

"Ethel would most likely rather have the chicken," Diggery said. "It's a deal."

"It's only a deal if you come back to town with me after you give Ethel her chicken," I said.

"You got my word," Diggery said.

Lula got the chicken from the car, handed it over to Diggery, and Diggery waved it in front of Ethel and led her back into the double-wide. After he got her into the trailer he slammed the door shut. Five minutes went by and there was no Diggery.

"Hey!" I yelled. "Simon!"

The door opened and Simon stuck his head out. "What?"

"Let's go."

"Go where?"

"You know where," I said. "We made a deal. You gave your word."

"Everybody knows my word isn't worth crap," Diggery said. And he slammed the door closed again.

"That really burns me," Lula said. "He took my chicken, and I didn't get no candy bar."

I blew out a sigh. This wasn't going to be easy. I was going to have to go in there and drag him out, all the while trying to avoid Ethel.

"I want my candy bar!" Lula yelled at the trailer. "You better not be eating my candy bar."

Nothing. No response from Diggery.

"That does it," Lula said. "He's not gonna get away with this. I was all set to have a tasty treat, and now I'm in a cranky mood. If there's one thing I don't tolerate it's a man who doesn't deliver on a dessert."

Lula stomped up to the trailer, climbed the rickety steps, and hammered on the door. "Open up," she said. "You better open this door and give me my Snickers bar or else."

"Waa, waa, waa," Diggery said on the other side of the door. "You're just a sore loser on account of I outsmarted you."

"Outsmart this," Lula said, hauling her Glock out of her purse and drilling seven rounds into the door.

About forty snakes rushed out from under the trailer and made off for the woods. I shouted at Lula to stop shooting. And Diggery wrenched his door open and glared out at Lula.

"What are you, nuts?" Diggery said. "You can't go around shooting up a man's home. This here's a respectable neighborhood. Look what you did to my door. Who's gonna pay to fix this door?"

"Where's my candy bar?" Lula asked.

"I don't have no candy bar," Diggery said. "I lied about the candy bar."

Lula leaned forward. "I smell Snickers on your breath. And you got a little smudge of chocolate stuck in your whiskers. You ate my candy bar, didn't you?"

"I was under stress," Diggery said. "I needed it. I could feel my blood sugar plummeting."

"Well, I'm not wasting any more time with you," Lula said. "I got better things to do. And now I got a craving for a Snickers."

Lula grabbed Diggery by his shirtfront, yanked him out of the double-wide, and kicked the door shut. She wrestled him down the stairs, lost her balance, and the two of them went to the ground. They rolled around a little. Lula got the top and sat on Diggery.

"I can't breathe," Diggery said. "How much do you weigh? Good thing for you I ate that candy bar. You don't need no more candy bars."

I got Diggery into plasti-cuffs, and Lula crawled off him. We lifted him to his feet and walked him to my car.

FOUR

IT WAS ALMOST noon by the time we left the police station. Diggery was in police custody, waiting for Vinnie to bond him out again, and I was in possession of a body receipt stating I'd recovered Diggery.

"I don't know why we bother doing this," I said to Lula. "It's just wasted time and energy. Vinnie bonds him out, he goes FTA, and we bring him in. And then it starts all over again. It's like we have a job doing nothing. Doesn't that bother you?"

"Nope," Lula said. "I'm in it for the money."

"The money sucks. Look at this car I'm driving!"

"Yeah, you must not know how to manage your money, because I have a kick-ass car."

"You make less than I do. You get a percentage of my percentage."

"True, but I'm also pulling a salary, and I do a little of this and a little of that."

I cut my eyes to her. "What's 'a little of this and a little of that'?"

"It's my entrepreneurial side. Like, I give hooker lessons on the third Saturday of every month. I help the girls who want to go into the profession. I teach technique. I was one of the few 'hos who could successfully do a thirty-second hand job for those customers in a time crunch. It was an adaptation of the Indian rope burn. And then I give advice on wardrobe, and I help them pick a corner. I tell them it's location, location, location. And then another enterprise I got going is my bedazzling skills. You'd be surprised how many people want shit bedazzled but don't have the time. I got business cards and everything."

"I had no idea you did all that."

"You bet your ass. I'm not just another pretty face. I got projects. That's why I got an appetite. It takes a lot of fuel to keep my brain operating. In fact, I'm probably not functioning at full power right now because I didn't get that Snickers bar."

"I feel like this is leading up to a stop at the 7-Eleven."

"Exactly. Not only could I get my Snickers bar, but we could get nachos for lunch."

I drove Lula to the 7-Eleven on Perry Street. We loaded up on nachos and backtracked to Lincoln. I crossed the railroad tracks, followed Chambers to Hamilton, and parked in front of the bonds office. Ranger pulled in behind me.

"It's like magic the way he always knows where to find you," Lula said.

It wasn't magic. It was GPS. He'd stuck trackers on my cars. I got out and walked back to him.

"I want to take you through the factory tonight," Ranger said. "They'll be cleaning until midnight. After that it will be empty except for security. Bogart employs a day guard and a night guard. They each make two rounds. The rest of the time they stay in the guard station at the loading dock."

"So someone had plenty of time to dip the HR guy in chocolate."

"You can draw your own conclusions when you see the plant. I'll pick you up at eleven-thirty."

Morelli wasn't going to like this. Ranger wasn't his favorite person. Ranger especially wasn't his favorite person when he was alone with me at eleven-thirty at night. Fortunately it was poker night, and Morelli would be doing his man thing with his cousin Mooch, his brother, Anthony, Eddie Gazarra if Shirley let him out of the house, and whoever else showed up with a six-pack of beer.

I watched Ranger drive away and joined Lula and Connie in the bonds office.

"What's up with the man of mystery?" Connie asked.

"Harry Bogart has hired Rangeman to manage security, and Ranger wants me to go undercover. I'm going to take a job on the line so I can look around."

"Are you shitting me?" Lula said. "You're gonna work in the ice cream factory? All my life I wanted to work in an ice cream factory. Maybe you could get me a job."

"I don't get to eat the ice cream," I said. "It's a job."

"Yeah, but I bet you get a discount. And suppose you

could score a job in the test kitchen? And, like, what happens when the gloppity gloppity machine screws up and doesn't fill the containers right? What happens to those screwed-up containers of ice cream? I bet they end up in the employee lunch room."

I gave Connie the body receipt for Diggery, took the outstanding FTA paperwork from my messenger bag, and read through the file. Eugene Winkle. Armed robbery and assault with a deadly weapon. Nineteen years old. Two priors. His address was on the fourth block of Stark Street. Not a good address. His mug shot wasn't good, either. He looked like an enraged bull. Smushed-in nose. Small, crazy, angry eyes. Thick lips parted enough to catch a glimpse of stainless steel caps. Undoubtedly could easily open a beer bottle with his teeth.

Lula was looking over my shoulder.

"Whoa!" Lula said. "That don't look human. What is that?"

"Eugene Winkle," I said. "He's FTA."

"And he's gonna stay that way," Lula said. "I'd rather face Diggery's snake."

"I was with Vinnie when he bonded him out," Connie said. "The picture doesn't do him justice. He's actually a lot uglier. He's about six foot five and weighs around four hundred pounds. Good news is that he probably can't run very fast. Bad news is . . . well, you can see the bad news."

"Maybe he's a nice person under all that ugly," Lula said. "He could be misunderstood. I bet he was bullied when he was a kid. They probably called him Winkie."

36

"He robbed his grandmother, shot her neighbor in the foot, and ran over the family dog," Connie said.

"That's terrible," Lula said. "What kind of person runs over a dog? I hope that dog is okay."

"I think it lost part of its tail," Connie said. "The grandmother put up Eugene's bond. She said he was too mean to be in jail. She said if she could find him she was going to set the dog loose on him."

"What kind of dog is it?" Lula asked.

"Chihuahua," Connie said.

"Hunh," Lula said. "Must be a vicious little bugger."

I looked at my watch. Damn. Too early to quit work and start drinking.

"Vinnie isn't back yet," Connie said, "so I suppose I'm going to have to go into town to bond out Diggery. Someone's going to have to babysit the office until I get back."

"I'll stay here," Lula said. "I got a new copy of *Star* magazine that I gotta read. It's got a article that Jennifer Aniston might get a tattoo of a unicorn."

Connie took her purse out of her bottom drawer and stood. "What about you?" she asked me. "Are you going after Winkle?"

"Eventually. Not alone. And probably not today. I'm still looking for Larry Virgil."

"Stephanie could stay here," Lula said. "Just in case we get a rush of desperados."

I cut my eyes to Lula. "'Desperados'?"

"It could happen," Lula said.

37

Connie looked over at me. "Good idea. Stay here and keep Lula from shooting the desperados if they show up. I won't be long. Court's in session. I should be back in an hour."

Connie and Vinnie always park in the small lot at the back of the building. The lot had parking for four cars and opened to a narrow alley that bisected the block. It was hidey-hole parking for Vinnie, and it allowed Connie to sneak cigarettes.

Connie left through the back door, and Lula turned to me. "I bet she's out there sneaking a smoke first. That alleyway and parking lot are like the safety zone for smoking without stinking up your personal environment."

"Seems like it would be easier to just quit smoking."

"You say that on account of you never smoked. Sure, it could shorten your life and give you lung cancer and heart disease and ruin your skin, but you ever see the look on someone's face when they take that first drag? It's like when you feel a orgasm coming on. Like you've been workin' and workin' at it and finally you know you nailed it and *zow!* you got yourself a orgasm."

"Were you a smoker?"

"Hell, yeah. I was a big smoker, but I'm not stupid. I got this beautiful chocolate skin and I'm not going all crone with it because of smoking."

"How did you quit?"

"I traded in my cigarettes for a vibrator. I got a dandy little battery job that I carry in my purse, and when I feel the urge to light up I just stick this thing against my lady parts and buzz myself into relaxation and happiness. Personally I don't get the whole e-cigarette thing. I mean, if you're going mechanical wouldn't you rather put those batteries to work on your pleasure bean?"

I was speechless. I was raised Catholic, and this was way outside my comfort zone. Okay, so I know about the pleasure bean, but the last thing I wanted to think about was Lula's pleasure bean. It was probably the size of a duck egg. I tried to shake the image out of my head, but it was stuck there. I was going to have to go home and pour bleach into my brain.

"So anyways," Lula said. "Do you think Jennifer Aniston should get a unicorn tattoo?"

I didn't have strong feelings about it one way or the other. I personally had never been a big unicorn person, but who am I to impose my views on Jennifer Aniston?

I settled into one of the uncomfortable plastic chairs in front of Connie's desk and looked over Larry Virgil's file. Nothing new jumped out at me, and the questions that arose weren't about Larry Virgil. They were about the truck and the frozen man. Surely by now the truck driver had been questioned. Was he a suspect? Had he known there was a dead guy in his truck? How the heck could this have happened?

"You look like you got a lot of thinking going on," Lula said. "You must care a lot about Jennifer Aniston."

"I was thinking about the frozen man. It really bothers me that he was dressed up like a Bogart Bar. I know this is weird, but it feels like a personal insult. Like someone disrespected the Bogart Bar."

"You don't know that for sure," Lula said. "Maybe it was a

homage to a Bogart Bar. Maybe the killer liked this man and wanted to make him look like his childhood favorite memory."

"The killer *killed* him! That's not something you do to someone you like."

"I see what you're saying, but maybe being turned into a Bogart Bar is one of the hazards of working in a ice cream factory. Not that I'd let it stop me on account of ice cream factory employment's on my bucket list."

"I didn't know you liked ice cream that much. I always thought of you as fried chicken and donuts."

"I'm a complex person," Lula said. "I got a lot of stuff going on. You haven't even seen the tip of my iceberg yet. One of my goals is to be a TV star."

"I thought you wanted to be a supermodel."

"Yeah, but that's all yesterday. It's about being a reality TV star now. It's only a matter of time before I have my own show. I got two ideas, and we're about to start shooting some demo reels. That's how you get on these shows. You gotta shoot a demo reel."

"What show do you want to be on?"

"Well, one is my own original idea and the other one is *Naked and Afraid*. I'm hookin' up with Randy Briggs."

Randy Briggs is thirty-six inches tall and has the personality of a junkyard dog.

"You hate Randy Briggs," I told Lula.

"Exactly. That's what makes it so good. There's instant drama, you see what I'm sayin'? We got the idea from *Saturday Night Live*. The sexy little guy from *Game of Thrones* did this *Naked and Afraid* skit with Leslie Jones, and it was dope."

"So you're going to rip off *Saturday Night Live*?"

"You got it. Brilliant, right?"

"Probably some people have already submitted reels for that."

"It don't matter, 'cause ours is so awesome. And we got a twist on it. Ours is *Naked and Afraid in Trenton*. It's gonna be the city version."

"I don't think you can go around naked in Trenton."

"Yeah, but we're only shooting at night. By the time we get reported to the police we'll be long gone, swallowed up in the shadows. Randy might have problems with that on account of he got pasty white skin and washed-out sandy hair, but I disappear real good in a shadow."

"What's your original idea?"

"I can't tell you, but it's huge. It's gonna way top *Naked and Afraid.* We don't want it to leak out, so I can only tell you it involves bathrooms. When we get ready to start shooting I might bring you along as a extra cameraperson. We don't want to miss a instant of reality. We could use a backup camera."

I'd rather be abducted by aliens than film a reality show involving bathrooms and Lula.

"Gee, look at the time," I said. "This doesn't seem to be a big day for desperados, so I should get moving on. I need to stop in and say hello to my mom. And then there's Larry Virgil still out there. And I might make a run to the supermarket."

"If I was you I'd be taking a nap this afternoon so I could keep up with Ranger on your midnight rendezvous."

"It's not a rendezvous. It's a workplace orientation."

FIVE

I LEFT THE bail bonds office in Chambersburg and drove the short distance to my parents' house. They live in a small two-story duplex that shares a wall with its mirror image. The mirror image is occupied by an elderly woman who bakes coffee cakes all day and feeds them to the birds that leave droppings all over her back stoop. My parents' house has a postage stamp front yard, a narrow front porch spanning the width of their house, and a bare-bones unused backyard.

There are three small bedrooms and a bathroom upstairs. Downstairs has a shotgun living room, dining room, and kitchen. The rooms are crammed with comfortable, unfashionable furniture. End tables are filled with photographs, candy dishes, and assorted treasures brought back from vacations at Seaside Heights, Atlantic City, and the Poconos. The kitchen has a little wooden table with four straight-back chairs, a ten-year-old Kenmore stove that turns out perfect pineapple upside-down cake, and enough room along one wall to set up the ironing board.

My Grandma Mazur lives with my parents. She moved in when Grandpa moved into Hotel Heaven, and she never moved out. Sometimes at the dinner table my father's knuckles turn white as he grips his fork and sneaks a look at Grandma, and we all keep a close watch on him that he doesn't launch himself across the table at her. I like Grandma a lot. Of course, I don't have to live with her.

I parked in front of the house, and Grandma Mazur appeared at the front door before I even got out of my car.

"I had this feeling," she said when she let me in. "I said to myself I bet Stephanie's going to stop by. And here you are."

"That's amazing," I said.

"It's not amazing," my mother called from the kitchen. "She's been standing staring out the door for hours."

"Well, you never know," Grandma said.

Grandma Mazur is a slightly shrunken, slack-skinned, gray-haired version of my mother. She keeps her hair short and curled. She wears bright lipstick and white tennis shoes, and she's one of only two women in America still wearing pastel-colored polyester pantsuits. She carries a purse that is big enough to hold her .45 long-barrel S&W.

"Did you already have lunch?" Grandma asked. "We got fresh olive loaf from Giovichinni's if you want a sandwich. And we got some cookies from the Italian bakery."

"Cookies," I said, hanging my messenger bag off the back of a kitchen chair. "I had lunch with Lula."

"The phone's been ringing all day," Grandma said, bringing

the box of cookies to the table. "And we had a photographer from the paper take a picture of the front of the house. You're famous. I wouldn't be surprised if you got a call from Geraldo."

My mother was furiously ironing a shirt.

"How long has she been ironing that shirt?" I asked Grandma.

"At least an hour," Grandma said. "She started just after the photographer showed up."

When my mother's blood pressure goes into the red zone she irons. Thursday morning is her usual ironing day. If you see her ironing any other time it's not a good sign.

"You ran over Eddie Gazarra's cop car," my mother said. "He's married to your cousin Shirley. You grew up with Eddie. What were you thinking?"

"It was an accident!"

My mother pressed the iron into the shirt, and a cloud of steam rose off the ironing board. "His mother called me this morning. She's all upset. She thinks you should be locked up in jail. She said you're one of those crazy cop-hater people."

"I wasn't even driving the truck," I said. "Lula was driving the truck, and she miscalculated the brakes."

"It was stolen," my mother said. "You stole an ice cream truck!"

I sat down and took a cookie from the box. "Actually Larry Virgil stole it. Lula and I sort of commandeered it."

"You should marry Joseph and have a baby," my mother said. "What are you waiting for?"

Good question. I didn't know the answer. I ate cookies

while I thought about it. After five cookies I still didn't have an answer. It was one of many questions without answers.

"If it was me I'd marry Ranger," Grandma said. "I go for those dark guys."

My mother flicked a glance at the cabinet over the sink. This was where she hid her stash of whiskey. I was sure my mother was thinking it was so close and yet so far. Too early for a drink. There were rules to be followed in the Burg. One didn't imbibe until four o'clock unless it was at a wake. Wake drinking began early in the morning. There were times when you wanted to kill someone just so you could have a Manhattan for breakfast.

"Ranger doesn't want to marry me," I said. "He has issues."

"What kind of issues?" Grandma asked.

"I don't know exactly," I said. "I think he's working on his karma."

"That's heavy," Grandma said.

"He's not the right person anyway," my mother said. "Joseph has a good job and a house."

This was true. Morelli had inherited a house from his Aunt Rose. It was less than a mile from my parents' house, and it was very similar. Long, narrow backyard. Small front yard. Three small bedrooms on the second floor and shotgun arrangement of rooms on the ground floor. Morelli had been working at making it his own, adding a half bath on the first floor and improving the kitchen. Aunt Rose's curtains still hung in two of the bedrooms, but the rest of the house felt like Morelli. Big flat-screen TV and comfy couch in the living room, billiards table in the dining room, king-size bed in the master bedroom. I especially liked the king-size bed. Plus Morelli had a dog and a toaster, and his mother regularly filled his fridge with lasagna and cannoli and mac and cheese.

"I ran into that little friend of yours today," Grandma said to me. "I was at the bakery picking out the cookies and he was buying a fruit babka. He said he was going into business with Lula."

"Randy Briggs?"

"Yep. That's the one. He had his hair all punked up with some kind of wax. He said he was getting ready to be a television star. I told him I wouldn't mind being a television star, and he should call me if they need someone to fill in."

"They're making a demo for *Naked and Afraid*," I told Grandma.

Grandma sucked on her dentures and thought about it. "I guess I could do that. I look pretty good naked," she said.

I smelled something burning and looked over to see my mother standing open-mouthed and glassy-eyed. The iron was resting on the shirt, and I could see the shirt material smoking and turning brown around the perimeter of the iron.

I moved to the ironing board and set the iron back on its stand. The shirt had a big iron imprint on it. My mother's mouth was still open.

"Maybe you need a drink," I said to her.

She was still staring off into space.

"That shirt's never gonna be the same," Grandma said.

I got the whiskey out of the cupboard, splashed some into

a juice glass, and handed the glass to my mother. She stared at the glass but didn't make a move to drink.

"Maybe she had a aneurysm," Grandma said. "Marie Sokolowski had one and now she calls everyone kiddo and she'll only eat soup. They tell me if you try to get her to eat something else she pitches a fit."

"Drink up," I said to my mother.

"Yeah," Grandma said, "come have a cookie. Give the ironing a rest."

My mother tossed the whiskey back and took a cookie from the box.

"There you go," Grandma said. "Feel better now?"

My mother nodded. "You wouldn't really go naked, would you?" she asked Grandma.

"Sure I would," Grandma said. "I got nothing to hide. I'm in pretty good shape. Although I guess I should take a look at myself when I get undressed tonight just to make sure."

"See," I said to my mother. "Nothing to worry about."

My mother held her glass out, and I poured some more hooch into it.

"Got to go," I said. "Things to do. People to see."

"You got an exciting life," Grandma said. "Always something new going on."

SIX

I LEFT THE Burg and drove through town to Stark Street. Stark Street starts at State Street and runs north. The first block is perfectly reputable. Bars, a couple small groceries, a nail salon, a hardware store, take-out pizza, fast food fried chicken, and a pawn shop at street level. Apartments on the second and third floors. The street deteriorates as the blocks progress until only nuclear rats and drugged-out crazies exist in burned and bombed buildings. Beyond the burned and bombed buildings is a half mile of neglected wasteland. And beyond the wasteland is a thriving junkyard.

Eugene Winkle lived on the fourth block of Stark. Not the worst location and not the best. If I left my car unattended on the street for more than ten minutes it would be gone with no hope of getting it back. If I wore the wrong gang colors I'd be dead or maimed for life. Since I was wearing jeans, a stretchy white T-shirt, and a gray sweatshirt I felt relatively safe. Not that it mattered, because I had no intention of stopping. I was just riding through to take a look around.

Eugene had listed a third-floor apartment as his home address. No employer was given. He listed his occupation as *entrepreneur*. Had to give him credit. At least he knew how to spell *entrepreneur*.

I drove past his building, made a U-turn, and drove past a second time. It was a three-story brownstone, decorated with gang graffiti. Third-floor windows were painted black. Trash had collected around the front stoop. There were two bullet holes in a ground-floor window, and the surrounding brick was pocked with bullet holes.

I didn't see Eugene out and about so I drove back down Stark to State Street and headed for home. I should have gone supermarket shopping, but I stopped at Giovichinni's Deli and Meat Market on Hamilton instead. It was more expensive but a lot easier.

I went straight to the deli counter and got sliced ham, sliced turkey, provolone cheese, a tub of broccoli slaw, a tub of homemade meatballs in red sauce, and a tub of three-bean salad. I grabbed a loaf of bread, a bag of chips, a jar of olives, peanut butter, milk, Froot Loops for snacking, granola for breakfast, mixed nuts for Rex. Hot dogs and rolls in case I needed to feed Morelli and he wanted a hot meal. Frying up a hot dog was pretty much the extent of my culinary skills. I added a large can of baked beans to my cart and went to check out.

Patty Giovichinni was at the register. She was my mother's age, and she was married to one of the many Giovichinni brothers.

She looked over the stuff on the belt. "No Bogart Bars?" she asked.

"Not for the rest of my life," I said, choking up a little at the thought.

"So what did the guy look like when he fell out of the truck? Was he really covered in chocolate and nuts?"

"Yeah. He was frozen."

"Did you get a picture?"

"No."

"Too bad. A picture would have been good."

I agreed. I should have thought to take a picture. Then again, did I really want to immortalize the horror? Truth is, I wanted to forget it. Blot it out of my mind. Erase the memory.

Mrs. Morganstern was behind me.

"I hear you tried to kill Eddie Gazarra," she said to me. "I think that's terrible."

"I didn't try to kill him," I said. "Lula accidentally hit his cop car. Eddie wasn't anywhere near it."

"Such a nice young man," Mrs. Morganstern said. "I hope they give him another car."

I carted my stuff back to my SUV and drove home. It was late afternoon, and the old folks who lived in my apartment building had taken all the good spots close to the back door. A lot of the spots were designated handicapped. Getting a handicapped card in Jersey is a badge of honor. You get to screw the system because you aren't really all that handicapped and at the same time you get a good parking place.

My hamster, Rex, was asleep in his soup can when I put the grocery bags on the kitchen counter. I tapped on his cage and told him I got Froot Loops, but he didn't come out.

"Your loss, Mister," I said.

Rex knew it wasn't a loss. Rex knew he'd get the Froot Loops on his terms. This was pretty much true for all the males in my life . . . rodents and otherwise.

I put the stuff away, and someone knocked on my door. I looked out the peephole and didn't see anyone. More knocking. I looked down and saw Randy Briggs.

Damn.

"I know you're in there," Briggs yelled. "I can hear you breathing."

I opened the door and looked out at him. "Now what?" I asked.

"You gonna let me in?"

I stepped back. "I suppose."

"Boy, that's generous. I come to visit you, and you got all this enthusiasm. I'm fuckin' overwhelmed."

"I'm sort of busy."

"Oh yeah? Doing what?" He looked around. "I don't see anything going on here."

"Is there an actual reason for this visit?"

"I'm getting to it," Briggs said. "I was just opening up the visit with some polite chitchat. How do you like the weather we're having? Blah, blah, blah."

I stared down at him. "And?"

"And I'm doing this project with Lula. We're auditioning for some television shows. Shooting some reels."

"I heard."

"Did you also hear that they're crap? She overacts on everything. And she's a screen hog. All you see is Lula, Lula, Lula. And between you and me, when you get the clothes off her she's not a pretty sight. You ever seen her naked?" He shook his head. "Not good."

"Is this going somewhere?"

"I thought you could talk to her. Explain to her that no one wants to see her fatness all over the screen. People are going to want to see me. I'm hot. And I'm little. Everyone wants to see hot little guys."

"I don't."

"And the other thing is I thought of a good angle. Every week it's the same thing on *Naked and Afraid*. It's a guy and some girl, right? So I'm thinking it would be more interesting if it was a guy and two girls. Get a little action going. Girl on girl and two girls on the guy."

"That would be the porno version of the show."

"Not necessarily. They always fuzzy out the private parts of the girl and the guy, so it's not like you'd see any of the good stuff."

"Have you talked to Lula about this?"

"No. I wanted to run it by you first. Give you first crack at it since you and Lula are so tight. And you're not real fat, so you wouldn't take up the whole frame."

"You want me to be the second naked woman?"

"Yeah."

"No."

Briggs looked shocked. "What do you mean, no? It's the chance of a lifetime. It could make you into a big TV star."

"No. Not going to happen. No way. No how. Never."

"You're going to pass up a chance to get naked with me?"

"Yeah."

"Why?" Briggs asked.

"You're cranky and disgusting."

"Okay, but besides that."

I pointed to the open door. "Go!"

"Aren't you going to offer me something to drink?"

"No."

"You got a lot to learn about hospitality," Briggs said.

I grabbed a bottle of water from the fridge and handed it to him.

"No wine?" he asked.

"You do realize that I have a loaded gun in this kitchen?"

"Your gun is never loaded," Briggs said. "You never even have any bullets. You keep the stupid thing in the cookie jar. You'd do better to throw your gun away and fill the jar with Oreos. At least you could offer your guests a cookie."

I gave him my squinty eye. "Don't push it."

He returned the squinty eye and left.

• • •

The lights from Ranger's black Porsche 911 Turbo swung into my parking lot precisely at 11:30 P.M. I was waiting in the lobby and, as always, I got a small rush when I caught sight of the car.

The car and the driver were perfectly matched. Lots of power and agility. Wicked fast. Dark. Sexy. Totally desirable and unobtainable. At least they were unobtainable for me. I couldn't afford a Porsche, and hitching my life to Ranger would also come with a high price.

I left the building, got into the car, and Ranger silently drove out of the lot and headed for north Trenton.

"Do you have any new information on the Bogart Bar man?" I asked.

"Arnold Zigler. Forty-two years old. Divorced. No kids. A sister in Scranton. Parents are deceased. Most of his co-workers seemed to like him. He'd been with the company for ten years as head of human resources."

"And the co-workers who didn't like him?"

"Nothing serious. No death threats. Mostly indifference. I haven't talked to any of them personally. This information has all come from Harry Bogart. You'll have a chance to find out more tomorrow when you mingle."

"I have to mingle?"

"Babe, I'm not putting you in there because you're good at making ice cream."

"I'm not sure I'm a good mingler."

"How much am I paying you?"

"You don't know?"

"It was a rhetorical question."

It was past my bedtime, and I wasn't in the best of moods.

I wasn't looking forward to being a snitch at the ice cream factory.

"Well, maybe I don't even want this stupid job," I said. "Maybe I'm doing this as a favor to you."

Ranger stopped at a light and looked over at me.

"I don't usually pay for favors, but if we're going in that direction I wouldn't mind turning this car around and taking you back to Rangeman for the night."

Yikes. Tempting but at the same time frightening. And then there was Joe Morelli. And the Catholic Church. And my mother.

"Well?" he asked.

"I'm thinking."

"Think faster, babe. The light just changed."

"Ice cream factory."

"It's only a matter of time," Ranger said.

I blew out a sigh. I knew this was true.

SEVEN

THE BOGART ICE Creamery was in a light industrial complex that had never developed beyond the ice cream plant. There were curbs and roads and empty lots, but no buildings other than Bogart's. The employee parking area was deserted. Streetlamps dropped pools of white light onto the blacktop. The big two-story warehouse-type building was dark with the exception of exterior lighting on the six-bay loading dock, and lights were blazing inside the small guardhouse.

Ranger parked by the loading dock, and we left the car and approached the guardhouse. There were two men on duty. One was in a green Harry Bogart uniform, and the other was in Rangeman black fatigues. Ranger nodded to both men and continued on to the back door. He tapped a code into the door lock, we entered the factory, and Ranger threw the main light switch.

Lights flooded the building, and it looked to me like the entire manufacturing process was essentially in one huge two-story room. Conveyor belts and stainless steel tubes snaked around the room entering and exiting large stainless steel boxes that performed who-knows-what. Heavy-duty refrigerator-type double doors were built into a far wall. I imagined the doors opened to a freezer. A series of small offices lined the wall on the opposite side of the room. The offices all had large fixed-frame windows that looked out at the line workers.

"Has it been determined how Arnold Zigler got crammed into the back of the truck?" I asked Ranger.

"No. The truck was loaded Monday morning. Half the truck was filled with pints of assorted flavors. The other half was filled with Bogart Bars. It should have left in the early afternoon, but the driver got sick and couldn't make his run, so the truck sat at the loading dock. It's speculated that the driver was poisoned. He's okay now, but he went down fast with food-poisoning symptoms. When the night guard made his first run at nine o'clock, someone took off with the truck."

"Virgil?"

"Don't know. Virgil is in the wind. Morelli will know more. He'll have access to CSI reports. My job isn't to solve the crime. My job is to make sure the crimes don't continue."

"Yes, but don't you need to solve the crime to do this?"

"It's not clear if this murder relates to the other crimes." Ranger pointed at three pipes with valves and dials on the far wall. "The cream gets pumped out of tanker trucks into refrigerated silos on the outside of the building. The silos empty into the pipes you see on the wall, and the cream flows into the pasteurization vat. After pasteurization it gets pumped through a homogenizer and then through a plate cooler and finally into another vat to be further cooled for storage. After that it's flash frozen to the consistency of soft-serve."

"What about the different flavors? And how does it get to be a Bogart Bar?"

"For the most part the flavors are added during the first cooling process. Bogart Bars have their own line. I'll walk you down to it. There's also a line that packages the ice cream. You'll see all that in action tomorrow."

The Bogart Bar line stretched almost the length of the room. Even without the machines running, the process was pretty clear. The soft ice cream was extruded into molds, and the molds were moved into a stainless steel box with a dial on the outside.

"The freezer, right?" I said.

"Right. The ice cream is flash frozen into bars. The bars move through the system to the chocolate machine where they're entirely encased in liquid chocolate. Excess chocolate drains off, the bars pass through the machine that covers them with nuts, and then they're frozen again."

I was standing next to the chocolate machine. "How does the chocolate get into this big contraption?" I asked Ranger.

"There's a ladder on the other side. The machine is sealed while it's running, but there's a hatch on the top for adding ingredients. And the entire lid can come off for cleaning."

"It seems to me that dunking someone in here would be at least a two-man job."

Ranger nodded. "And it would be messy."

"So maybe the dead man was chocolate coated somewhere else?"

"That would be my guess."

"Like at a rival ice cream baron's plant?"

"I haven't seen Morris's setup, but I doubt he would contaminate his own chocolate vat by dumping a dead man in it."

"Good point. So maybe Harry Bogart didn't need to scour his whole plant."

"He had no way of knowing if any of the equipment had been compromised." Ranger pointed to the row of offices. "Bogart has the large corner office. He also has offices elsewhere in the building. The deceased was four offices down from Bogart. The test kitchen is in the double office at the far end. There are more offices and storage in a separate wing. The main entrance and reception area are also in that wing."

"So you're thinking that Zigler, the human resources guy, was shot and frozen someplace off-site. Then he would have been chocolate covered and sprinkled with nuts and put back in a freezer."

"Correct."

"The killer has a really big freezer."

"The deceased was five feet ten inches. There are some home chest freezers that could hold him, but it's more likely the killer had access to a commercial freezer."

"The killer also had access to the freezer truck."

"Everyone had access to the freezer truck. It was sitting at the loading dock, plugged into electric with the freezer unit running."

"I imagine you're suggesting he install a gated, razor-wire fence."

"Razor wire would be an option, but the area around the loading dock should definitely be fenced and gated. And he needs security cameras not only for security but also for liability."

"And he's willing to spend the money?"

"Apparently. He's resisted in the past because he's been afraid it would tarnish the innocent image of his ice cream."

I was all in favor of keeping the image of ice cream innocent. Unfortunately, that ship had sailed for me when the head of human resources for Bogart Ice Cream was murdered and covered in chocolate. As much as I wanted to wipe the image of the dead man from my mind, I also wanted to find the person who killed him. Murder is ugly. And this murder felt especially ugly to me. It felt personal. I was there when Arnold Zigler fell out of the truck and crashed to the ground. I saw him covered in chocolate and nuts, and I didn't like it. The more I thought about it the angrier I got. It was disrespectful to Arnold Zigler, and I know this is shallow, but some immoral creep had ruined a childhood treasure for me. Bogart Bars were now tied to a vision of a grisly murder.

The human resources office had yellow crime scene tape stuck to the locked door. Ranger peeled the tape off and used a slim lock pick to open the door.

"The police have already combed through this office, but they don't always look for the right thing," Ranger said. "You take the desk, and I'll go through the file cabinet."

We pulled on disposable gloves and went to work. I rifled the desk drawers and found that the HR guy chewed nicotine gum. He used nicotine patches. He vaped e-cigarettes. And he smoked Marlboros. If he hadn't been shot he wouldn't have lasted much longer anyway. He preferred fine-point Sharpies. Had sticky pads in a variety of sizes and colors. And he kept a collection of porno mags in his bottom drawer. I guess after all that nicotine he had to relax himself from time to time.

"Are you finding anything?" I asked Ranger.

"Nothing dramatic. There are several large files for unhappy employees. A couple more for problem employees. I've copied them for you to read through. It wouldn't hurt for you to check them out. There's also a file here with nothing more than a name. 'J. T. Soon.' Did you find anything in the desk?"

"Just the usual stuff. Pens and sticky pads and porno."

He glanced over at me. "Anything I should see?"

"No. I imagine you've seen it all."

"Babe," Ranger said.

"Zigler has a folder here with a bunch of loose papers. Job applications, health insurance forms, and a handwritten note to run a full background check on J. T. Soon."

"Anything else on Soon? Was he one of the people applying for a job?"

"No. There's just this note. Nothing else."

We stepped out of the office, relocked and closed the door, and replaced the crime scene tape. We peeled our gloves off and tossed them in the trash.

"I have one last show-and-tell," Ranger said.

I followed him through the double doors that led to the other wing. We walked a short distance down the hall and pushed through another set of double doors into a storeroom. Rows of metal shelves filled the warehouse. The shelves were stacked with paper booties, jugs of vanilla, toilet paper, chocolate syrup, powdered milk, large plastic bags of crushed nuts, towers of empty ice cream containers, cases of strawberries packed in air-tight bags, pallets of shrink-wrapped Bogart Bar wrappers.

"CSI hasn't released an analysis of the nuts and chocolate coating the deceased," Ranger said, "but Bogart feels pretty certain they came from his plant. He uses a proprietary mix of specially chopped nuts. So we're thinking it might be an inside job. And we're looking for someone who had access to the storeroom and could walk off with a couple gallons of chocolate syrup and not be noticed."

Ranger wrapped an arm around my shoulders and moved me out of the storeroom. "Let me know when you find him."

"Do I get a bonus?"

He grinned and kissed me on the top of my head. "Yeah. You'll get a bonus."

I had a pretty good idea about the nature of the bonus.

"How much?" I asked him.

"It'll be priceless."

"Oh boy."

We were standing in the hallway that led to the manufacturing plant. Ranger pushed me against the wall and leaned in. "Would you like to know the details?"

There was no space between us. I could feel him pressed into me. His lips skimmed the rim of my ear when he asked the question, and I felt the rush of heat buzz in my brain and flash through every part of me. The heat curled into my hoo-ha with a spasm that was a blink away from an orgasm.

He kissed me, and our tongues touched. The kiss deepened, his hand caressed my breast, and my hand went south on him in search of the bonus.

Somewhere far off a door opened and closed, and we both paused. It was the night guard making one of his rounds.

I guess I should be grateful. I might have been condemned to hell if it had gone any further. It was one thing to have a relationship with two men. It was a totally other thing to have them simultaneously.

I looked around. "So is there anything else to see?"

"Not tonight," Ranger said.

EIGHT

IT WAS AFTER one o'clock when I crawled into bed with mixed emotions about the next day. I wanted to rush in and root out the killer, and at the same time I felt completely incompetent at doing the job. I set my alarm for seven o'clock, giving me a half hour to shower and whatever, and a half hour to drive to the ice creamery.

. . .

The alarm went off, and I hit the snooze button and pulled the pillow over my head. Five minutes later the alarm went off again, and I dragged myself out of bed and into the shower.

I wasn't sure what one wore to work in an ice cream factory, so I dressed in my standard uniform of jeans, a red short-sleeved V-neck jersey, and running shoes. I scarfed down a cold meatball sandwich for breakfast and poured my coffee into a to-go mug. As I chugged out of the parking lot, I got a phone call from Lula.

"Are you there yet?" she asked. "What kind of job did you get?"

"I just got on the road. I don't have to be there until eight o'clock."

"Well, you better hurry. You don't want to be late on your first day. People hate that."

"Are you at the office?"

"Hell, no. I'm in my closet deciding on who I want to be today. I mean, I'm always Lula, but I got a multifaceted personality."

"Talk to you later," I said. And I hung up.

I drove two blocks, and I got a call from Morelli.

"Big day today," he said.

"How so?"

"You have a new job. Are you on your way to the ice cream factory?"

"Yeah."

"Are you excited?"

"Are you?"

"Not at the moment," Morelli said.

"Do you have any news on the Bogart Bar man?"

"Nothing interesting. It would help if we could find Virgil. Maybe you could keep your eyes open for him."

"In my spare time."

"Boy, you're cranky today. Probably because you didn't see me last night."

"How was the poker game?"

"I lost my shirt. I think Anthony cheats."

Morelli's brother, Anthony, cheats on everything, including his wife. Aside from that one major character flaw he's a fun guy.

"If you ask me nice I might come over for dinner tonight," Morelli said.

"Sure. Hot dogs?"

"I heard you got meatballs at Giovichinni's."

"I ate them for breakfast."

"I'll bring dinner," Morelli said.

"Deal. I have to go now. I have to concentrate on my driving."

Mostly what I had to do was whip up some enthusiasm for Harry Bogart ice cream.

By the time I walked through the front door and up to the receptionist I had almost convinced myself I could do the job. I could learn how to make ice cream. I could mingle. And maybe I could find the killer.

"I'm Stephanie Plum," I told the woman behind the desk. "The employment office is expecting me."

"The employment office is in a bit of disarray," the woman said, "but Mr. Bogart will personally speak with you. He's in his office just down the hall. Go through the double doors and turn left."

Okay, I told myself. I get to meet Mr. Ice Cream. I get to talk to the inventor of the Bogart Bar. It could be cool, right?

I walked the hall and came to the little gold plaque on the wall that said "Harry Bogart." The door was open so I peeked in at the man behind the massive oak desk.

"Hell-o-o-o," I said. "Knock, knock."

"For God's sake just come on in," Harry Bogart said. "Who the hell are you?"

"Stephanie Plum."

"Who?"

"I work for Rangeman. I'm supposed to assume a job on the floor so I can look around at your operation."

Harry Bogart was a big man. Big blockhead with buzz-cut gray hair. Close-set blue eyes, bushy gray eyebrows, ruddy cheeks, thick lips, jowls. Not entirely attractive. I guessed he might be six feet tall and about fifty pounds overweight. He was wearing a tan suit, white dress shirt, brown-and-blue-striped tie. He fit the suit like an overstuffed sausage.

"You don't look like much," Bogart said to me. "Is this how you come to a job interview? Do you smoke dope?"

I told myself to keep thinking about the bonus and how I was going to avenge the sullying of the Bogart Bar. Telling Bogart he was a bloated ass was pointless, since he undoubtedly already knew this.

"It wasn't my understanding that this was an interview," I said, giving him my best kiss-up smile. "I was told I would be working on the floor."

"I don't want you talking to anyone. If anyone even suspects you're a snitch you're out of here."

I felt my eyes involuntarily narrow and knew it wasn't doing a lot for the smile still plastered to my face.

"Maybe you want to review this plan with Ranger," I told Bogart.

Bogart leaned forward and squinted at me. "What's with the black? Why is he always wearing black?"

"It's easy. Everything matches."

"That's nuts. What the hell's wrong with him? Even his underwear?"

"Getting back to your security problem," I said.

"Someone's out to get me," Bogart said. "I think it's that skunk Morris."

"Do you think he killed your human resources man?"

"I wouldn't put it past him. He's sneaky. Always looking like such a goody-goody do-gooder, but you turn your back on him and he's a sneak."

"Okay."

I looked around the office. It was a cluttered mess. Stacks of files and magazines. Bowling trophies. Photographs on every surface. Harry Bogart with kids, dogs, politicians, and a monkey eating ice cream.

"Am I supposed to be working now?" I asked him.

He pressed a button on his multiline phone and yelled at it. "Kathy!"

A moment later a fifty-something woman stuck her head in the open door to Bogart's office. "Yes?" she asked.

Bogart gestured at me. "This is what's-her-name. She's going to be working the line. Get her suited up and take her to Jim."

There was the sound of activity in the hall, and the

receptionist and Lula shoved themselves past Kathy and stumbled into the room.

"I tried to stop her," the receptionist said to Bogart.

"This receptionist woman don't know nothing about political correctness," Lula said to Bogart. "She didn't want me to come in here because I'm a black woman of a certain size."

"I didn't want you to come in because you don't have an appointment," the receptionist said.

"Yeah, but you prejudged me," Lula said. "And anyways, I do have an appointment. I'm with Stephanie."

"Who's Stephanie?" Bogart asked.

"I'm Stephanie," I told him.

"That's right," Lula said. "And I'm with her. We're a team."

"I don't know anything about a team," Bogart said. "I wasn't told about this."

"Well, lucky you," Lula said. "You get the two of us. In my former profession as a 'ho it was considered a treat to get two women."

Bogart's ruddy cheeks had turned purple, and it seemed to me he was having difficulty breathing.

"Do you know this woman?" he asked me.

"No," I said. "Don't know her."

"I'll take care of it," Kathy said, herding Lula and me out of the office. "I'm sure Jim can find jobs for them."

We followed Kathy down the hall, into the main production area and through a door marked "Ladies' Locker Room."

"You can have lockers 17 and 18," Kathy said. "You can get suited up and leave your personal possessions in the lockers."

"Say what?" Lula said.

"Everyone working on the floor needs to wear a sanitary cap, booties, and a jumpsuit," Kathy said. "You'll find them in your lockers. I'll tell Jim you're here, and he'll meet you just outside the locker room."

Lula looked at the jumpsuit assigned to her. "I picked out a special celebratory ice cream outfit for today, and this is going to ruin everything. I don't see where this is going to contribute to my experience."

I shrugged into the jumpsuit and covered my sneakers with the booties. I didn't care a lot about it since I hadn't worn a special celebratory ice cream outfit. I put the yellow disposable shower cap on, and Lula looked horrified.

"You look like a idiot," she said. "You look like a giant deranged minion from that movie *Despicable Me.*"

"Are you getting dressed? Or are you going home?"

"I'm thinking about going back and demanding a office job. It would be something more suited to my wardrobe and unique talents."

"What talents are we talking about?"

"Office worker talents. I got a lot of them. And I got a good chance of getting a excellent office job because I got cards. You gotta take what they give you, because you got almost no cards. You got the woman card, but it's about worthless on account of you're thin and white. I'm a plus-size black woman. *Bam!* That's three cards. It's like I hit the political-correctness jackpot. Only thing better than what I got is if I lost a eye or a leg to police brutality."

"That's horrible."

"No way. It's using what God give you. I got a personal relationship with God, and I know he'd be disappointed in me if I didn't use my gift cards."

I guess she could have a point with using her gift cards, but I didn't think those cards were going to help her when she had to figure out how to read a spreadsheet.

"I have to go to work," I said to Lula. "I'll try to hook up with you at lunch."

"They give us ice cream for lunch, right?"

NINE

JIM WAS WAITING at the locker room door. He looked like he drank a lot of beer and was ready for retirement.

"So," he said. "You want to make ice cream?"

I adjusted my shower cap. "Mostly I want to make money."

"I hear you. We'll start you out on the cup dropper and filler. It's a real no-brainer. You watch the empty cups when they come on line and make sure they're straight. If they aren't straight you fix them. Then you watch that the ice cream goes in them okay. If it doesn't go in perfect you pull the screwup off the line. If it happens three times in a row you shut the machine down by hitting the big red button that says 'Stop.' A buzzer will go off and I'll come over to take a look."

I gave him thumbs-up and he walked away. A minute later the machine went into action. After forty-five minutes of watching the cups go by I was hypnotized. I jumped up and down, stamped my feet, and sang "Happy Birthday" to myself. After an hour and a half I was afraid I was going to go into a catatonic stupor and face-plant into a pint of mint chocolate chip.

A young woman tapped me on the shoulder. "You get a fifteen-minute break," she said. "I'll watch the machine."

I shuffled off to the break room next to the locker room and went straight to the coffee machine. Two women were at a round table that seated six. I got my coffee and sat at the table with them.

"I'm Tina, and this is Doris," one of the women said. "How's your first day going so far?"

"I'm having a hard time concentrating. All those cups going by one after the other. It's hypnotic."

"You get used to it," Tina said. "You need to drink a lot of coffee. And if that doesn't work I've got some red pills that'll perk you up."

"Aside from the boredom it seems like an okay job," I said.

Doris drained her coffee cup. "Yeah, as long as you don't get turned into a Bogart Bar."

I leaned forward a little. "I heard about that. Did you know him?"

"Sort of," Tina said. "He was here every day, but he mostly kept to himself. He'd come in and get coffee and take it back to his office. I guess when you're the guy who has the power to promote or fire you can't get real chummy with the folks."

"Why do you think he was killed?"

"Someone didn't like him," Tina said.

"Did you like him?" I asked her.

"He seemed okay. I didn't have much to do with him."

"What about Mr. Bogart? I met him for the first time today, and he seemed grumpy."

"He huffs and puffs around the floor a couple times a day. Doesn't say much to anyone. Everything goes through Jim."

"Bogart is big on image," Doris said. "Everyone has to look happy when he's on the floor. We get suited up in yellow because he thinks it's a happy color. His slogan is 'Happy ice cream made by happy people.'"

"Is everyone really happy?" I asked her.

She shrugged. "I'm happy."

"Me too," Tina said.

I looked at my watch. My break was over. I went back to my station and stared at the cups for two more hours. Every once in a while I had to straighten one. At precisely one o'clock the young woman came back and sent me to lunch. The break room was filled with second-shift lunch people. They were all brown baggers. Harry Bogart didn't operate a cafeteria. There was free coffee and tea, and there were vending machines.

I went to my locker and called Lula.

"Where are you?" I asked her. "Did you get an office job?"

"I'm here with Connie. They said they didn't have no office jobs available, and it don't matter anyway because cheap-ass Bogart don't give away free ice cream to his employees."

"What's going on at the bonds office? Am I missing anything?"

"We got cupcakes instead of donuts this morning. And a

new copy of *Star* magazine came out. I didn't get a chance to read it yet, but it got a guy on the cover that looks like one of the Property Brothers, but I think it might just be a look-alike. Imagine three guys out there lookin' that good. And the real Property Brothers can even sing. You ever hear them sing?"

"No."

"I think they should be on *Live at Daryl's House* and then I could see my two favorite shows at one time."

"I thought your favorite show was *Naked and Afraid*."

"I got a lot of favorite shows. Mostly the common ingredient is hot men. Daryl got a real dope band, and the best part is Daryl's hair. He's got one of them blond flip-back things going. If I was white I'd want hair like Daryl. He's like Farrah Fawcett only with a lot of testosterone."

"Anything happening at the office besides cupcakes and the *Star*?"

"Vinnie came in, and he was on a rant over Eugene Winkle. How long you gonna be working at the ice cream fun factory? Vinnie's not gonna be happy to hear you're moonlighting."

"I'll go after Winkle tonight."

"Are you nuts? The man is a bridge troll. How are you gonna bring him in?"

"Do you want to help?"

"No!"

I disconnected, pulled a couple dollars out of my pocket, and fed them into one of the vending machines in the break room. I got a packet of peanut butter crackers, a candy bar, and more coffee. I sat at a table with four women and introduced myself.

"I see you're going for the high-protein vending machine diet," one of the women said to me. "I'm Betty, and this is Miranda here to my right."

"I didn't pack a lunch," I told them. "I thought there might be a cafeteria."

"Honey, you're working at the wrong ice cream factory," Betty said. "That would be Mo Morris across town. He's got a cafeteria, and his wife makes the sandwiches."

"Yeah, and everyone gets free ice cream over there," Miranda said.

I unwrapped my crackers. "So why are you all working here?"

"It's impossible to get a job at the Morris plant," Betty said. "No one ever leaves."

"There's not much turnover here either," Miranda said. "Of course, there's a human resources job open."

"I noticed they still have the crime scene tape up," I said. "It's a little creepy. When I came in this morning the receptionist took me to see Mr. Bogart. Didn't the human resources guy have an assistant?"

"Nope. It was just him," Betty said. "This isn't such a big operation. Evelyn has the office next to HR. She does the clerical work for everyone, including Arnold. He's the deceased. Arnold Zigler."

"Who's Evelyn?" I asked.

The round-faced chubby woman sitting across from me raised her hand. "I'm Evelyn."

"Oh, wow," I said. "I'm sorry. You must have been friends with . . . Arnold."

"He was a nice man," Evelyn said. "Quiet. Kept to himself. Took his job seriously. I didn't know him beyond work." She pressed her lips together. "He hated Bogart Bars. He was allergic to nuts. Not so bad that they bothered him in the plant, but he couldn't eat them."

"What happened if he ate them?" I asked.

"Hives," Evelyn said. "I never saw them firsthand. He kept Benadryl in his desk just in case."

I didn't know what to say. I guess it could have been an ironic coincidence, but it seemed especially nasty that he'd been covered with something that made him sick.

"Do you have any idea who killed him?" I asked.

Evelyn shook her head. "No."

Everyone else had the same response.

"Terrible," I said. "I heard the nuts came from here. It had to have been done by someone who works here and knew him. Remember Jeffrey Dahmer, the serial killer who worked in a candy factory? Maybe there's a serial killer at loose here."

"So far only one person has been killed," Betty said. "You need to kill a bunch of people to be a serial killer."

"This could be the beginning," I said. I looked around the table. "Do any of you know anyone who looks like a serial killer?"

"Marty," Betty said. "He's at the end of the line working the wrapper. He has shifty eyes. They look in different directions."

"He told me about that once," Evelyn said. "He has a glass

eye. He poked his real eye out with a clam shucker. He said he'd been drinking."

There was a moment of silence.

"Anybody got any weed?" Evelyn asked.

"I have some in my locker," one of the other women said.

Evelyn perked up. "I'll trade you for an egg salad sandwich."

"Is it on sourdough?" the woman asked. "Do you have pickles?"

"Of course."

"Deal."

So now I thought I might be understanding everyone's happiness.

. . .

My shift was over at four o'clock. I peeled the yellow jumpsuit off and dragged myself out of the ice cream factory. I got into my SUV and stared at the windshield.

Wake up! I thought. Snap out of it.

Someone knocked on my side window. It was Evelyn.

"See you tomorrow," she said.

I nodded and forced a smile. The people were nice. The job was deadly. All those cups. The hum of the machines. The overhead fluorescent lights. And the smell of vanilla beans was stuck in my nose. Did I accomplish anything? No. I wasn't the world's best spy.

There was still plenty of daylight, so I pointed my car toward Stark Street. The plan was to ride past Eugene

Winkle's address and hope I didn't see him. If I did see him I'd call Ranger and ask for help. This plan had the additional advantage of being able to pop into the 7-Eleven on State Street at the end of Stark and get some nachos. Morelli was bringing dinner, but he wouldn't be around until six o'clock and I was starving.

I connected with Stark Street on the fifth block and turned left. Traffic was minimal. A couple weary-looking hookers had staked out a corner. An old man was curled up like a cat asleep on a stoop. Fast food drink cups and burger wrappers littered the sidewalks and banked up against the curbs. No gargantuan snub-nosed guy in sight.

I continued on down Stark, looking for Winkle, trying to stay alert for trouble. I didn't want to get caught in gang-related crossfire. I didn't want to accidentally run over a drugged-up homeless person. I didn't want to look like I was trolling for dope. I recognized a hooker on the corner of block three. Her name was Sharelle Jones. Vinnie had bonded her out several times, and she was friendly with Lula. I pulled over and rolled my window down.

"Hey, girl," Sharelle said, leaning in. "You lookin' for a good time?"

"No," I said. "I'm looking for Eugene Winkle. Have you seen him?"

"Haven't seen him. Don't want to see him. Don't need that kind of trouble. Dude's ugly inside and out."

I wrapped a twenty around my business card and handed it to Sharelle. "Let me know if you hear anything."

"Will do," Sharelle said. "Tell Lula I was askin' on her."

I drove the length of Stark and pulled into the 7-Eleven. I was on my way out when I ran into Larry Virgil.

"Oh crap!" Virgil said. And he took off running.

He tried to cross State Street and ran out of luck halfway when an orange Subaru plowed into him, knocked him into the oncoming lane, and three cars ran over him before all traffic came to a screeching stop. I called 911, but I didn't think they needed to be in a big rush.

A lot of people ran to Virgil and huddled around. I stayed on the outskirts. I didn't think I could help in any way, and I didn't especially want to see the carnage.

A fire truck was the first to arrive. Two cop cars were close behind. Within five minutes the road was clogged with emergency vehicles, and police were diverting traffic.

Eddie Gazarra got out of a cop car and walked over to me.

"I see they gave you a new car," I said to him.

"They tried to put me on a bicycle, but my ass didn't fit on the seat." He looked at the container of nachos still in my hand. "Are you going to eat that?"

I shook my head. "My stomach isn't feeling great. I bought these before . . . you know."

"Looks like they gave you extra cheese glop. Be a shame to waste it."

I handed the nachos over to Eddie. "Enjoy."

"If I had to take a guess I'd say you bumped into Virgil on your way out of the 7-Eleven, and he ran across the road trying to get away."

"Your guess would be right."

"It's not your fault," Eddie said.

"It feels like my fault."

"He chose to run. You didn't make him run into the street, did you?"

I blew out a sigh. I knew Eddie was right, but I still felt bad.

"No," I said. "I didn't make him run into the street, but I was a catalyst. It's like I'm always there when disaster happens."

"I hear you," Eddie said. "You think you're in a lousy spot? You should have my job."

"How do you manage?"

"I walk the dog, and I think about my retirement pension."

I helped myself to one of the corn chips and scooped up some cheese goo. "There has to be more."

"For as long as I could remember I wanted to be a cop. It's not exactly the way I thought it would be, but I think I'm a good cop. And sometimes I get to help people. And it's never boring. The 'never boring' is important because I have a short attention span. I'm ADD."

As were his kids and his dog.

"I suppose I have to talk to someone," I said.

Eddie looked back at the knot of people around Virgil. "I think Manny Rogezzi has this. You remember Manny? He was a year ahead of you in high school. He married Marilyn Fugg." He finished the nachos and handed the empty container back to me. "Stay here and I'll send him over."

After what seemed like an eternity Manny made his way through the crowd to where I was standing.

"How is he?" I asked. "He was killed, wasn't he?"

"Yeah. From the tire tracks on him I'd say he was killed at least three times. Did you see him run into the road?"

"I was coming out of the store and I bumped into him. He panicked and ran. I don't think there was any way the cars could have avoided hitting him." I gave an involuntary shudder at the memory. "He was FTA."

"He was more than FTA," Manny said. "I heard he was driving the Bogart ice cream truck with the frozen Bogart Bar guy inside. At least, he was driving it until you and your sidekick got hold of it."

"I think he must have come across the truck abandoned, or maybe it was a spur-of-the-moment hijacking. He for sure wasn't a Bogart employee. It's unfortunate that he's dead, because he would have been able to fill in some blanks on the murder."

Manny cracked a smile. "Did you really total Gazarra's squad car?"

"Lula misjudged the brakes on the truck."

Manny gave a bark of laughter. "Life is good." He cut his eyes back to the road. "Sometimes. Sometimes not so good."

"Anything else?"

"No. I'll send you an accident report to verify."

"And I'll need a body receipt so Vinnie can collect his bond."

"I'll leave it at the back desk," Manny said. "Give me a day. This is going to be a lot of paperwork."

TEN

IT WAS A little after six o'clock when I got home. Morelli and Bob were already in my apartment. The table was set for two, and the kitchen smelled like Morelli's mother had been cooking in it.

"Have you been here long?" I asked him.

"Nope. Just got here. I've got my mom's lasagna in the oven, and there's bread from the bakery."

I was so relieved I almost burst into tears. I wrapped my arms around Morelli and relaxed into him. He was warm and solid and comforting. Bob jumped off the couch and nosed his way in between us.

"Bad day?" Morelli asked.

"The worst. The ice cream plant people are really nice, but I'm all wrong for the job. And then after work I stopped at 7-Eleven and ran into Larry Virgil."

"I heard," Morelli said. "Eddie called me. He said you were shook up."

"I saw him get hit. I can still hear the sound. It was horrible. And then a bunch of cars ran over him."

Morelli wrapped his arms around me. "It's not your fault."

"That's what Eddie said."

"In the interest of mental health I'm suggesting you move on to something more positive . . . like sex or lasagna."

"Lasagna!"

"I knew I shouldn't have given you a choice."

I went to the fridge, grabbed two bottles of beer, and gave one to Morelli. "Anything new on the Bogart Bar man?"

"The truck was stolen at nine o'clock Monday night. It's unlikely the human resources man was on the truck at that time. And it's unlikely that the crime was committed at the plant. Everything indicates the HR man was killed, frozen, and coated in chocolate off-site."

"Could Virgil have been the killer?"

"Hard to believe. Probably Virgil happened on the truck and hijacked it. Thought it was his lucky day."

"Someone went to a lot of trouble to make Arnold Zigler into a Bogart Bar."

"Yeah. It showed motivation."

Morelli pulled the lasagna out of the oven and brought it to the table. I poured dog kibble into a bowl for Bob, and brought over the bread and two more bottles of beer.

"Do you guys have any persons of interest?" I asked Morelli.

"No." He looked across the table at me. "Do you?"

"No."

Morelli served the lasagna, and we all dug in. Morelli's mom was an amazing cook. My mom was good, but Morelli's mom was a pro. Her lasagna noodles were always perfect. Her red sauce was a family secret. She used just the right amount of ricotta, mozzarella, and Italian sausage.

"This is fantastic," I said to Morelli.

He smiled. "You always say that."

"I wish I could cook like your mom."

"You have other talents."

I wasn't going to pursue this. If I asked about my other talents we'd never finish dinner. We'd be in the bedroom. Don't get me wrong. I like sex. I like it a lot. I just don't like it as much as I like Morelli's mom's lasagna.

"Do you have any lab reports back?" I asked.

"It looks like the chocolate and nuts came from the Bogart plant. Time of death seems to be late Friday. DNA will take longer."

"Prints?"

"Nothing on the body. The truck was covered with them, including yours. Lots of people come in contact with that truck during a normal business day."

My phone buzzed with a text message from Ranger.

"I'm working the loading dock tomorrow," I told Morelli. "I'm supposed to report to the foreman at eight o'clock. And I'm supposed to wear sensible shoes."

"Walk me through the purpose for this job one more time," Morelli said.

"Ranger's been hired by Harry Bogart to improve his security. Bogart thinks someone is trying to sabotage his business. So Ranger hired me to go inside and look around."

"And the Bogart Bar guy?"

"It's not clear if the two problems are related."

"Did you learn anything from your first day?"

I helped myself to another chunk of lasagna. "Nothing useful. It's a pretty bland group. Not a lot of gossip. And I only came in contact with a few people. It sounds like Mo Morris runs a more employee-friendly plant, but no one seemed especially unhappy to be working for Bogart. This could be because Bogart doesn't do drug testing. He's got a bunch of mellow ladies working for him."

"Do I need to send someone in there?"

"Probably not necessary. Ranger will straighten it out when he takes over security."

"That'll be popular."

"Yeah, I imagine they'll have some employee turnover." I looked toward the kitchen. "Is there dessert?"

Morelli grinned.

"Not that!" I said. "I know there's that. Jeez Louise, don't you ever think of anything else?"

"It's on my mind a lot," Morelli said.

"Even when you're working?"

"Not so much when I'm working. I'm a homicide cop. I almost never get a hard-on when I'm looking at a body filled with bullet holes."

"So is there dessert?"

"Yeah. There's ice cream."

I collected the plates, took them into the kitchen, and went to the freezer. It was filled with Bogart Bars.

"Are you kidding me?" I said. "You got Bogart Bars?"

"They were on sale."

ELEVEN

AT 7:45 A.M. I parked in the employee lot at the ice cream plant and found the employee entrance. It opened up onto a hall that led to the locker rooms. Because I was working on the loading dock I didn't need to get suited up, so I left my messenger bag and lunch in a locker and went in search of my foreman.

I was directed to a wide hallway with polished concrete floors and harsh overhead lighting. Double doors to the freezer were at one end of the hall and double doors to the loading dock were at the other. I pushed through the loading dock doors and looked around, happy to be outside. It was a cloudless blue-sky day. Perfect for September. Warm in the sun and chilly in the shade. Hardly any stench from the chemical plant in the neighboring industrial park and only a slight haze of air pollution.

A young guy slouched against one wall, and an older man was talking on his phone. A refrigerator truck was backed up to the high concrete platform. It was a box truck about half the size of the eighteen-wheeler Lula and I commandeered. A much smaller ice cream truck decorated with pictures of Bogart Bars and Kidz Kups was parked by the ramp leading down from the platform. It was the beloved Jolly Bogart truck. It was one of the few ice cream trucks that still drove through neighborhoods, rain or shine, summer or winter, selling ice cream to kids and their moms.

The older man put his phone away and stood hands on hips, looking me over. He blew out a sigh and shook his head. Not happy.

"What the hell am I supposed to do with you?" he said.

I didn't know the answer to that. "I assume you're the foreman."

"Yeah. Gus. And you're what?"

"Stephanie."

"Well, Stephanie, we gotta load this truck up with ice cream. The stupid-looking guy standing over there with his thumb up his ass is Butchy."

"Haw," Butchy said, and he lit a cigarette.

"Last time Butchy loaded up a truck it had a dead guy stuffed into the back of it," Gus said.

"Not my bad," Butchy said. "I didn't put him there. And when I loaded the truck there wasn't no room for a dead guy. That truck was full up to the doors. Someone got away with some ice cream. My thinking is that Zigler was just a placeholder. He was put there to take the attention away from the fact that someone's stealing ice cream."

"Right, and maybe it was aliens stealing the ice cream," Gus said.

"Exactly," Butchy said. "It was most likely them Mexicans just come over the border."

Gus and I exchanged glances.

"This is what I got to work with," Gus said. "He's dumb as a box of rocks."

Butchy sucked on his cigarette. "Haw," he said, blowing out a cloud of toxic smoke.

Gus gave me a list of ice cream orders. "You can read, right?"

"Yep."

"I always gotta ask these days. You never know. We have to pack the truck for delivery, and we have to put the ice cream in according to drop-off order. It's all color-coded, and if you start at the top of the list you can't go wrong. Sometimes the trucks go out to warehouses for fulfillment. When we do those trucks we load pallets, and we use the forklift. This truck is doing local deliveries, so the orders have been shrink-wrapped and we gotta move them on dollies. You're gonna take a dolly into the warehouse freezer and stack it up as best you can with your orders. Then you're gonna push it out here, and Butchy is gonna load it into the truck. We got two dollies, so while he's loading you can go back and get more orders. When he turns blue from being in the freezer truck you'll swap jobs with him until he thaws out."

There was a yellow forklift parked on the far side of the loading dock and two things next to it that I assumed were the dollies. They looked like something from the Home Depot garden section. A wide, flat shelf on heavy-duty castors with handles attached to both ends.

I stuffed the list of orders into my jeans pocket and took a dolly for a test drive. I wrestled it around to the door leading to the hallway and shoved it down the hall to the freezer. The freezer door had a numerical lock on it. Bummer. I returned to the loading dock and asked Gus about the lock.

"Just punch in zero, zero, zero, zero," Gus said.

"That's the code?"

"Yup. Think you can remember it?"

"Me and everyone else."

"Now you're catching on. We try to keep things simple here. Otherwise I gotta do everything myself."

"I can't get locked in the freezer, can I?"

"Good question. No. The door opens from the inside."

I returned to the freezer, punched the code in, and rolled the dolly through the door. The door closed behind me, and my heart did a little flip. I tried the door and it opened. Good deal. I wasn't going to freeze to death. Three-quarters of the freezer was devoted to shrink-wrapped ice cream on pallets. The remaining space contained smaller quantities of the color-coded shrink-wrapped orders. I started at the top of the list and loaded the dolly. By the time I got the dolly loaded my fingers were cold and aching, and my nose was running. I towed the dolly out of the freezer and paused for a moment, stamping my feet and rubbing my hands together. I needed Uggs and gloves and a sweatshirt. I'll be better prepared next time, I thought. The follow-up thought was that I hoped there wasn't a next time.

I pushed the dolly down the hall, maneuvered it through the loading dock door, and handed it over to Butchy. I got the second dolly and repeated the drill. Butchy didn't seem inclined to swap jobs, so we kept going until the last order was placed in the truck a little before eleven.

"Now what?" I asked Butchy.

Butchy lit up. "Now we hang out and wait for Gus to come back. He's got a bad prostate. He takes lots of pee breaks. He says it just dribbles out. Pathetic, right?"

"I wish I didn't know that."

Butchy sucked on his cigarette. "I go like a racehorse. I got a real fire hose."

Butchy was a scrawny guy with an eagle's beak nose, bad skin, bad teeth, and a bad haircut. He was in his late teens to early twenties. The fact that I now knew he had a fire hose did nothing to enhance my opinion of him.

The hallway door opened, and a man came out dressed in a bright green clown suit. He was wearing an orange wig that was a cross between Ronald McDonald and Carrot Top. His nose was covered in red greasepaint. He was the Jolly Bogart clown. When I was a kid he was the highlight of my day. Even if I didn't get ice cream I loved to hear the truck come down the street playing the Jolly jingle.

"Hey," Butchy said to him.

"Yeah," Jolly said. "Where's my shit? Is it in the truck?"

"Gus hasn't come out with it yet," Butchy said. "He's trying to drain the lizard."

"Cripes, how long's he been in the can?"

Butchy looked at his watch. "Half hour."

Jolly blew out a sigh, and his shoulders slumped. "This is gonna mean an extra fifteen minutes in the clown suit. Could it get any worse?"

"The clown suit looks comfortable," I said.

"Right," Jolly said. "Nice and baggy. Gives my boys room to breathe, which is a good thing because the only fun they have is knocking against each other. You know what it's like to try to get laid when you're a clown? It's not easy. The greasepaint won't come off my nose. I glow in the dark. And you know what I gotta do all day? Smile at the rotten, smelly, snot-nosed little kids. I hate kids."

"Why don't you get another job?"

"Lady, I've been a clown for twelve years. You think I'm going to get hired to do brain surgery?"

"At least you're not a Bogart Bar," Butchy said. "Haw."

Jolly grinned. "True. That honor went to Zigler. It brightened my day a little. Someone looked more ridiculous than me. It's a shame there wasn't a picture in the paper. That part was a disappointment."

Gus pushed a loaded dolly through the hall door. "Someone give me a hand getting this down the ramp."

Butchy and I helped Gus, and Jolly followed. We wrangled the dolly up next to the Jolly Bogart truck, and packed the truck with Bogart Kidz Kups and Bogart Bars. Jolly got behind the wheel and drove off.

"You might as well take an early lunch," Gus said to Butchy and me. "We have a truck coming in at one."

. . .

Butchy went off to take a nap in his tricked-out F-450 pickup, and I went to the deserted break room. I got coffee and ate my sandwich while I looked through the employee files Ranger had copied for me. There were five in total.

PeeWee Stutz had been accused of sexual harassment six months ago. He'd received a warning and been referred to group counseling. That seemed to be the end of it.

Maureen Gooley had a long history of lunchroom altercations. She worked on the floor and was fired three weeks ago after she sucker-punched Lucinda Keever. Maureen was sixty-three years old and was rumored to have a drinking problem.

Stan Ducker had the thickest file of all. It was filled with requests to transfer. Job description simply said "Truck driver." I read further and realized this was the Jolly Bogart clown. Each request was very neatly stamped "Declined." No other explanation given. It seemed odd that you would turn the Jolly Bogart truck over to someone who hated kids. Maybe once Stan got out on the road and rolling he perked up.

Sylvia Mook also had a file filled with requests to transfer. She was working on the floor and wanted an office job. She'd been at the plant for five years.

Maria Ortiz was unhappy with the machines in the break room. She wanted Coke, and only Pepsi was offered. She also didn't like the brand of toilet paper in the ladies' room. She thought there should be assigned parking in the lot so you could find your car more easily. She worried about the air quality throughout the plant. And she wanted a transfer from the housekeeping crew to a job on the floor. There were seven requests for transfer. All neatly stamped "Declined."

I used my phone to check my email. I called Morelli but got his voicemail. I glanced over at the vending machines. Maybe I needed to treat myself to a giant Reese's Peanut Butter Cup. Peanut butter is healthy, right?

I was scrounging in my bag, looking for loose change, when a text message came in from Ranger telling me my snooping days were over. I'd been recognized and reported to Bogart, and Bogart wanted me out of the plant.

Thank God. I wanted to find the man who'd murdered Arnold Zigler and the Bogart Bar. I truly did. And I wanted to do a good job for Ranger. But Jeez Louise I hated working the line and the loading dock.

I shoved the files back into my messenger bag, tossed my trash, said adios to the break room, and headed for my car.

TWELVE

IT WAS ALMOST noon when I walked into the bonds office. Lula was on the fake leather couch with her laptop. No Connie.

"What's up?" Lula asked.

"I got outted. Someone recognized me, and Bogart gave me the heave-ho."

"Did you get any ice cream?"

"No."

"Bummer. Next time you need to negotiate a better deal. You should have had one of them golden umbrellas."

"I think you mean *golden parachute*."

"Say what?"

"A golden parachute lets you gently float down to earth."

"Mary Poppins could do that with a umbrella," Lula said. "What about Mary Poppins?"

The thing about Lula is that when she gets things wrong they frequently make sense.

I heard the door open behind me and saw Lula's eyes go wide. I turned and bumped into Ranger.

"Babe," he said, his hands at my waist to steady me.

Even if I'd had my eyes closed I would know I was smashed up against Ranger. He always smells great. He uses Bulgari Green shower gel, and the scent clings to him. I've used it and it's gone by the time I'm done toweling off.

His hand moved to my wrist, and he tugged me outside. "I'm on my way to talk to Bogart," Ranger said, "but I wanted to talk to you first. Did you pick up anything useful while you were at the plant?"

"I didn't get to talk to a lot of people, but the general attitude is mostly mellow. No one seems to be overly concerned about the freezer meltdown, the tainted ice cream, or the Bogart Bar guy. I read through the five files you gave me, and nothing really jumped out. Three files were thick because of requests to transfer. You might ask Bogart about that. I didn't see anything in the employment histories as to why the requests were consistently turned down. No reasons were given. It occurred to me that we might want to take a look at new hires. If Mo Morris sent someone into the plant to sabotage stuff it would have been just before all the bad things started to happen."

"I'll check on it," Ranger said. "Anything else?"

"Did you just take a shower?"

"This morning."

"You smell nice."

A smile twitched at the corners of his mouth. He leaned in and kissed me. Our tongues touched, and I curled my fingers into his shirt.

"Criminy," I said.

He gave me a light parting kiss. "You have my number."

Oh yeah.

I watched him drive away, and I went back into the office.

"Criminy," Lula said.

I nodded agreement. "So true. Where's Connie?"

"Courthouse, covering for Vinnie. I'm babysitting the office but nothing's going on, so I'm working on my reality show. We're gonna shoot it tonight. We did some preliminary test runs but this is the real thing. I'm just going over the script one more time."

"I thought reality shows were unscripted."

"They're scripted unscripted. Not a lot of people know that. Just us on the inside," Lula said. "You want to hear my script?"

"No."

"Why not?"

"I don't want to have to think about you and Briggs naked."

"Yeah, I could see where that would be a problem with Briggs. He's not real attractive once you get his clothes off him. Not a lot to look at, if you know what I mean."

"Did we get any new FTAs?"

"A shoplifter and a mime."

"What did the mime do?"

"He pooped in the middle of the street. Right at the corner of Hamilton and Broad."

"Get out."

"Cross my heart. You can look on his arrest sheet. Everybody was taking pictures. Traffic was stopped all over the place. He was trending big on YouTube when it happened, but it's dropped off some now. I'm surprised you didn't know about it."

"Why did he do you-know-what in the middle of the street?"

"He said it was performance art. He said he was making a statement about our repressive society. Problem was, he repressed traffic because he was posing too long with his art, so he got arrested."

"What were the charges against him?" I asked Lula.

"Obstruction of something and making a general nuisance of himself. Personally, if it was me, I couldn't see myself pooping in the middle of the street. Even if I had to go real bad. I'd be afraid I'd get run over. I mean, even dogs know enough not to poop in the middle of the street. You ever see a dog poop in the middle of the street? I bet a turkey wouldn't poop in the middle of the street, and I hear they're real dumb."

I agreed. Turkeys were known to be dumb.

"So, about the reality show," I said. "Where are you doing this?"

"Mill Street. I got a map worked out. We're going to start on the second block and work our way up to no-man's-land."

"Are you insane? You'll die."

Mill Street ran parallel to Stark Street, one block over. It wasn't as bad as Stark, but it was still pretty bad. Residential in a crack house kind of way for a block or two and then mostly warehouses.

"We got a plan," Lula said. "We're shooting two blocks, and

then we're faking the rest. I mean, it's dark out, right? Nobody's gonna know where we are. We can just keep running around the same two blocks and do some creative camera work. And the good part is the cops won't go anywhere near there so we haven't got no worries about the naked thing. Nobody's going to care we haven't got clothes on. All the people wandering around there are hallucinating anyways."

"Good to see you've thought it through."

"I got a mind for this," Lula said. "I'm one of those underestimated people."

"How are you going to film in the dark? Do you have lights?"

"You know Handy Howie, right? He's the guy sells the handbags out of his Eldorado in the projects? Well, he's doing the cinematography. He's got a infrared camera. He's always wanted to make movies, so we're gonna give him a film credit and then after we're done with this he can use it as a demo."

"Wasn't he arrested for invasion of privacy?"

"He explained that to me," Lula said. "He'd just got his first infrared and he was learning how to use it, and he accidentally filmed some people in their bedroom. They were doing the nasty, and Howie said it was a shame the police confiscated that camera on account of it would of made a good documentary."

"But he got another camera?"

"Yeah. Howie has connections. Handbags are his bread-and-butter business, but sometimes other stuff falls off a truck, if you know what I mean."

The back door opened and slammed shut, and Connie walked in. She dumped her handbag into her bottom drawer and kicked her five-inch platform stilettos off.

"These shoes are freakin' killing me," she said.

"Your problem is you haven't got the right balance to your body to wear shoes like that," Lula said. "You gotta balance out your boobs with your bootie. Like, take me for instance. I got just the right proportion of boob to bootie. I could walk all day in those FMPs and never tip over. You got a imbalance of boob. It's one of them genetic things. Italians can grow boob, but they're deficient in bootie. I got a advantage with my African tribal background and taste for macaroni and cheese."

I wasn't getting involved in this, but I suspected the tribal background wasn't the big player in the bootie development. If I ate like Lula I'd have a lot more bootie. Anyone would have more bootie.

Connie swiveled her head to take a look at her ass.

"So you think that's my problem?" Connie asked.

"Either that or you bought your shoes too small," Lula said.

Connie took two files off her desk and handed them to me. "These just came in. They're low bonds, but they shouldn't be hard to clear out."

"I already told her about them," Lula said. "I told her about the performance art guy."

"He won't be hard to find," Connie said. "He does standup at the comedy club on Route 1 at night, and he works as a mime during the day. Usually he's hanging around the coffee shop by the State House."

I read through the file. Bernard Smitch. Thirty-four years old. Graduate of UC Berkeley. Address listed as "Under the bridge." I knew this was bogus because the comedy club on Route 1 operated at a pretty high level. If Smitch lived under the bridge he wouldn't smell all that good, and he wouldn't be let into the comedy club. I'd been under the bridge and it wasn't pretty.

"Where does Smitch *really* live?" I asked Connie.

"With his mother in Princeton," Connie said. "His father is a state representative. I think there might be a conflict there."

"Especially when he pooped in the street," Lula said. "That's not politically correct."

"I'm heading out," I said. I looked over at Lula. "Do you want to ride along?"

"You going after Smitch?"

"Yep."

"I'm in," Lula said. "I'm all about supporting the arts."

"We aren't supporting him," I said. "We're dragging him back to jail."

"Yeah, but we might support him at a later date when he gets out. I could go watch him perform."

• • •

I drove down Hamilton to Broad, went north on Broad, and turned onto State Street. The coffee house was on a side street off State. It was a perfect September day, and people were sitting outdoors. The mime was working, but no one was paying attention.

I parked in a metered space across the street, and Lula and I watched the mime. He was dressed in classic mime attire of whiteface, black-and-white-striped long-sleeved T-shirt, and slim black pants. He pretended to walk on a tightrope. He pretended to be stymied by a glass door. He poured himself a drink and pretended to be drunk. He rebooted and went back to the tightrope routine.

"You watch this long enough and you get to wishing he'd take a poop," Lula said.

We got out of my SUV, and I hung cuffs from my back pocket and stuck a small canister of pepper spray in the other back pocket. Lula was wearing a poison green spandex miniskirt that didn't have any back pockets, but she had her purse hanging on her shoulder and God-knows-what-all she had in that purse.

I approached the mime and asked him if he was Bernard Smitch. He put his finger to his head and looked like he was thinking. While he was thinking I snapped the cuffs on his right wrist. He looked at the cuffs and mimed with a stiff middle finger.

"Now, that's not nice," Lula said to him. "That's rude miming."

He turned and mooned Lula and spanked his bare ass. Lula pulled her stun gun out of her purse, pressed the prongs to the mime's butt, and gave him a couple hundred volts. *Zzzzt.* The mime went down like a sack of sand.

"Mime that," Lula said.

There was a smattering of applause, and then everyone went back to drinking coffee and eating their pastries.

We snapped the other cuff on the mime, pulled his pants up, and carted him across the street. We maneuvered him into the backseat, and I drove to the police station.

"That was easy," Lula said. "Another day and another dollar."

"It would be best if you don't mention to anyone that you stun-gunned the mime since that's a little illegal," I said.

"Yeah, but he was being disrespectful."

"It doesn't matter. It's still illegal."

I pulled around to the police station back door that led directly to the holding cells and the booking desk. I pressed the intercom button and told them I had a drop-off. Moments later the back door opened, and a guy in uniform came out. I'd seen him around. His name was Gary. I couldn't remember his last name.

"What have you got?" Gary asked.

"Bernard Smitch," I said. "He's FTA."

I pulled my papers out of my messenger bag and handed them over.

Gary grinned. "I know this guy. He pooped in the middle of Broad Street."

Lula and I got out and more or less dragged Smitch out of the backseat and propped him up against my SUV.

"Is he okay?" Gary asked.

"He's a mime," Lula said. "He's miming a seizure. It's one of his most popular routines."

"Looks to me like he might be miming that he got zapped with a stun gun," Gary said.

"It's possible," Lula said. "There's a similarity between the two experiences. And you never know with a mime."

We dragged Smitch into the building and cuffed him to a bench. I got my body receipt, and Lula and I returned to the bond office.

"Done and done," Lula said to Connie.

"You guys are hot," Connie said. "You got Virgil, Diggery, and Smitch. Vinnie's going to be happy."

Lula looked over at Vinnie's open door. "Where is the little perv? How come he's not here?"

"Good question," Connie said. "Don't know the answer. He tends to wander into murky waters when Lucille goes out of town."

"I hope he's not looking for another duck," Lula said. "I try to be open-minded about people's needs, but that was disturbing. I doubt that duck was consensual."

"Gosh, look at the time," I said, checking my watch. "I need to get home in case Morelli wants me to make dinner for him."

"Me too," Lula said. "I gotta get ready for my filming. I gotta glitter up my eyelids. And I want to go over the script one more time."

Connie wrote me a check for the mime catch. "What are you making for dinner?" she asked me.

"Hot dogs."

"Can't go wrong with hot dogs," Lula said. "What are you going to serve with them?"

"Beer."

"That'll do it," Lula said.

A text message from Ranger dinged on my cellphone.

"Now what?" Lula asked.

"I'm supposed to meet Ranger at Mo Morris Ice Cream tomorrow at eight o'clock."

"That's the good ice cream place," Lula said. "That's where they give you free ice cream."

"Why are you going to Mo Morris?" Connie asked. "I thought you were at Bogart's solving security issues."

"Harry Bogart thinks Mo is behind all the disasters at his plant. Ranger's sending me in to see if I pick up any bad vibes."

"How's he going to get you in there?" Lula asked. "I thought it was impossible to get a job at that plant."

I shrugged. "Don't know. It's not my problem."

"Yeah," Lula said, "your problem is trying to look good in a shower cap and paper onesie."

I squelched a grimace, took the check from Connie, and headed out. Truth is, I wasn't going home to get ready to wow Morelli with my culinary skills. I was going home to take a nap and reassess my life.

THIRTEEN

REX WAS IN his soup can when I walked into my kitchen. I tapped on the cage and said hello. Nothing. I dropped a peanut into his cage, he rushed out of the can, stuffed the peanut into his cheek, and rushed back into his can. Okay, that was fun. I ate some olives and a couple handfuls of Froot Loops. I lifted the lid on my brown bear cookie jar and looked in at my gun. Probably Briggs was right. I should get rid of the gun and buy some cookies. I wasn't opposed to gun ownership. I just didn't feel comfortable shooting people. And it would be nice to have cookies.

Morelli showed up at four-thirty with Bob. We took Bob for a walk, came home and fried up the hot dogs, and downloaded a movie. Domestic bliss. At nine-thirty we were about to migrate to the bedroom and take the bliss up a notch when my mother called.

"Is your grandmother with you?" she asked.

"No. Is she supposed to be with me?"

"I was brushing my teeth, and I heard the front door open and close. I looked out the window and saw your grandmother get into a red car that looks like the one Lula drives."

Oh boy.

"I hope she's not going to another one of those Chippendales shows with Lula," my mother said. "She almost got arrested last time when she got up onstage to dance with them."

"I don't think the Chippendales are in town."

"Well, you need to go find your grandmother and bring her home before she gets into trouble."

"No problem," I said. "I'll track her down."

Morelli looked at me with one eyebrow raised. "I don't like the sound of this."

"Lula is shooting her reality demo tonight, and I think Grandma has volunteered to be part of the production team. My mother said Grandma just got into a red car that looked like Lula's Firebird."

"Is that so bad?"

"They're doing a demo for *Naked and Afraid* . . . the Trenton version."

Morelli cracked a smile. "You're kidding. Who's going to be naked?"

"Lula and Randy Briggs."

"Whoa!"

I got my messenger bag from the kitchen, and Morelli followed me.

"I'll ride along with you," Morelli said.

"No way. You're a cop. You'd have to arrest Lula for being naked."

"Where are they shooting this?"

"Across town," I said. "Don't worry. I won't be long. I'll go get Grandma, bring her home, and be back in a jiffy."

I took the stairs and ran to my car. I wanted to get to Mill Street before they started filming. Not only didn't I want Grandma near Stark Street, I was afraid Grandma would be the second naked woman. There was minimal traffic, but I hit every light going across town. By the time I got to Mill Street I was white-knuckle on the steering wheel. I'd tried calling Lula, but she wasn't picking up.

It was a cloudless sky with a sliver of a moon. Not a lot of light on Mill. Streetlights had been shot out long ago, and most of the buildings were shuttered at night. There were rooming houses on the lower blocks, but eventually they gave way to commercial-use warehouse-type structures. Lula had said they'd be filming on the edge of the residential area. I found them on the third block. They were huddled beside a van. Lula's Firebird and a silver Honda Civic were also parked there. They were in front of a graffiti-spattered three-story building that had at one time been apartments but was now boarded up.

I parked in front of the Civic and walked back to the van. Howie was there with a handheld camera. A large woman with cornrows and braids halfway down her back stood next to Howie. She was wearing an apron with a lot of pockets.

When I got closer I saw that they were stuffed with makeup brushes and assorted cosmetics. One of the pockets held a large can of hairspray. Another pocket held a large nickel-plated semiautomatic. The gun caught the moonlight and sparkled like a piece of jewelry.

Grandma, wearing black Pilates pants, a black sweatshirt, and a fanny pack, was holding a flashlight and standing next to the makeup woman. The barrel of Grandma's .45 stuck out of one end of her fanny pack.

Lula and Briggs were naked. They were listening intently to Howie.

"This is the big opening scene," Howie said. "You're going to stand on the stoop of this apartment building, and you're going to look excited, anxious to start your adventure. Grandma's going to highlight you with the flashlight, and I'll pan in for a close-up."

"Excuse me," I said. "My mother sent me to get Grandma."

"Good thing you're here," Lula said. "Laurene didn't show up, and we need someone to work the clacker."

"What's a 'clacker'?"

Howie handed me a small chalkboard. "It's this thing," he said. "You write the number of the scene on it, and then you say 'Scene one, take one,' and you clack the wooden frame down."

"It's a real important job," Lula said. "It keeps everything in order."

"I'm not staying," I said. "I just came to get Grandma."

"I can't go," Grandma said. "I have to shine the flashlight during close-ups."

"We're losing time," Howie said. "Everybody on their marks."

Lula and Briggs went to the stoop.

"You gotta scooch down a little," Howie said to Lula. "I can't get both of you in the frame."

"How about if I just pick the little dwarf up?" Lula said.

"You touch me and I'll be on you like a badger ripping apart a rodent," Briggs said.

"That's good!" Howie yelled. "Already we got drama. Grandma, get the flashlight on them."

"We can't start yet," Grandma said. "Nobody did the clacky thing."

Everyone looked at me.

"Oh, for crying out loud," I said. "Scene one, take one." And I clacked the clacker.

Grandma rushed in with the flashlight, Howie shouted "Action!" and Lula and Briggs mugged for the camera.

"Cut!" Howie yelled. "Grandma, you're supposed to be shining the light on their faces. You're shining it on Randy's dick."

"It's one of them uncontrollable things," Grandma said. "I can't stop staring at it. I never get to see men's parts anymore."

Lula looked down at Briggs. "There's not much to see."

"Yeah," Grandma said. "I remember them as being bigger, but it's still hypnotic the way it's moving around."

"I'm excited, okay?" Briggs said. "This is what happens when I get excited."

"Now that everyone called attention to it, I find it distracting," Lula said. "I can't do my best emoting under these circumstances."

"Cripes," Howie said. "Now you have me staring at it."

"Maybe it would help if you put some powder on it so it's not so noticeable in the moonlight," Grandma said.

"It's not the moonlight," Briggs said. "It's the stupid flashlight."

The makeup woman rushed in and powdered Briggs's dick.

"Hold it still," she said. "I can't do nothing with it bobbing around."

"Listen up," Howie said. "We're all going to ignore the dick."

"I'm good with that," Grandma said. "I've seen enough."

"Here's the plan," Howie said. "After I get a close-up of Lula and Randy they're going to start on their way around the block. I'm going to follow them as they creep forward. When they move to the next block with the burned-out warehouse they get more wary. This is where they're on alert for urban dangers. I got a couple dangers planned out, but they're going to be a surprise."

"I don't like snakes and dead people," Lula said to Howie. "You better not have any of them in your plan."

I rubbed out "Take 1" on my chalkboard and wrote in "Take 2."

"Yada yada," I said. And I clacked the clacker.

"Action!" Howie yelled.

Lula and Briggs walked down the street. They were bare-assed and barefoot, and it was dark. Mostly the only thing visible was the little red light from the infrared camera following after them.

"I don't like this," Briggs said. "I can't see where I'm going, and I don't know what I'm stepping in. I just stepped in something squishy."

"Waa, waa, waa," Lula said. "You gotta get tough. We got a rocky road ahead of us. We gotta find our way out of this urban jungle."

"Get ready," Howie whispered to Grandma. "The first life-threatening danger is coming up. You have to get some light on their faces."

Lula and Briggs were creeping along. I saw movement in a doorway to Lula's left, and a woman threw a cat out at them. It bounced off Lula and landed on its feet.

Gurrhr, phffft, RAAAWR!

"What the freaking Sam Hill!" Lula said. "That sounds like a wild cat. It's one of them vicious killer wild cats."

Lula was jumping around, waving her arms in the air, not sure which direction to run. She stepped back, crashed into Briggs, and knocked him on his ass.

Grandma flashed the light on Lula and then on the cat. It was a fluffy white cat with a pink collar.

"It don't look like a killer cat," Grandma said. "It's a pussycat."

"Well, I hate cats. I'm allergic to cats," Lula said. "And anyways you never know which one of them is a killer."

She bent down to pick Briggs up, and she farted.

"Cut!" Howie yelled.

"What do you mean 'Cut'?" Lula asked. "You keep yelling 'Cut' and we're never gonna get done with this thing."

"You farted," Howie said.

"It's a human dilemma," Lula said. "You telling me you don't fart?"

"Not on camera," Howie said.

"Well, excuse me," Lula said. "It was my body releasing all my pent-up frustration. It's not like this here's a perfect filming experience for me. Every time I turn around, Short Stuff got his nose in my business. But I'm not acting like some prima donna and complaining about it."

"Maybe I don't like that your business is always in my face," Briggs said. "You ever think of that?"

A woman came out from the doorway and scooped up the cat.

"Good kitty," the woman said. "Good job." She looked over at Howie. "Will you need Snowball any more?"

"No," Howie said. "We're done with Snowball."

"I think I skinned my ass when Sasquatch knocked me over," Briggs said. "Someone look and see if I'm bleeding."

"Excuse me for knocking you over," Lula said, "but it was a frightening experience. Just like it was supposed to be. It was supposed to point out the dangers of moving around in a city where you got cats and shit. I bet we got some good film on that. Like I had fear going. That's genuine emotion."

Howie ran the footage back. "What I got is Grandma on camera saying it's a pussycat."

"Maybe we could put a sex spin on it," Lula said.

"It's Grandma," Howie said. "We're not supposed to see her or hear her. You ever hear or see any of the crew on the real show? No! It's gotta look like people are out there alone . . . naked and afraid."

"You told me to light their faces," Grandma said. "How am I supposed to do that if I don't move in?"

"You put the light on the cat," Howie said.

Grandma narrowed her eyes and stood her ground. "I thought people would want to see it."

"Could we get on with this?" Briggs said. "I'm getting cold. Between the cat fiasco and the night air I'm getting shrinkage."

"Gee, look at the time," I said. "I have to be running along with Grandma now. I promised my mom. And Morelli is waiting for me. We wouldn't want Morelli to come out here to get me. He might have to arrest the naked people."

"Who's going to work the flashlight if I leave?" Grandma asked.

"It's gonna be a problem. We got a skeleton crew," Howie said. "Give your flashlight to the makeup 'ho. I guess she can do it."

Grandma handed the flashlight over and followed me to my car.

"Sorry I had to ruin your night," I said to Grandma, "but Mom was worried about you."

"It's okay," Grandma said. "The flashlight was running out of batteries anyway. It was getting real dim. And if you ask me I don't think anybody back there knows what they're doing."

• • •

I dropped Grandma off and returned to Morelli.

"How'd it go?" he asked.

"Mission accomplished. Grandma's home safe and sound. Anything interesting happen here?"

"No, but if you didn't show up soon I was going to start without you."

"After seeing Lula and Briggs in the altogether I'm not feeling especially romantic."

"Cupcake, when you see what I've got to show you it'll all be forgotten."

"That sounds promising."

"The first thing we have to do is get your clothes off."

"Wait a minute," I said. "I thought you were going to show me what you've got."

"Even better," Morelli said.

He got rid of his shoes and socks, stripped off his shirt, and shucked his jeans. He was wearing blue plaid Calvin boxers. He cuddled me up close against him and let me look inside the Calvins. He was right. Poof! No more Briggs.

FOURTEEN

MORELLI WAS GONE by the time I made my way to the kitchen Friday morning. I was supposed to meet Ranger at eight o'clock. That meant I had to leave my apartment at seven-thirty at the latest. I wasn't sure how to dress so I'd chosen dressy black jeans, a blue V-neck sweater, a black blazer, and black Skechers. It was one of my go-to outfits when I worked for Rangeman. I gave Rex fresh water and a couple hamster crunchies. I looked at my watch. It was seven-thirty. I grabbed my messenger bag and a frozen waffle and took off.

Ranger was waiting in his Cayenne, toward the back of the Mo Morris Ice Cream lot. I parked beside him, and we both got out to talk.

"How's this going to happen?" I asked him. "I hear it's impossible to get a job here. No one ever quits."

"Morris is also interested in increasing security in his plant.

He's approached me to take a look. And he's very vocal about playing no part in the problems across town. He's agreed to let you come in undercover. All he asks is that he's kept in the loop. He wants to know if we find hard proof that someone in his organization has gone to the dark side."

"Does this mean I'm a double agent?"

"Think of yourself as an investigative operative."

I thought the title was kind of fancy for someone who was probably going to be wearing a shower cap.

"How do I get started?" I asked Ranger.

"Park your car up front in visitor parking. Use the front entrance and ask at the reception desk for Vicky. She'll be your inside contact. You'll work the line today. Morris runs his plant six days a week, so Vicky will find a job for you tomorrow as well."

"Did you ever find out who told Bogart about me and got me kicked out of the plant?"

"It was one of the women on the line. You went to school with her daughter and she knew you worked as a bounty hunter. She thought you were in there looking for a skip. Bogart was never comfortable with an undercover operative and used it as an excuse to get rid of you. Things should be different here. Morris was in favor of putting someone in place to look around."

His watch buzzed, and he glanced at the message.

"I have to go," Ranger said. "I'll be in touch."

He gave me a quick kiss and took off.

I licked my lips. I really was going to have to stop the

Ranger kissing. Maybe tomorrow. Maybe next week. I got back into my car, drove to the front of the building, and parked in visitor parking.

The front of Morris's plant was nicely landscaped with flower beds and shrubs. The grass was green and perfect. I looked more closely and saw that it was artificial. Fake grass, fake flowers, fake shrubs. I liked it. It gave the building a theme park quality.

I pushed through the large glass door into the lobby and went to the desk. Everything was bright and colorful in the lobby. Orange couches, white tile floor, lamps that looked like six-foot ice cream cones. And an old-fashioned ice cream pushcart filled with ice cream cups that were free for the taking. The Mo Morris theme was written in large red letters across one of the walls. "Our Ice Cream Is Mo Better!"

There was a young man behind the desk. He was dressed in a white ice cream vendor uniform. I told him I was there to see Vicky, and moments later Vicky appeared. Vicky was also wearing the white ice cream vendor uniform. I followed her down a hall to the women's locker room. She assigned a locker to me and gave me the key.

"I understand you have experience with the cup dropper and filler," she said, "so I thought we'd start you there. That way you can look around without the pressure of learning a new job."

I felt my eyes glaze over at the thought of the cup dropper and filler. I nodded and attempted a smile.

"Oh boy," I said. "The cup dropper and filler."

"Of course, everyone on the floor wears a sanitary uniform," Vicky said. "You'll find one in your locker. Once you're suited up just go through the door labeled 'Yummytown.' It opens to the manufacturing area. I'll be waiting on the other side."

The Mo Morris uniform was almost identical to the Bogart uniform, but it was orange. The slogan printed in black over the door to Yummytown said "Orange you happy to be working in an ice cream factory!"

If I opened the door and saw Oompa-Loompas working the line I was going to run like hell and never come back.

I peeked out and saw that it looked a lot like the Bogart factory. One large warehouse-type room with a lot going on. No Oompa-Loompas in sight. Vicky led me to the cup dropper and filler machine and said she'd be back at ten so I could take a break.

After an hour of looking at the cups going by I found myself dozing off on my feet. I jumped around a little and I sang the Pharrell Williams "Happy" song. Vicky came over and asked if I was okay because she'd noticed I was clapping my hands and dancing. I told her I was being happy, and she went away.

Three cups came down crooked. I fixed them and realized that they were all coming down crooked. I couldn't set them right fast enough, and down the line the ice cream was plopping onto the side of the cup and oozing over onto the conveyor belt and onto the floor. I looked for the red button that stopped the line and called the foreman, but there was no red button. There were a bunch of switches and a green button.

"Hey!" I yelled. "Yoo-hoo! Somebody?"

No one could hear me over the machinery. I held my breath and flipped the first switch. The line sped up. Cups were coming down one after another and moving along the belt at warp-speed. Ice cream was flying all over the place. The floor was inches deep in ice cream.

A large woman rushed over, threw a switch on the side of the conveyor belt, and everything came to a grinding halt.

"What on earth?" she asked.

"There's no big red button," I said.

A man hurried over. He was dressed in one of the white vendor uniforms, and he had a medal pinned to his jacket. He slipped on the ice cream and went down to one knee. He got up and I saw that the medal said "Big Shot." I guess that meant he was a boss of some sort.

"No red button," I said to him.

He looked confused.

"She keeps saying that," the woman said. "She keeps saying there's no red button."

Vicky ran in. "She's new," Vicky said. "My bad. I assumed she knew how to run the machine."

"There's no big red button," I said to Vicky.

"No problem," Vicky said. "I was coming to get you anyway. There's a man here to see you."

Ranger was waiting for me in the break room.

"Babe," he said, his attention focusing on the orange shower cap.

"If you so much as crack a smile I'm going to hit you."

"I have good news and bad news. The good news is that you can lose the orange after today. You're going back to Bogart."

"Gee, I just got here."

"Yeah, I know you're broken up about leaving, but we have a situation across town. The bad news is that the loading dock foreman was found dead in the freezer this morning."

I felt myself go into suspended animation for a beat. Disbelief that another Bogart employee was frozen. A sense of dread that it was true and that I knew the man.

"Gus?" I asked.

"Yes. You worked with him yesterday."

There was still disbelief. "How did it happen?"

"The ME didn't see any sign of trauma. It looks like Gus got locked in and froze to death."

"That's impossible. The freezer door always opens from the inside."

"Someone tampered with the lock. There's no cell reception in the freezer, but Gus left a message on his phone. He said he went in to do inventory and couldn't get out. The time on the phone was five-ten."

My heart was beating hard. It could have been me! "I was in and out of that freezer all morning. The door was working perfectly."

"It was also working perfectly for most of the afternoon. A truck came in at one o'clock, and it took three hours to load it. No one had any problems with the door."

"No one noticed that Gus was missing?"

"Butchy clocked out at four-thirty P.M. The Jolly clown clocked out at seven P.M. He said he tried to put his unsold ice cream back in the freezer but the number code wouldn't work, so he used a small auxiliary freezer in the storeroom."

"He didn't think it was odd that he couldn't get into the freezer?"

"He thought it was inconvenient but not odd. He said it wasn't the first time he couldn't get into the freezer. He said Gus was an idiot, and Bogart was a cheap bastard who never fixed anything. And he wondered who he should see to apply for the foreman job."

"He's been trying to get out of the clown suit for years."

"Not going to happen. I asked Bogart about the denied requests to transfer. It's company policy straight from Bogart not to move people around. No exceptions. He hires from the outside for new jobs or he promotes within departments. The clown is a department of one. He isn't going anywhere."

"What about Gus's family?"

"He lived alone. Divorced. Two kids that live out of state."

"I hate this," I said. "It's ugly and horrible and sad. And I'm in the middle of it. And I can't even eat a Bogart Bar and feel happy."

"Babe," Ranger said.

I blew out a sigh. "Criminy."

Ranger wrapped his arms around me and held me close. "It's what we do. We wade in and try to make things a little more safe."

"I know, but I'm having a shortage of happy."

"I could fix that."

"Your fix would create a whole other set of problems for me." I stepped away. "So how do I fit in across town?"

"Bogart wants you back. He's scared. This is the second employee death. And it looks like another murder."

"I don't see where I'm doing anything helpful. I'm not good at the spy thing. I hardly get to talk to anyone."

"Keep your eyes open. You're getting jobs that don't require a lot of concentration. Look around. Look for things that don't make sense. An employee with too much money. Someone who's out of place. Someone who has all the right access to the trucks, the freezer, the storeroom."

"That would be everyone. Bogart runs a very loosey-goosey operation. Everyone has access to everything."

"I have the list of new hires," Ranger said. "There are only three in the appropriate time period."

I looked at the list. Gina Slater was hired and placed on the line six months ago. Maureen Gooley joined the housekeeping crew at about the same time. William ("Butchy") Boone was placed on the loading dock a little over a year ago.

"I'd like to see more on Boone," I said to Ranger.

"I'll have a full report sent to you. Tomorrow Bogart's plant production line is closed. CSI will be crawling all over it. The only one working will be the Jolly Bogart clown. You can ride along with him."

I slid a glance at the door to the plant. "It's sort of a mess in there. One of the machines malfunctioned."

"That would explain the ice cream all over your orangeness."

I looked down at myself. "There was no big red button."

"Babe."

. . .

I ditched the orange suit and explained to Vicky that I'd been reassigned. She gave me a pint of ice cream and said everyone would miss me and they were sorry I couldn't stay longer. She made an admirable effort, but underneath it all I knew she was relieved to see me go. I mean, really, who wouldn't be?

I took my ice cream to my car, chugged out of the Mo Morris Ice Cream parking lot, and drove to the office.

"I thought you were at Mo Morris today," Lula said when I walked through the door.

"It didn't work out, but I got some ice cream."

"That's my kind of job," Lula said. "Work a couple hours and get some ice cream. What flavor?"

"Vanilla."

"I like vanilla," Lula said.

I got spoons for Lula, Connie, and me, and we finished off the ice cream.

"How'd it go last night?" I asked Lula.

"It went pretty good. There were a couple things that didn't go exactly right . . . like when we were supposed to find shelter for the night and we picked a abandoned building and Randy got bit by a rat."

"Omigod!"

"At least we think it was a rat. It was dark, and we couldn't get a good look at it. It was one of them bite-and-run things. It didn't sound big enough to be a crackhead."

"Is Randy okay?"

"Yeah, he was all hysterical for a while, but he calmed down after we took him to the clinic and got him a shot."

"Anything else go wrong?"

"While we were making our way to our final destination and going around the block someone stole Howie's van. We should have seen that one coming. It wasn't as bad as it might have been on account of it turns out Howie stole it in the first place. It's just that it had all our clothes in it."

"How'd you get home?"

"We called a Uber car but it wouldn't let us in naked, so me and the makeup 'ho walked over to Stark Street, and the makeup 'ho traded some services for a ride."

"Good thing you had a makeup 'ho on the team," Connie said.

"Truly," Lula said. "Otherwise I might have had to come out of retirement."

"But you got your demo film, right?" I asked.

"Yeah. Howie is editing it for us and then we'll send it in. We got some real good stuff on it. Those *Naked and Afraid* people would be nuts not to sign Randy and me up for their show, but just in case they don't like this reel I got a backup idea. Naked bungee jumping. I figure we could go off the bridge over the Delaware. The one that says 'Trenton Makes, and the World Takes.'"

Connie and I were mouths open, eyes glazed. I actually felt my mind go numb for a beat.

"I bet nobody's sent them a demo for naked bungee jumping," Lula said.

My cellphone buzzed with a text message. It was from Sharelle. *Just saw Winkle having lunch in Fat Dave's.*

"Saddle up," I said to Lula. "Eugene Winkle is in Fat Dave's."

"And?" Lula said.

"And we're going to bring him in."

"How are you gonna do that? You got an elephant gun? You got Ranger in the trunk of your car?"

"I have you. I'm going to send you into Fat Dave's and you're going to charm Winkle."

"That might not be a bad idea," Lula said. "I am charming. I could charm the ass off him."

"Exactly. And then we convince him that once we get him rebonded he's going to have a really good time."

"He might even know my reputation," Lula said. "I was known for doing quality work back in the day. Of course, we aren't really going to show him a good time. Unless he got some hot qualities. Then I might think about it."

FIFTEEN

FAT DAVE'S IS a hamburger joint on the second block of Stark. It's dark and dingy and has grease running down the walls. It also makes the best burgers in Trenton.

I was on Stark, looking for a parking place, hoping I wasn't too late to catch Winkle.

"You know the secret to Fat Dave's burgers?" Lula said. "It's duck fat. Not many people know that on account of it's a secret. He slicks his griddle up with duck fat, and it imparts that excellent gamey taste. And then he uses extra salt. Salt brings out the flavor of shit."

I found a parking place on the third block, and Lula and I walked back to Fat Dave's. We looked in through the large plate glass window and saw that Winkle was still there. We could tell by his gargantuan body overflowing the counter stool.

"You go in first," I said. "You do your thing, and then I'll come in and close the deal."

Lula sashayed in and sat next to Winkle. I gave her five minutes, and then I went in and joined them. I had plasti-cuffs stuffed into my jeans waistband, hidden by my sweatshirt, and a canister of pepper spray in my sweatshirt pocket.

"Well, look who's here," Lula said. "It's my friend Stephanie."

Winkle gave a sound that was like a bull snorting. He had an empty plate in front of him, and there was ketchup everywhere. He was working on a basket of French fries.

"This is my new friend Eugene Winkle," Lula said to me.

Eugene gave another snort and shoved French fries into his mouth.

"Is Eugene ready to party?" I asked Lula.

"Eugene's thinking about it," Lula said. "He's gotta finish his fries first."

"Did you tell Eugene about the deal?"

Eugene looked at me. "What deal?"

"Lula likes handcuffs."

"Yeah," Lula said. "I'm thinking about going into dominatrixing. I like to give a little and then I like to get a little."

"Oh yeah?" he said. "What do you like to get?"

"I'm pretty much into spanking," Lula said. "Are you any good at that?"

"Do I have to get spanked first?"

"Yeah."

"And then I get to spank you?"

"Yeah."

He shoved a wad of French fries into his mouth. "Let's go."

"First we have to cuff you," I said.

He threw a twenty down on the counter and held his hands out. "Do it. This is going to be good. I'm going to spank you hard when it's my turn."

"I like that," Lula said. "Nothing I like better than a hard spanker." She looked over at me. "Make sure you pull those plasti-cuffs real tight."

I had them around Winkle's wrist, and I went for a second. "I'm doing double."

"What are you going to use?" he wanted to know. "Are you going to use a switch or a paddle?"

I looked at Lula and read her mind. She was thinking she would use a couple thousand volts of electricity.

We walked Winkle to my car and secured him into the backseat. He had his hands double cuffed behind his back. Lula was in the front seat with her hand wrapped around the stun gun in her purse. I had one eye on the road and one eye on Winkle in my rearview mirror. If he somehow managed to get out of the cuffs I was going to stop the car, jump out, and run like hell.

"Where are we going?" he asked.

"I got a place on Clinton Street," Lula said.

"I don't like Clinton Street," Winkle said. "That's where the police station is. Hey, wait a minute . . ."

"Drive faster," Lula said to me. "A lot faster."

"I think you tricked me," Winkle said. "You don't want to get spanked. I bet you're cops. I don't like this. I don't like being tricked."

Lula reached over the seat with her stun gun and Winkle

head-butted her. Lula knocked against me, I jumped the curb, and crashed into a streetlight. By the time I fought my way free of the airbag, Winkle had disappeared.

Lula and I got out and looked at my car. The front was smushed in where it'd hit the pole.

"It's not so bad," Lula said. "The wheels look okay. And so far as I can see it's not leaking anything. You probably could drive it."

I got behind the wheel, backed off the sidewalk, and slowly drove away.

"Just like new," Lula said, "except for that big dent in the front and the mold smell coming from the backseat."

"Winkle has a high bond. If I could bring him in I might be able to buy a car."

"I could help you," Lula said. "I'm good at picking out cars. And I got connections."

"Winkle is out here somewhere," I said. "Eventually he'll go home. I'm going to ride around a little and then stake out his house."

"I don't think I can charm him again," Lula said. "I got a headache. I bet I got a big bump on my forehead."

"If we find him we won't fool around. We'll rush him, and stun him right away. After we get him trussed up like a Sunday goose I'll call for help transporting him."

"Remember how you told me it was illegal to stun gun someone?"

"Extenuating circumstances," I said. "And we're going to lie about doing it."

"You bet your ass," Lula said.

I was two blocks from the police station. A low-income residential neighborhood sat between Winkle's Stark Street apartment and me. Streets followed no logical pattern, and it was easy to get lost in the maze of modest two-story houses that were smashed together on tiny lots.

"He had to cut through this mess of houses," Lula said. "You need to turn here."

After ten minutes I was completely confused.

"We're going around in a circle," Lula said. "I keep seeing the same houses."

"I don't know how to get out of here. It doesn't matter if I turn left or right, I still get back to here."

"You need to pull your map up." Lula looked at my dashboard. "Hold on here. You haven't got a map. You haven't got no screen at all. How old is this car?"

I stopped at a cross street. "You should be able to get a map on your smartphone."

"Okay, I have us on the map. We're the little red dot. Looks to me that you turn right at the next street and go as far as you can until you come to a T intersection."

I turned right at the corner, and half a block away it looked like King Kong was lumbering down the street.

"That's Winkle!" Lula shouted. "Run him over."

"I'm not going to run him over. I'm going to drive up behind him. We'll jump out of the car and take him by surprise."

"How about you?" Lula asked. "Do you have a stun gun with you?"

"It's in my messenger bag."

She got my stun gun out of my messenger bag and handed it over to me.

"Power up," Lula said.

Winkle had freed himself from the plasti-cuffs and was ferociously huffing along, eyes focused forward. I jerked to a stop about twenty feet behind him. Lula and I jumped out and ran. I reached him first and tagged him with my stun gun. He turned and looked at me. Surprised.

"What the . . ." he said.

Lula pressed the prongs of her stun gun against Winkle's arm. *Zzzzzt zzzt!*

"That stings," Winkle said. "Stop it."

He grabbed the stun gun from Lula and threw it across the road.

"Hey, you big moron," Lula said. "That's an expensive stun gun. It's not like they grow on trees."

Winkle backhanded her and knocked her off her feet. I shoved my stun gun into my sweatshirt pocket and pulled out the pepper spray.

"Hey!" I said to Winkle.

He turned to look at me, and I sprayed him in the face at close range. I jumped back away from the toxic cloud, catching a small amount of spray. Uncomfortable but not incapacitating.

"*Yow!*" Winkle yelled, hands to his face, rubbing his eyes, making it worse.

He staggered back off the curb, lost his balance, fell into the street, and started rolling around. Lula and I were standing back, not sure what to do with him. Unless she shot him or I ran over him, I couldn't see any way to get the plasti-cuffs on him.

A black Rangeman SUV pulled up beside us, and Hal got out. Hal was a good guy who looked a little like a stegosaurus. He was one of Ranger's most competent men unless he saw blood. Hal tended to faint at the sight of blood.

"What have we got here?" Hal asked.

"He's FTA," I said. "I gave him some pepper spray, but I can't get him cuffed."

"No prob," Hal said.

Hal got cuffs and shackles from his SUV and brought them to Winkle, who had managed to get to his feet and was bellowing like an enraged bull gone nuts.

Hal kicked Winkle's feet out from under him and had him hog-tied in fifteen seconds. Winkle's eyes were red and watering, and he was covered in snot. Hal hoisted him to his feet and held him at arm's length.

"Do you want me to take him in for you?" Hal asked.

"Yes," I said. "That would be great. Thank you. We'll follow you and take care of the paperwork."

"Lucky us that you came along," Lula said.

Hal jerked Winkle over to the Rangeman SUV, trundled him into the back, and secured the ankle shackles to iron rings bolted onto the SUV's floor.

"The control room saw that you kept going around in circles and asked me to check on you," Hal said. "I was doing a patrol in the neighborhood anyway."

. . .

We stopped at Cluck-in-a-Bucket on the way back to the office. I got a Hot and Crunchy Clucky Meal and Lula got a Supersized Bucket of Cluck with the Works. The Works included mashed potatoes and gravy, biscuits, coleslaw, fried okra, and an apple turnover.

"I feel much better now that I have a good meal inside me," Lula said. "That whole Winkle thing was a depressing experience." She swiveled in the booth and looked back up at the menu that was over the counter. "I might need some ice cream as a palate cleanser."

She got a giant cup of soft serve, and we headed out.

"I still got a headache, I chipped some of my nail varnish, and I think I got a bruise on my derriere," Lula said. "I'm leaving early today."

"Are you okay? Do you need a ride home?"

"I'm not going home. I'm going to get my nail varnish repaired."

I parked in front of the bail bonds office, told Lula I'd see her on Monday, and took my body receipt in to Connie.

"I just got off the phone with Carolyn Freeda," Connie said. "Her son Mickey is an EMT, and he was at the ice cream plant this morning. Did you know another guy got frozen?"

"Ranger told me. The man's name was Gus. He was the foreman on the loading dock. I worked for him yesterday."

"The whole thing gives me goose bumps. I have an uncle who whacks people for a living, so I'm not exactly squeamish about murder, but there's something really disturbing about these ice cream killings."

"Did Carolyn have any information on how it happened?"

"Just that the door lock had been jammed somehow. One of the people on the line tried to get into the freezer this morning, and the code wouldn't work. I guess eventually they forced the door open somehow, and that's when they found this poor guy frozen solid. Mickey was one of the first responders. He said there was nothing anyone could do."

I couldn't help grimacing when I asked the question. "Did Mickey say if the man was covered in chocolate and nuts?"

"That was the first question I asked too," Connie said. "No. No chocolate or nuts. Just frozen."

Okay, I felt a little better about it all. It was sad that Gus got frozen, but at least he wasn't turned into a Bogart Bar.

"If I was working at that ice cream factory, I'd quit," Connie said. "There's a homicidal lunatic running around loose. And I for sure wouldn't go near the freezer."

I was going to do exactly the opposite. I was showing up for work at the ice creamery tomorrow, and I'd probably be in and out of the freezer. And I was doing it because that's the way it is. . . . Ranger and I wade in and try to make things a little more safe. Morelli did that too. Not to mention that I was pissed off at the whole Bogart Bar issue.

"Lula went home with a headache and a chipped nail," I said to Connie. "I'm taking off too. I have some homework to do."

I got my check from Connie, and I drove my dented piece

of junk back to my apartment building. I said hello to Rex, got a beer from the fridge, powered up my MacBook Air, and downloaded Ranger's report on Butchy.

William Boone, better known as Butchy, was twenty-two years old. He was born and raised in Barre, Vermont. His mother was a cashier in a supermarket. His father was an unemployed auto mechanic. Butchy graduated from high school and disappeared for three years. Interviews with relatives suggested he was in Nashville, trying to break into the music industry. He resurfaced in Trenton and got a job at Bogart Ice Cream. He had no arrest record. His credit score was nonexistent. He bought his F-450 six months ago and he'd paid cash. It was estimated that with the custom additions the truck was worth in the vicinity of $60,000. He was making $20 an hour at the ice cream plant. Clearly Butchy had supplemental income. He was high on my list of suspected homicidal lunatics. He had all the right access. He had unexplained money. And it was hard to believe he was as stupid as he seemed . . . because he seemed unbelievably stupid.

According to Butchy's employment file and Ranger's research, Butchy lived on the edge of the Burg. He was renting a house on King Street. I couldn't place its exact location, but I knew the area. It was typical Burg. Mostly blue-collar. Small cottage-type houses on tiny lots.

It was Friday night, and I traditionally had dinner with my parents. Morelli had a standing invitation to join us, but he usually begged off. I couldn't blame him. At some point during the dinner the inevitable question of marriage would arise. I had no good answer.

My mother called at four-thirty. "Is Joseph coming to dinner?" she asked.

"I'm pretty sure he has to work," I said. "I think it's only going to be me."

"It's just as well. Your grandmother invited some stranger. She said she met him at Bertha Webster's viewing, and he might be the man of her dreams."

Okay, I know this sort of thing drives my mother nuts. She worries about my grandmother. I don't worry about Grandma so much as I do about the rest of the world. It seems to me Grandma is livin' la vida loca. Truth is, I'm a little jealous. It looks to me like she's having more fun than I am.

SIXTEEN

I LEFT MY apartment at five o'clock and drove to the Burg. I wound around the jumble of streets and finally found King. Butchy's place was a little box of a house in the middle of a block. One floor. Probably two bedrooms and one bath. Detached single-car garage. It wasn't a total shambles, but it wasn't in immaculate condition either. The paint was peeling around the windows. The postage stamp front yard was clean but barren. No shrubs, flowers, gnomes, or plaster statues of the Virgin Mary. Butchy's truck was in the driveway.

I stared at the truck for a bunch of beats. It was chilling to think that it might belong to a killer. Even more creepy that the killer might be Butchy. Butchy wasn't on my radar when I was working the loading dock, but he was a big blip on the screen now.

I slowly cruised down the street and made my way to my parents' house. I parked in their driveway because the front of my car was less visible there than it would be at the curb. My mother was at the door with my grandmother when I stepped onto the porch.

"What happened to your car?" my mother wanted to know.

"It got a little smushed," I said. "It doesn't matter. I'm getting a new one."

"What kind are you going to get?" Grandma asked. "Are you going to get a Corvette? I think you should get one like Ranger. His cars are hot."

"I haven't thought about it," I said. "I'll have to see what I can afford."

A chopper slowly rumbled down the street and parked in front of my parents' house. The rider was in full black leather with a long gray ponytail sticking out from under a black Darth Vader helmet.

"There's my honey," Grandma said.

My mother went pale.

"He could be okay," I said to my mother. "He's probably a lawyer."

"Nope," Grandma said. "He tends bar at Kranski's in north Trenton. His name's Bertie. And he's got tattoos all over the place."

Bertie took his helmet off, hooked it onto the back of his bike, and walked toward us.

"He reminds me of someone," my mother said.

"Willie Nelson," I told her. "But I think he's older than Willie. Willie's only in his eighties."

"Bertie isn't that old," Grandma said. "It's that the smoke in the bar's aged him. He's still a handsome devil, though. Wait until you see him up close. He's got bedroom eyes. The one bedroom eye you can't see so much on account of it's behind the cataract, but the other one is a beaut."

We all said hello to Bertie and moved inside to the living room where my father was in his favorite chair, watching television.

"This is my honey, Bertie," Grandma said to my father.

My father looked over at Bertie. "Are you going to marry her?" my father asked.

"Not tonight," Bertie said.

My father gave up a sigh and turned back to the television.

"Dinner is ready to go on the table," my mother said. "We have pot roast."

We all shuffled into the dining room and took a seat. I helped my mother with the pot roast, potatoes, green beans, gravy, and red cabbage. There was red wine, beer, and a pitcher of water on the table.

"It's too bad Joseph couldn't come to dinner tonight," Grandma said. "We would all be couples." She turned to Bertie. "Joseph is Stephanie's boyfriend. He's a homicide detective."

"That's got to be a pretty interesting job in Trenton these days," Bertie said. "Was he assigned to the Bogart Bar murder?"

I shook my head, no. "He wasn't working that night," I said.

"Stephanie was there," Grandma said. "She saw the whole thing. The Bogart Bar man fell out of the freezer truck, right at her feet."

Bertie looked impressed. "No kidding! How did you manage that?"

"I was involved in a car accident," I said. "It was a coincidence."

My father was at the head of the table, barely tolerating the conversation, waiting for the food to be passed to him. My mother always put the meat platter directly in front of him, but the rest of the food was distributed along the length of the table.

"Potatoes," he barked, leaning forward, knife in one hand, fork in the other.

Everyone jumped in their seat, and Grandma handed him the potatoes.

"I heard another Bogart worker got frozen," Grandma said. "And it doesn't look like they have any suspects."

"It's obvious to me," Bertie said. "They should talk to Kenny Morris."

"Who's Kenny Morris?" I asked him.

"He's Mo's kid," Bertie said. "He's a regular at the bar where I work. He's got a real grudge against Bogart. Gets a snootful and all he can talk about is how he hates Bogart and wants to ruin him."

"Why does he hate Bogart?"

"He had a thing for Bogart's daughter. Asked her to marry him and she turned him down. He blamed it on her father. He said her father wouldn't have her involved with a Morris."

"Gravy," my father said.

Grandma passed him the gravy.

"That's so sad," Grandma said. "It's just like Romeo and Juliet, but instead of Romeo and Juliet dying, Romeo turns some people into Popsicles."

"It seems like a stretch," I said. "Did he ever say anything that would make you think he killed the two Bogart men?"

"Not directly," Bertie said, "but he hated Bogart Bars. He said they were his father's idea, and Bogart stole it. And he said he had a plan to get even. He said that a lot. Personally, I think he turned that Bogart worker into a Bogart Bar to torture old Harry. And I think one day it's going to be Harry Bogart who gets dipped in chocolate and nuts."

"You should be a detective," Grandma said to Bertie. "You have this all figured out."

"People talk to bartenders and barbers," Bertie said. "Occupational hazard."

"What about the man who was frozen today?" I said. "He wasn't turned into a Bogart Bar."

"Yep," Bertie said. "That presents a dilemma."

"You'll have to ask Kenny about it when you see him next," Grandma said.

My experience is that drunks aren't especially reliable. Fact and fiction tend to intermingle, stories get inflated, emotions run amok. So I wasn't going to immediately decide Kenny Morris was a killer. I wasn't going to dismiss it either.

"How often does he come into the bar?" I asked Bertie.

"Couple times a week. Always on Saturday night. Guess that's a low point in his week since he's not seeing the Bogart girl."

Bertie had his plate heaping with food, and he poured gravy over everything.

"This gravy rocks," Bertie said.

"The trick to good gravy is that you have to burn the meat," Grandma said. "Only on the bottom, of course. That way you get the nice dark color."

"I was married once," Bertie said. "Seems like that marriage went on forever. When you have kids you stick it out even if it makes you sick."

"Did it make you sick?" Grandma asked.

"Gave me an ulcer. She was always talking, talking, talking."

"I don't talk all that much," Grandma said. "Mostly I watch television."

"And she couldn't cook," Bertie said. "Couldn't make gravy. Couldn't come close to this gravy."

"I bet her gravy had lumps," Grandma said.

"Yeah," Bertie said. "It had big, ugly lumps. Disgusting."

My father had his head up. The conversation was starting to interest him.

"Edna is a great cook," he said. "Some man is going to be lucky to get her. She makes French toast."

"It's one of my specialties," Grandma said. "I use real vanilla and a touch of nutmeg."

"See, that shows you take pride in your work," Bertie said. "You add that extra touch of nutmeg. I'm like that when I tend bar. Every drink is special. Like when I make a mojito I use a mortar and pestle so I get the mint leaves just right."

"Gives me goose bumps when you talk about it," Grandma said.

"Me too," my father said. "You want more pot roast, Bertie?" He looked down the table at my mother. "Maybe you need to reheat the gravy for Bertie."

Grandma jumped up. "I'll do it. I'm real good at reheating."

"So, Bertie," my father said. "It sounds like you have a real job and everything. I bet you even have a house."

"The wife got the house," Bertie said. "I have an apartment over the bar."

"I bet it's a nice apartment," my father said.

Bertie forked into his pot roast. "Suits me. I don't have far to go after work. When I want to take off there's no maintenance to worry about."

Grandma brought the gravy to the table. "That's important, because Bertie's a free spirit, like me."

"Yep," Bertie said. "That's why Edna and I get along. We understand each other. We're a couple rollin' stones."

We all looked over at Grandma. She didn't usually roll very far. Mostly to the bakery and the funeral home.

"Bertie and I are thinking about taking a vacation on his chopper," Grandma said. "We might go to Mexico."

"That's a long way to go on a chopper," I said. "Have you ever ridden on the chopper?"

"No," Grandma said, "but we're going out tonight after dinner. Bertie's going to take me for a ride."

"You're going to love it," Bertie said. "There's nothing like it."

My mother looked into her glass. It was empty. "I might need more iced tea," she said.

. . .

We all stood on my parents' small front porch and watched Grandma mount the chopper in her powder blue polyester pantsuit and white tennies. She put a big black helmet on and wrapped her arms around Bertie.

"Woohoo!" Grandma said. "Here we go."

"She's going to die," my mother said.

My father looked hopeful.

Bertie fired up the bike, and it gave a lurch and rolled down the street.

"She'll be fine," I said to my mom. I didn't totally believe it, but it seemed like the thing to say.

"You should follow her," my mother said.

"I'll keep my eyes open for them," I told her, taking my car keys out of my messenger bag.

It was true that I would watch for them, but I wouldn't follow them. They were out of sight, and I had no idea where they were going. And I had plans of my own. I wanted to ride by Butchy's house one more time.

I had my usual bag of leftovers in the crook of my arm and my messenger bag hanging from my shoulder. I marched to my car and settled myself behind the wheel. So far so good. No one made a parting comment on the dent. I waved to my parents as I backed out of the driveway. My father was smiling

146

and shaking his head. My mother was grim-faced, lips pressed tight together. I sighed and drove away.

It was twilight when I got back to King Street. Not yet dark enough to creep around Butchy's house and peek in his windows. I parked on the opposite side of the street, two houses down, and waited. Butchy's truck was still in his driveway. Lights were on in the front room. A light went on in another room toward the back of the house, and I guessed Butchy had gone to the kitchen. All the other houses on the street were lit too. Traffic was minimal. Every driveway had a car parked in it. Garages in the Burg were for the most part used to store items that should have been thrown away ten years ago. Cars with dead batteries and flat tires, rusted bicycles, the sofa the dog chewed up and the cat peed on. Plus there were lawn mowers, snow shovels, Costco economy packs of bottled water and paper products, hoses and sprinklers, and cases of motor oil.

I checked in with Morelli. "What's up?"

"I couldn't get the game in on your television, so Bob and I are at my house. Did your mom pack a leftovers bag for me?"

"Pot roast for sandwiches, Italian bread from the bakery, half a chocolate cake, plus some stuff in the bottom of the bag. I think she threw in some apples."

"You're coming over, right?"

"Right. Give me a half hour."

I waited ten more minutes, left my car, and walked to Butchy's house. There were two windows on the driveway side, which was now in deep shadow, so I walked toward them. Probably bedroom windows. I stood on tiptoes and peeked in. The shades weren't drawn, but the room was dark and I couldn't see much. I went to the garage and tested the door. Locked. I circled around to the window on the side. It had security bars on it, and the glass had been painted black.

I had an instant image of a large freezer sitting inside surrounded by empty jugs of chocolate syrup and chopped nuts.

I moved on to the back of the house, crept quietly onto the back stoop, and looked in the back-door window at the kitchen. Part of the room was given over to an eating area with a table and four chairs. There was a large cardboard box on the table. I couldn't see the contents. There were a couple dishes and some glasses in the dish drain by the sink. Dated electric stove and refrigerator freezer. Small toaster oven on the counter. A roll of paper towels. A loaf of supermarket bread, a jar of peanut butter, and an open package of Chips Ahoy! cookies were lined up next to the paper towels. I thought to myself that Butchy kept a Spartan kitchen, and then I realized it looked a lot like mine. This dragged another sigh out of me.

I left the back of the house and carefully avoided the side window in the front room. Butchy was watching television. I didn't want him catching movement on the other side of the glass.

Ten minutes later I parked in front of Morelli's house. Bob rushed at me when I walked in and knocked me against the wall. I held the food bag over my head. Morelli gave me a fast kiss and took the bag off my hands.

"You don't usually stay this long at your parents'," he said, taking the bag to the kitchen.

"A guy that I worked with on the Bogart loading dock rents a house in the Burg. I wanted to look around a little."

Morelli set the cake on the counter and put the rest of the bag in the fridge. "And? Did you look around?"

"Yes. He doesn't make a lot of money, but he has an expensive truck. He parks it in the driveway, not in the garage, and the garage is locked with the window barred and painted black."

"You're talking about half the Burg. None of that is criminally unusual."

I got two forks, and we attacked the cake.

"I guess that's true, but he feels off," I said. "He's too dumb. And he's too much in the right place. And he has unexplained money."

"He could be in debt up to his eyeballs."

"I ran him through the system. He's debt free."

"So you think he's doing wet work? Connie's uncle won't be happy to learn there's a competitor."

I carved out a piece with maximum frosting. "I think it would be more like industrial sabotage."

"I'll pass this along. In the meantime I want you to promise me you'll keep your distance."

"Sure," I said.

Morelli looked at me. "That's a fib, isn't it?"

"Pretty much." I watched him shoveling in cake. "Aren't you supposed to be avoiding gluten?"

"I'm taking probiotics, and I'm better as long as I don't get carried away."

"What about your mom's lasagna?"

"If my mother makes it, the gluten doesn't count."

"And what about this cake?"

"Your mom made it. Close enough."

I didn't want to burst his bubble, but I didn't think he was close enough at all. It seemed to me that being engaged to be engaged wouldn't count for much in the gluten protection plan.

"Okay, so if it wasn't Butchy, who do you think killed the two Bogart men?" I asked him.

"I don't know, but I think this killer is psycho. Killing someone and running away from the crime is normal. Killing someone and trying to hide the crime is normal. Killing someone and making him into a Bogart Bar isn't normal."

"He only did that once."

"Yeah," Morelli said. "He probably ran out of chocolate."

SEVENTEEN

IT WAS SATURDAY, and I woke up next to Morelli. This was a luxury that didn't often happen. Even when he didn't have to be at an early briefing, he was still up before the sun. He made coffee. He showered. He walked Bob. He surfed the news. This morning he was in bed and the sun was outside, shining without him. That meant Morelli wanted something.

"This is nice," I said. "You're usually long gone by the time I wake up."

"I'm trying something different."

I looked over at the bedside clock. It was eight o'clock, and I didn't have to be at the ice cream plant until ten-thirty. I had time for something different.

"I'm game," I told him, snuggling closer. "What did you have in mind?"

"Originally I was going to treat you to brunch, but I've

been waiting for three hours and I think we might be looking at a fast cup of coffee."

. . .

I rushed into my apartment at ten o'clock. I said good morning to Rex, gave him fresh water, and filled his cup with hamster food. I changed into clean clothes and was back in my junker car twenty minutes later.

Stan Ducker was waiting for me when I screeched to a stop at the loading dock. He was suited up and standing by his Jolly truck.

"They told me I had to take you with me," he said. "Like my life isn't bad enough."

"Sorry," I said. "This wasn't my idea."

"You need to get dressed. I've got an extra wig and suit for you. You can put it all on over your clothes."

"Nobody said anything about getting dressed."

"This is the Jolly truck. If you ride in it you gotta look like a Jolly Bogart clown. I'm not supposed to give rides to down-on-their-luck bimbos."

"Are you implying I'm a down-on-my-luck bimbo?"

"Let's just say you don't look like the queen of England." He hooked his thumb toward his truck. "The suit and wig are on the seat. We need to get moving. The nasty little brats are out there waiting for their Booger Bars."

Jeez Louise. If this was how he started his day, what was he going to be like at the end of it?

I stepped into the clown costume and tugged the wig on. "Okay," I said. "I'm ready to roll."

"Not yet," he said, handing me a can of red greasepaint. "You gotta do the nose."

I smeared the stuff all over my nose and thought I was beginning to understand why Ducker was so grumpy. If being a clown wasn't your lifelong ambition, this wasn't the job for you.

We chugged out of the parking lot and headed for north Trenton.

"I heard about Gus," I said. "People are saying he was deliberately locked in the freezer, and it looks like another murder."

"I don't know about that, but I always worried about it happening to me. There was an emergency call box in there, but it broke and was never fixed. That's the way it is in this plant. Bogart cheaps out on everything. Him and his jolly, jolly, jolly crap. Everything has to look all sunshine and roses for the morons who snarf up his ice cream, but it's not so jolly inside this fucking clown costume."

"You really need to find a different job."

Ducker turned onto Oak Street. "Not now, sweetie pie," he said. "It's finally getting to be fun. Bogart has to jolly his way through two murders. Jolly, jolly, jolly my ass."

"Why do you suppose someone would want to murder Gus? He seemed like an okay guy."

"Maybe the killer is just some nutcase. Gets his jollies from freezing people." Ducker smiled. "Did you catch that? Gets his *jollies*?"

"I would expect you to be more upset."

"My happy disposition is chemically enhanced."

"I'm seeing a lot of that at the plant. Seriously, do you think the two murders are drug related?"

"Don't know. Don't care." He pushed a button on the dash, and the Jolly Bogart song blasted out of the loudspeakers. "Showtime," Ducker said.

We crawled along, stopping when people appeared. The drill was that Jolly would spring out of the truck, put on his happy face, and conduct business. He'd get back into the truck and mutter something about the dumb little fuckers. After an hour of this his mood had turned even more sullen.

"What time is it?" he asked me.

"It's almost one o'clock."

"Damn! We're behind schedule. Hang on."

Ducker stomped on the gas. The truck chirped its tires and shot forward. He blew through a stop sign, took a corner on two wheels, and raced down Central Avenue.

"What's going on? Where are we going?" I shouted at him.

"The soccer games are over at one o'clock. Whoever gets the parking place by the gate gets to sell all the ice cream. The only other parking place is half a block away, and no one goes there."

"Is it critical that you sell all your ice cream?"

"Yes! If I sell it all early I get to go home early. I don't have to finish out the route."

He turned onto the street that ran along the playing fields, and his face got as red as his nose when he saw the Mo Morris truck parked by the gate.

"Sonnovabitch! That sonnovabitch!" he yelled. "He knows that's my spot. I hate that sonnovabitch."

Ducker drove past the Mo truck and gave the driver the finger, then wheeled around and parked nose to nose with him.

"You're in my spot!" Ducker yelled. "Get out of my spot."

"I got here first," the Mo driver said. "It's my spot today."

Ducker reached under his seat, hauled out a big semiautomatic, and pointed it at the driver. "You want to play Mister Tough Guy?"

The Mo driver went pale, backed his truck out of the parking space, and drove away. Ducker returned the gun to its hidey-hole under his seat and got out to sell ice cream.

So I'm thinking that now I might have three suspects. Ducker was a raving lunatic. He was also in the right spot at the right time. I had his employment record, but I didn't have any of his financials. I thought it wouldn't hurt to take a closer look at him.

I called Connie and asked her to run a report on Stan Ducker and Kenny Morris.

"Do you want me to email them to you, or do you want to pick them up here?" Connie asked. "I'll be here until three o'clock."

"I'll pick them up. If I don't get there by three just leave them by the back door. Is Lula working today?"

"She's here at the office. I wouldn't go so far as to say she's working."

I hung up with Connie and called Eddie Gazarra.

"Do you still need a babysitter for tonight?" I asked him.

"No, it's a wash," Eddie said. "My youngest woke up with a stomach bug and is running a fever. I'm not all that unhappy. We were supposed to go to a baby shower. I'd like to get hold of the idiot who thought it was a good idea to have men invited to baby showers."

I murmured condolences to the youngest and congratulations to Eddie. I disconnected, swiveled in my seat, and looked out at Ducker. He was surrounded by people wanting ice cream.

"Do you need help?" I asked him.

"Yeah. Try to get them into a line before I get trampled."

I got everyone lined up, and Ducker collected the money and handed out the ice cream. The last person in line got the last Bogart Bar. He wanted two Bogart Bars, but there was only one left, so Ducker gave him a Bogart Kidz Kup for free.

"Done and done," Ducker said, getting up behind the wheel.

"You sold everything?"

"We sold all the Bogart Bars, and there aren't enough Kidz Kups left to worry about. Now we just have one more stop. I always get a lottery ticket when I'm done on Saturday. It's a ritual. I go to the deli on Beverly Street, and I get a hot dog and a lottery ticket."

I thought a hot dog and a lottery ticket sounded like a good idea. I was familiar with the deli. It was half bakery and half deli. Besides a hot dog and a lottery ticket I could also get a fresh-filled cannoli.

Ducker drove to the cross street and turned right onto Beverly. The deli was in the middle of the block, squashed between three-story row houses. Across the street was an empty lot that served as a repository for bags of trash, a discarded couch, and God-knows-what that lurked in the weeds and rubble of a demolished building.

He parked the ice cream truck at the curb in front of the empty lot. I hiked my messenger bag onto my shoulder and we crossed the street to the deli.

"You go ahead and get what you want," Ducker said. "I have to use the men's room."

I got a cannoli and a hot dog and I went to the register. I bought a lottery ticket, paid for everything, and went to the door. I was about to walk outside when the truck blew up.

BAROOOM!

It was a sturdy truck, but the doors flew off and the whole thing jumped a couple feet off the ground. The deli's plate glass windows rattled, and I felt the force of the explosion in my chest. An instant fireball consumed the vehicle. Clouds of black smoke billowed off the flames, and the acrid scent of burning tires penetrated the deli.

I was gobsmacked. I stood frozen at the door with my hot dog in one hand and my cannoli in the other.

Ducker came up beside me. "What the fuck?" he said.

"It was sitting there all by itself and it blew up," I said.

I was actually having trouble breathing. My heart was

pounding, and I was trying to push air out of my lungs. If the explosion had occurred fifteen seconds later I'd be dead. Morelli was right. I should stay far away from everything associated with ice cream.

"Someone blew up my truck," Ducker said.

He sounded stunned, but when I turned to look at him he was grinning.

"Some sonnovabitch blew up my truck," he said, dancing around in his clown suit. "This is my freaking lucky day. I'm golden. I'm hot." He stopped dancing. "I need a lottery ticket. I gotta go buy a lottery ticket."

The clerk was the only other person in the deli, and he was flat on the floor behind the counter.

"We've been bombed," he said.

"Not exactly," I told him. "It was the ice cream truck. I think you can get up."

"I need a lottery ticket," Ducker told the clerk. "And a hot dog."

I could hear sirens in the distance, and people were venturing out of houses and businesses to check out the fire.

"Has it occurred to you that someone probably just tried to kill you?" I asked Ducker.

"I don't think so," Ducker said. "I'm the Jolly clown. Everyone loves me. I think someone was trying to kill *you*. You're a bounty hunter. Everyone knows about you. And probably no one likes you. Except me. I like you *a lot* because you got my truck blown up."

Bummer.

I called Lula and asked her to pick me up. There were

police cars and fire trucks and ambulances in the street, so I told her I'd meet her at the corner. I ate my hot dog and cannoli, peeled off my clown suit, and got rid of the wig. Ducker stood in the street, talking to a couple cops. I didn't see any reason for me to join in the discussion. I could give a statement some other time. So I left the deli and walked to the cross street to wait for Lula.

I couldn't get the Jolly Bogart jingle out of my head. It had played on a constant loop the whole time I'd been in the truck. I looked back down the street and wondered if it was still playing. "Jolly, jolly, jolly, jolly." Another pleasant memory from my childhood shot to hell. I'd only been in the truck for three hours, but after the initial shock of the explosion wore off there was some relief that it had been destroyed.

Lula's Firebird pulled up in front of me. I tossed the clown suit into the back and got in next to Lula.

"There's a story here," Lula said.

"I had to ride around with the Jolly Bogart clown today. We sold all the ice cream, so we stopped at the deli for a hot dog and the truck blew up. End of story."

"Same old, same old," Lula said. "What's with the red nose?"

I put my finger to my nose, and it came away red. I flipped the visor down and looked at myself in the mirror.

"Greasepaint," I said.

I got a tissue out of my messenger bag and scrubbed my nose. Some red greasepaint came off onto the tissue, but my nose was still bright red.

"That's not attractive," Lula said. "People are gonna call you Rudolph."

"I need makeup remover."

"There's some at the office. I keep it there in case I need to change my look halfway through the day. Sometimes first thing in the morning I'm feeling like blue eye shadow and then after lunch I might want to warm up my color palette and go more to the pink tones. We can get your car and then get you fixed up."

EIGHTEEN

CONNIE WAS PACKING up to leave when we walked in. "I have the two reports you wanted," she said. "What's wrong with your nose? It's red."

"It's more like what's wrong with her life," Lula said. "She rode around with the Jolly clown this morning until his truck got blown up."

Connie handed the reports to me. "Was anyone hurt?"

"No," I said. "We were in the deli on Beverly Street when it happened. Fortunately the truck was parked in front of an empty lot, and no one was walking by when the explosion occurred. I think it must have been a bomb on a timer."

I shoved the reports into my bag and went to the restroom. I used Lula's makeup remover, and I tried hand soap. My nose was still red. I dabbed concealer on it and gave it a light dusting of powder. It was toned down to a rosy glow. I returned to the office.

"This is as good as it's going to get," I said.

"It's not so bad," Lula said. "I bet if it was nighttime you'd hardly notice it at all."

Something to look forward to.

"If you're depressed over your nose we could do something fun like go car shopping," Lula said. "I know a guy that could fix you right up, and you wouldn't have to drive that ghetto car no more."

I stared out the window at my car. It was leaking something.

"Okay," I said, "but I can't go over five thousand dollars, and the car has to be legal. I don't want a stolen car."

"Boy, you got a lot of rules," Lula said. "I think you might have to compromise on one or the other."

"Where is this car person located?"

"Just follow me," Lula said. "He operates out of his house."

We took Hamilton to Broad, crossed the Delaware River into Pennsylvania, and headed north on River Road to Yardley. Lula turned away from the river into a wooded area, and I stayed close behind. I was hoping we got to this guy soon because I wasn't sure what was leaking from my car, and I worried what would happen when it stopped. Lula put her blinker on, and we left the road and followed a single-lane dirt drive that opened into a large field. A split-level house sat in the middle of the field. There were several cars lined up on the grass by the house. Lula found a place to park by the front door, and I pulled up alongside her.

A wiry little black man with close-cropped hair and a skinny mustache looked out at us. He was wearing a red satin tracksuit and fancy basketball shoes.

"Lula," he yelled. "You lookin' for work?"

"Hell, no, you nasty-ass moron. I'm looking for a car for my friend."

He left the house, walked over to us, and gave Lula a hug. She was wearing over-the-knee boots with five-inch heels, and when the little guy hugged her, his nose got buried in her Grand Canyon–size cleavage.

"This is my friend Stephanie," Lula said to him. "We gotta find her a good car."

He pulled his nose out of her cleavage and turned to me. "Gaylord Brown," he said. "It's the perfect name because I'm gay and I'm brown."

"Since when are you gay?" Lula asked him.

"It comes and goes," he said. "I like to keep an open mind. So what kind of car does Sugar Cookie want?"

"Well, as you can see the one she's got isn't in perfect condition," Lula said.

Gaylord looked at the car and grimaced. "Tragic," he said.

"Exactly," Lula agreed. "So she needs something right away. We don't want something leaking vital body fluids like this one. And we don't want something with a big dent in it like this one. And it would be desirable if the backseat wasn't a mold factory."

"No problem so far," Gaylord said.

"She works with me in the bounty hunter business, so she needs four doors so she can chuck the bad guys into the backseat. It could be a sedan or a SUV."

Gaylord nodded. "Noted."

"She don't want it too old, and I ride around in it sometime so it should be shiny and have a good sound system."

"Goes without saying," Gaylord said. "You got a color in mind?"

"I'm partial to red," Lula said, "but I guess we could be flexible on that one."

"And how much you got to spend?"

"She don't want to go over five thousand."

"Okay, I might have to work a little, but I might find something."

"Gaylord is a specialist middleman," Lula said to me. "You tell him what you want and then he finds it for you."

"Anything else?" Gaylord asked.

"She wants it legal," Lula said. "You know, with a VIN and papers and all that shit."

"All my cars come with papers," Gaylord said. "And we'll make sure it has everything looking legal."

"What did I tell you?" Lula said to me. "He's a sweetie, right?"

I noticed he'd said everything would *look* legal, and it occurred to me that looking legal might be different from being legal. I glanced back at my SUV and gave an involuntary shiver. It would never make it back across the river. It was a miracle I'd been able to drive it this far. Okay, so he looked like a nice man. And if I harp on the legal issue he might get insulted, right? I wouldn't want to insult one of Lula's friends. And, honestly, did I even care? I gave up a sigh. Of course I cared. I didn't want to be involved in a crime, and I didn't want to encourage crime. On the other hand, I needed a car. And who was I to prejudge this businessman?

"What about my current car?" I asked. "What's it worth?"

Gaylord cut his eyes to the Explorer. "Fifty."

"Fifty dollars?" I said. "That's all you'll give me for a trade-in?"

"No," he said. "That's what I'll charge you to haul it to the junkyard."

"So when can we expect her new car?" Lula asked.

"I'll get Wayne working on it right away," Gaylord said. "Where do you want it delivered?"

"You could call my cellphone, and I'll let you know where we're at," Lula said.

"We need full payment when we deliver," Gaylord said to me. "And I only take cash. Eliminates overhead, if you know what I mean."

Oh boy.

I emptied out the Explorer, and Lula drove us back to Trenton.

"Now what are we going to do?" Lula wanted to know.

"I need to get cash for my capture check and my bank is closed."

"No problem. I know someone who can fix that too if you don't mind a twenty-five-dollar transaction fee."

• • •

It was a little after five when I walked into my apartment. I dropped the envelope with $5,000 in cash onto the counter, grabbed a cold beer from the fridge, and made myself a peanut butter sandwich for dinner. Rex came out of his soup can and looked at me, whiskers twitching, eyes bright. I gave him a corner of my sandwich. He stuffed it into his cheek and scurried back into his can.

I called Ranger and gave him the details on the ice cream truck explosion. I told him about Kenny Morris. I told him the Jolly Bogart clown was a lunatic.

"Babe," Ranger said.

"Dude," I said back at him.

I thought I sensed him smile, but I could be wrong.

We disconnected, and Morelli called me. "Were you the second clown in the ice cream truck?" he asked.

"Yes."

"Are you okay?"

"I can't get the red greasepaint off my nose, but aside from that I'm good."

"Do we have a plan for tonight? Are you babysitting Gazarra's kids?"

"Babysitting was canceled, but I have some errands to run."

"'Errands'?"

"Work related. I should be home around eleven o'clock. Also, if anyone finds a semiautomatic in whatever is left of the ice cream truck they should run a ballistics test against the bullet taken out of Arnold Zigler."

"Are you kidding? You think the Jolly Bogart clown killed Zigler?"

"All I'm saying is that he had a gun, and why not test it if it turns up?"

"Fair enough."

I pulled the two reports out of my messenger bag and took them to my dining room table to read. There wasn't much on Ducker. He lived alone in a one-bedroom apartment in a large apartment complex in Hamilton Township. He drove a leased Kia. He had a bunch of credit cards. He had no arrest history. He was a high school graduate. After high school he'd enlisted in the Army and served for three years. Never saw combat. Was unemployed for almost a year after the Army. Eventually was hired by Bogart. Never married. His parents lived in Newark. His father was a butcher.

Kenny Morris graduated from Lafayette College and went to work in his father's ice cream business. He worked on the floor for a year and then moved to a corner office, where he presided over the test kitchen. He'd been in the corner office for two years. He was twenty-five years old. His two older brothers weren't interested in ice cream. One was a lawyer in Philadelphia with a wife and two kids. The other was a graphic designer, working in Silicon Valley. Kenny also had no arrest history. His credit rating was top-notch. He drove a black Jeep Wrangler Rubicon Hard Rock, which I thought was a badass car. He lived at home with his parents. And he was in love with Bogart's daughter. Connie had included Kenny's college yearbook picture. Blond hair, blond eyebrows, shy smile. A little bland looking.

I opened my computer and was about to check my email when I got a call from Lula.

"Gaylord got a car for you," Lula said. "They're getting it detailed now, and then it'll get brought over to your building. Wayne's got all the paperwork, and all you gotta do is give him the money."

"What kind of car is it?"

"Don't know," Lula said. "I forgot to ask, but Gaylord said it didn't have no dents and it wasn't leaking nothing."

"I need to go to Kranski's Bar in north Trenton. Do you want to tag along?"

"Sure. We were going to do a filming but it got canceled, so I got the night free."

"Was this another *Naked and Afraid* episode?"

"No. It was this other idea I had where I say I feel like I'm a guy today, and I go into a public men's room. And then we film my positive experience. Only problem was I did a test run this afternoon and there were already a bunch of women in there with the men. The men were all standing back, looking confused, and the women were taking selfie videos of themselves trying to use the urinals. It was a ugly scene. Those women weren't having any luck with those urinals. I like to think I'm a open-minded person, but I don't see where this whole unisex thing is going to work. It don't even make good television. I mean, if you can't make a decent reality show out of a situation, what's the point of going there?"

This was wrong on so many levels I almost had a seizure

from rolling my eyes, and yet in the end her point was sort of valid.

"I'll pick you up at nine o'clock," I said. "Hopefully I won't have to spend a lot of time at Kranski's, because I'd like to also take another look at Butchy's house."

"What kind of bar is Kranski's? I need to know so I make the appropriate wardrobe choice."

"I've never been there, but I think it might be a small neighborhood dive. And if we get lucky and Butchy isn't home we might try to break into his garage, so dark colors would be good."

· · ·

Wayne delivered my car at seven-fifteen. He was excessively polite and neatly dressed in a three-button collared knit polo shirt and dress slacks. He handed me an envelope with my registration and bill of sale, plus information on Bua's Takeout Chicken, Renee Nails, Fancy Dan's Detailing, and Kitty's Escort Service.

"I'd like to see the car first," I said.

"Of course. Let's go take a look."

We took the stairs to the parking lot. Wayne led me over to a black Lexus GS F and gave me the keys.

I was speechless for a full minute. "This is it?"

"It's not new," Wayne said. "It's a 2013, but it's in excellent condition."

"What's wrong with it?"

"It has a little scratch on the left rear quarter panel, but you can hardly see it. I know Lula said she liked red, but this car came available and Gaylord thought it suited you."

"It's hot, isn't it?"

Wayne smiled, showing a lot of really white teeth. "It will be with you in it."

"I mean it's hot like stolen."

"Would that be a problem?"

"Yes!"

"Then it's definitely not stolen."

"Good to know," I said.

Crap! It was for sure stolen.

"We've attached your plates and taken care of all the title transfers. The nonstolen VIN number is displayed wherever required. And we've given you a full tank of gas."

I handed him an envelope with my $5,000 in cash.

"Enjoy," Wayne said.

A Cadillac Escalade pulled up, Wayne got in, and the SUV drove off.

Little black dots floated in front of my eyes, and there was a roaring sound in my ears. I put my hand out onto the Lexus to steady myself and sucked in air.

Okay, so he said it wasn't stolen. And he was very nice and neatly dressed. And he thought I'd look hot in the car. True, it was a $30,000 car that I got for $5,000, but there were reasons for the discrepancy, right? Like low overhead and sales incentives. And it had a scratch. And best not to dwell on how the title transfer was accomplished on a Saturday night.

When the vertigo cleared and my breathing was more or less normal, I got into the car and drove it around the parking lot. It was a great car. And even if it was stolen, chances were good that by the time the police caught up with me, the car would already have been flattened by a cement truck. My cars didn't last all that long.

NINETEEN

I DRESSED IN black jeans, a black V-neck stretchy T-shirt, and a black hoodie. It was the perfect outfit for breaking and entering, with the exception of my nose, which was shining like Rudolph's. I told Rex I'd be home later, I hiked my messenger bag onto my shoulder, and I left my apartment. It was almost nine o'clock, and the sun had set. I got into my new car and drove to Lula's apartment.

"Girlfriend," Lula said, "look at you! This is an excellent car. It isn't red, but it's excellent all the same."

"I think it's stolen."

"You don't know that for sure," Lula said, belting herself in. "Mostly Gaylord deals with insurance scamming. He takes a car off a lot and the insurance company pays."

"That's still stealing."

"I guess, but it's an insurance company, and everyone hates those people."

"I don't hate them."

"Well, you're weird," Lula said. "Do you like the car?"

"I love the car."

"There you go. And by the way, you might want to put a dab of concealer on your nose."

Kranski's Bar was on the corner of Mayberry Street and Ash. This was a neighborhood very similar to the Burg, but the houses were a little larger, the cars were newer, the kitchen appliances were probably stainless. I parked in the small lot beside the tavern, and Lula and I sashayed into the dim interior. Bertie was working behind the bar that stretched across the back of the room. A bunch of high-top tables were scattered around the front of the room. Two women sat at one of the tables, eating nachos and drinking martinis. At one end of the bar four men were drinking beer and watching the overhead television. I spotted Kenny Morris at the other end. He was alone, nursing what looked like whiskey.

Bertie caught my eye, tilted his head toward Kenny, and I nodded back.

"I guess that's the guy you're looking for," Lula said. "You want to tag-team him?"

"No. I just want to talk to him. I'll go it alone."

Lula hoisted herself onto a barstool by the four men, and I approached Kenny.

"Anyone sitting here?" I asked him.

"No," he said. "No one ever sits there."

"Why not?"

"The television is at the other end."

"But you're here."

"Yeah, I'm not into the team television thing."

He looked a lot like his yearbook photograph. His hair was a little longer. He was slim. Medium height. Pleasant looking. Wearing jeans and a blue dress shirt with the top button open and the sleeves rolled.

He was staring at my nose with an intensity usually displayed by dermatologists during a skin cancer exam. I couldn't blame him. I'd smeared some makeup on it, but even in the dark bar it was emitting a red glow.

"It's a condition," I said. "It comes and goes. It's not contagious or anything. Do you come in here often?"

"Couple times a week."

I got Bertie's attention and ordered a glass of wine.

"I was supposed to meet someone here, but I think she might be a no-show," I said to Kenny.

He knocked back his drink. "Women. That's the way they are. No show."

Bertie brought my wine and another glass of whiskey for Kenny.

"It sounds like you've had women problems," I said.

"Make that singular. One woman. No backbone. No mind of her own. Has to do what her asshole father wants her to do. I can't believe I got mixed up with her and her stupid family."

"Sounds like you're still mixed up with her."

"I'm working at it." He chugged his drink and held his finger up to Bertie for another.

I had no idea where to go with this. I wasn't a brilliant

conversationalist. I had no clue how to pick up a man at a bar. And here was another reminder that I sucked as Nancy Drew.

"Do you have a name?" he asked. "A job?"

Bam! I was back in business. "Stephanie. And I work at the Bogart Ice Creamery."

"I hate Bogart ice cream."

"I've only worked there a couple days."

"Well, you should quit. Bogart is evil. And his ice cream is crap. Did you know the Jolly Bogart truck got blown up today? Good riddance. Too bad the clown wasn't in it. That would have been good. Not as good as the guy who got turned into a Bogart Bar, but still pretty good."

"I'm told they don't know who did it."

"Whoever it is, he deserves a medal. I hope more people get frozen."

"Most of the people working there are nice. Maybe not the clown, but most of the people."

"Then they should leave, because that factory is going down. Someone is out to destroy it."

"Would that be you?" I asked him.

"I wish," he said. "If it was me I'd do it differently. I'd cut off the head. Literally. And maybe I will someday."

"Bogart?"

"He should die."

"Have you ever thought about talking to someone about anger management?"

Bertie brought Kenny another drink. "Last one," Bertie

said. "This is your limit. You want something to eat before I call a car for you?"

"Nachos. Extra cheese."

I leaned toward Kenny a little and lowered my voice. "Were you serious? Would you really cut off Bogart's head?"

"In a heartbeat."

"What's stopping you?"

"No guts. Haven't got the right sort of knife. And I faint at the sight of blood."

That got a smile out of me. I was liking Kenny Morris. From the corner of my eye I saw Lula get off her barstool and head for us.

"I'm trying to decide if I should order food," Lula said to me. "What do you think?"

"Is this the person you've been waiting for?" Kenny asked.

I dropped a twenty on the bar and stood. "No. We're going to go looking for her. It's been nice talking to you. I hope things work out."

. . .

"He seemed okay," Lula said. "One of them preppy individuals."

"He's having a personal problem."

"Well, we all got them. What are we doing now? Are we gonna snoop around Butchy's house?"

"Yes."

I drove across town, keeping my eyes open for police officers who might be under the mistaken impression that I was driving a stolen vehicle. I relaxed a little when I reached the Burg without getting pulled over. Lights were off in Butchy's house. His truck wasn't in the driveway.

"Nobody home," Lula said.

I parked three houses down on the opposite side of the street, and Lula and I walked back to Butchy's house. I had a big Maglite, and Lula had her purse.

"What are we looking for?" Lula asked.

"I don't know exactly. Evidence of chocolate syrup and chopped nuts. A huge freezer. Bloodstains."

"The usual stuff," Lula said.

We stood across the street in front of the house for a couple minutes and watched for movement, then crossed to the driveway and went directly to the garage. It was overcast with not even a sliver of moon showing. The garage was lost in deep shadow.

"I can't see where I'm walking," Lula said. "Last time we did this in the dark I stepped on a dead person. I still get nightmares."

I had a small penlight besides the Maglite, but I didn't want to use it in the yard. Lights were on in the houses flanking Butchy's place. Last thing I wanted was for someone to call the police or send out a killer dog.

We circled the garage but didn't see a way in. There were bars on the only window, and the door was locked. I took a closer look at the front of the garage and found a keypad. I tapped in 0000, and the door opened.

"Boy, you're good," Lula said. "I would never have figured that out."

We stepped in, and I hit the button that closed the door.

When the door was entirely closed I flipped the light switch next to the garage opener, and the garage was flooded with light.

One wall was lined with boxed microwave ovens. They were four boxes deep and seven boxes high, running the length of the garage. Large cartons of Nike shoes lined the other wall. And there was an island of toaster ovens.

"This boy has a lucrative sideline going," Lula said.

I looked around. "I don't see any chocolate syrup or blood."

"No, but he has a freezer."

I walked to the large chest freezer that was under the window on the side wall. It was about five feet long and three feet wide.

"Do you suppose he has another body in there?" Lula asked.

"It would have to be someone short."

"Not necessarily. You could fold him up and freeze him and then when you take him out you could hit him with a hammer and straighten him out."

"I wish you hadn't shared that," I said to Lula.

"Just sayin'."

I held my breath, opened the freezer, and we looked in. It was filled with Bogart Bars.

"I'm thinking he didn't buy all these," Lula said.

"I'm thinking you're right."

I was also thinking it could be the ice cream that was removed from the truck to make room for Arnold Zigler.

I closed the lid on the freezer. We took one last look around and left the garage. We walked around the house, looking in windows, but it was too dark to see anything.

"Do you want to get in?" Lula asked. "I got a knack for getting in."

Her knack for getting in was to break a window or door.

"No breaking in," I said. "I don't want him to know someone was snooping around."

We were on the side of the house, and my heart skipped a beat when Butchy's truck drove up. He turned into the driveway and cut the engine.

Lula and I froze, not sure if we'd been seen. I heard the driver's door open and close, and I held my breath. I couldn't see the driveway or the front of the house, but I heard Butchy's footsteps. He walked from the truck to the front door, the door opened and closed, and a light flashed on in the living room. A moment later a light flashed on in the kitchen. I crept closer to the window, and I saw Butchy go to a drawer next to the sink and take out a gun.

Crap!

"Feet don't fail me," Lula said, and she took off running.

I turned and took off at the same time. We reached the end of the block, and ducked behind a parked car a beat before Butchy came out his front door. He looked up and down the street, walked out to the sidewalk, and looked up and down again. He wheeled around and went back inside his house.

Lula and I scurried across the street and jumped into my car. I made a U-turn and took off.

"You'll notice how I used restraint and didn't shoot him or

nothing," Lula said. "Only reason I ran was because I knew that's what you wanted. Ordinarily I wouldn't run."

"Running was the right thing to do," I said.

"I bet he's the killer," Lula said. "He's got a freezer and a gun."

I turned onto Broad Street. "He's on the list."

"Do you think he saw us?"

"He saw something, but I don't think he recognized us. It was pitch-black, and we were against the house."

I dropped Lula off and drove home on autopilot. My cellphone rang when I pulled into my parking lot.

"Babe," Ranger said. "Your car has been in Pennsylvania all afternoon, but your messenger bag has been all over the place."

"I got a new car. The old one was leaking stuff."

"Who were you visiting in the Burg?"

"Butchy from the loading dock. Turns out he's got a large chest freezer and a collection of what I suspect are hijacked shoes, toaster ovens, and microwaves in his garage. And he's got a gun in his kitchen drawer."

"And the bar in north Trenton?"

"I was socializing with Kenny Morris. He's very angry."

"Does he have a gun and a freezer?"

"Don't know. It didn't come up in conversation. I suspect he has a freezer because he lives at home, and his father owns an ice cream factory. Do I have an assignment for Monday?"

"I'd like you at the Bogart factory. It'll be your last day there. I have technicians working today, and on Tuesday I'll have the cameras up and running."

"There's no way I'm getting back into the clown suit."

"I'll work around it."

I said good night to Ranger and trudged into my apartment building and up the stairs to my apartment. Morelli was asleep on my couch. Bob was asleep on the floor beside him. Bob opened an eye and looked at me and went back to sleep. Morelli woke up and took a couple beats to focus.

"And?" he asked.

"Butchy from the loading dock has a gun."

"Cupcake, everyone you know has a gun." He sat up and squinted at me. "Your nose is red."

TWENTY

MONDAY MORNING I presented myself at the ice cream factory and was assigned to the floor. I was back at the cup dropper and filler machine. I felt comfortable doing this since it had a big red button.

Three Rangeman techs were on the floor adjusting and programming the newly installed cameras. Their purpose was to keep everyone safe, but I suspected their presence was a constant reminder of danger.

I was relieved at ten-thirty, and I went to the break room for coffee. Three women were at one table, and two were at another. I didn't know any of them. No one looked up and invited me to join them. The atmosphere in the room was subdued. Two murders and an explosion were taking a toll. Things were no longer so jolly. I got coffee and a candy bar and sat by myself. I didn't want to intrude on the women, and I didn't think they would tell me anything useful.

Bogart's assistant, Kathy, found me and told me I was being reassigned to the loading dock. A truck needed loading and they were short a man.

I stripped off my yellow floor outfit and stuffed it into my locker, checked my email, grabbed my sweatshirt, and made my way to the loading dock.

Butchy was packing a small truck with shrink-wrapped orders of assorted ice cream. He stopped packing and ambled over when he saw me.

"I'm guessing you're my helper," he said. "Play your cards right and you might get to be foreman, being that I don't want this job."

"Why don't you want the job?"

"Too much work. I'm an easygoing guy. I'm a responsibility shirker."

"But for now you're the foreman?"

"Looks that way. I got Noodles helping me load this truck, and when it gets loaded there's a big rig coming in. Meantime, I need someone to load the Jolly junker over there by the guardhouse."

I looked toward the guardhouse and saw the old, rust-riddled, faded-glory Jolly Bogart truck.

"We pulled her out of retirement," Butchy said. "Bogart had her sitting on a hill looking out at Route 1 for the past ten years. Like an antique billboard. We put a new battery in her, and damned if she doesn't still run. There were some squirrels living in her, but we cleaned it all up except for the one seat that's a little chewed."

"Who's driving it?"

"Stan's driving it."

"Does he know this?"

"I didn't talk to him personally, but someone told him to come to work, so I guess he got it figured out."

Oh boy.

"Anyway," Butchy said. "We gotta get the old girl filled with Kidz Kups and Bogart Bars."

"I'm not going to get locked in the freezer, am I?"

"Hard to tell around here what's gonna happen next."

I grabbed the hand truck and pushed it down the hall to the freezer. I punched the code in, and propped the door open with the hand truck. A lot of frigid air was rushing out of the freezer, but I didn't care. I was taking precautions. I loaded the hand truck and exited the freezer. The door closed with a click behind me, and I gave an involuntary shudder.

I had the Jolly truck almost filled when Stan burst out of the loading dock door. He wasn't in his clown suit, but his nose was bright red and his hair was every which way. He was waving his arms, and his eyes were bugged out of his head.

"Are you freaking kidding me?" he yelled. "Goddamn, motherfucker, holy shit, and fuck me. Where is it? Where's the piece-of-shit truck they dragged out of hell to make my life an even worse misery?"

"By the guardhouse," Butchy said. "How come you're not in your clown suit?"

"I've been reasonable about this," Stan said. "I went out and did my job while I patiently waited. Well, no more. The gloves are off. No more jolly, jolly, jolly. You want to see jolly? Jolly fucking this!"

He pulled a gun, I ducked behind the guardhouse, and he fired off about fifteen rounds at the truck.

"That's whack-a-doodle," Butchy said to Stan when he stopped shooting.

"I hate this plant," Stan said. "I hate this second-rate ice cream. I hate every shitty Bogart Bar that was ever made. And I especially hate Harry fucking Bogart."

"I hear you," Butchy said, "but you should chill. You want a joint?"

"I need more than a joint," Stan said.

"I got some of that too," Butchy said.

Stan wheeled around and marched back into the building.

"Someone should go after him and make sure he doesn't do more shooting," I said.

"He'll be okay," Butchy said. "He just had to do some venting. And besides, he emptied his clip." Butchy lit up. "I guess you gotta take the truck out," he said to me.

"No way."

"Somebody's gotta do it."

"Not going to be me," I said. "I'm not getting into the clown suit. I'm not smearing the greasepaint on my nose. I'm not driving the truck. Suppose he decides to shoot up the truck again with me in it? And anyway last time I went out in a Jolly Bogart truck it got blown up."

"Yeah, but you weren't in it, so it's all good, right?"

"You take the truck out."

"I can't. I'm the foreman. I gotta stay here."

"I'll be the foreman."

"It don't work that way. Mr. Bogart gotta make you the foreman. And anyway you'd be the foregirl. *Haw!* Foregirl. Who ever heard of a foregirl?"

"Okay. Fine. I'll take the stupid truck out, but I'm not wearing the clown suit."

"I don't give a fig about the clown suit," Butchy said. "Personally it always scared the holy whatever out of me."

I tossed the remaining ice cream into the truck, got my messenger bag out of my locker, stomped back to the loading dock, and climbed behind the wheel. I turned the key, and the engine sputtered and cranked over.

"I'm not happy," I said to Butchy. "I'm totally not happy."

I stomped on the gas, and the truck jerked forward. I drove out of the parking lot and headed for the first neighborhood. After a couple miles the truck coughed and died. I thunked my head on the steering wheel. "Why me?"

I got out and looked at the truck. It was leaking something. Déjà vu. The story of my life. I called Lula and asked her to pick me up. I ate a Bogart Bar while I waited, and I called Ranger and gave him a recap.

"They recommissioned an old Jolly Bogart truck," I said. "Stan Ducker went nuts when he saw it. He emptied a clip into it and stormed off. I got stuck taking the truck out, and it broke down after a couple miles. Lula's coming to get me, but someone needs to get the truck. I don't have any numbers associated with Bogart, so I'm calling you."

"Lucky me," Ranger said.

I gave him the address, disconnected, and helped myself to another Bogart Bar. Ten minutes later Lula pulled up next to the truck.

"This here truck is full of bullet holes," Lula said.

"It had a hard morning."

"Do you got Bogart Bars?"

"I have a truck filled with them."

"I'll take two. It's almost lunchtime and I don't mind starting with dessert."

I gave Lula the Bogart Bars, and we waited until the tow truck showed up. I handed over the keys and abandoned the Jolly Bogart truck.

"It's sad to see a broken-down ice cream truck full of bullet holes," Lula said. "What's this country coming to?"

• • •

I retrieved my car from the Bogart lot and followed Lula back to the bonds office.

"I ordered pizza on my way here," she said. "It should get delivered any minute now. I got a extra-large pie with the works, and I got a extra-large pie with extra cheese. I'm celebrating because I expect to hear from the *Naked and Afraid* people today. I could be catapulted to instant fame on that show. It's a highly rated show."

I pulled a chair up to Connie's desk, took Stan Ducker's file out of my bag, and read through it one more time. There was nothing to indicate he was batshit crazy. I suspected it was the Jolly jingle. A person could only take so much of the

Jolly jingle. After a week of working as the Jolly Bogart clown I'd probably empty a clip into the truck too.

"Hold on," Lula said. "I just got a email from *Naked and Afraid*. It says they think me and Briggs got potential, but . . . say what?"

Connie and I leaned forward.

"And?" Connie said.

"They regret to inform me that the film we sent wasn't sufficiently compelling for them to go forward with the process and they wish us the best of luck."

"Did they say anything else?" I asked.

"They thought the white pussycat was adorable."

The pizza delivery car stopped in front of the office, and the delivery kid got out with the pizzas.

"Hurry up," Lula yelled at him. "Can't you see I'm in need of a pizza? You think I got all day? I received bad news and I gotta console myself. I'm one of them comfort eaters."

She took the two pizza boxes, stuffed some money into the kid's hand, and brought the pizza to the desk.

"I knew it was a mistake to have that cat in the film," she said. "He was a scene stealer, and it was hard for people to tear themselves away from him so they could see me showing my mix of terror and bravery all at the same time."

Lula took a piece of the extra-cheese pizza and sunk her teeth into it.

"Good thing I got a backup plan," Lula said. "I thought something like this might happen on account of you never know if people got any taste. It could have been some intern who knows nothing that got my film. Or she could have had a bad day. Like she might have got up this morning and found she had a STD. That could affect the way you think all day."

I helped myself to a piece of the extra-cheese and Connie took from the box with the works.

"I suppose you're wanting to know what my next audition tape is going to be," Lula said. "Remember I told you about naked bungee jumping? Only it won't be for *Naked and Afraid* because it don't fit their format. I'm thinking we send it to CNN. They got that Anthony Bourdain show, and me and Briggs would be the perfect lead-in. We could do a travelogue of naked bungee jumping all over the world. Problem is, Bourdain might look lame after people get to watching me and Briggs. Bourdain might have to up his game."

"Why would you do it naked?" I asked.

Lula took a second slice of pizza. "That's our thing. Like, it's our trademark. Anybody can go bungee jumping, but how many people go naked? You see what I'm saying? We could bungee jump off that bridge in London or off some crazy rope bridge in Africa. And then I was thinking for the second season we could do naked zip-lining."

I had a mental image of Lula zip-lining through a jungle, screaming like Tarzan. Hilariously funny and utterly awful.

"My problem is I gotta find a place to bungee jump here in Trenton," Lula said. "After I get to be famous I imagine they'll let me jump from anywhere, but this first film could be tricky."

"Are you jumping at night or during the day?" Connie asked.

"Most likely at night," Lula said. "We got the infrared

camera, and I'm thinking it adds drama to the event. Plus I noticed the dimples in my ass don't show up on infrared."

"You have a double problem," Connie said. "You have to find someplace they'll let you jump, and then you have to figure out a way to do it without getting arrested for indecent exposure."

"It pretty much rules out all the bridges," Lula said. "And there's some big buildings going up, but I've taken a look at most of them, and they don't lend themselves to bungee jumping. Some people use them big skyhook cranes for jumping. We could do that if I could find one in the right spot."

"What about the junkyard?" Connie said. "They have that catwalk running between the control tower and the giant magnet that picks the cars up and puts them in the crusher."

Lula's eyes got wide. "That's perfect. I don't know why I didn't think of that. I even got a good relationship with the asshole who runs the junkyard. We go way back."

I looked over at Connie and gave her a "What, are you nuts?" gesture.

"That's a terrible idea," I said to Lula. "You're going to die. You don't know anything about bungee jumping."

"I Googled it," Lula said. "I'm pretty sure I could do it. And anyways, I'm sending Briggs off first."

. . .

I drove to Hamilton Township and found Ducker's apartment complex, which consisted of eight two-story blocky redbrick buildings arranged around a parking lot. Entrances were flanked by fake white columns. Landscaping was minimal. I'd been here before, and I knew everyone had either a patio or a balcony in the back. Not high-end luxury but not ghetto either. More than I could afford.

Ducker's silver Kia was parked close to his building. Probably he was in his apartment, cleaning his gun and plotting his revenge on Bogart. It didn't seem likely that he had a massive freezer, so turning Bogart into a Bogart Bar might be difficult.

I was here because I was curious. I didn't expect the visit would accomplish anything beyond confirming Ducker was tucked away in his apartment and not out hunting down Bogart. Not that I cared a whole lot about Bogart. I didn't want to see him dead, but I wasn't liking him either. And I could feel my initial outrage about the Bogart Bar crime fading. It looked as if I was done snooping for Ranger. Good riddance to that job. My nose still glowed in the dark.

I sat in the lot, watching Ducker's building. Not sure why. It was like a boring book that you keep reading because there's the promise that something astonishing might happen on the next page. After an hour with nothing astonishing happening on the Ducker front, I gave it up and drove home.

TWENTY-ONE

BRIGGS WAS SITTING on the floor in the hallway, his back to my front door. I was tempted to turn and run, but he saw me exit the elevator, and he would have run after me.

"Cripes," he said, "where were you? I've been here forever. You gotta help me."

I had my keys in my hand, but I wasn't opening my door. If I opened my door he would follow me in.

"What are you doing?" he asked. "Aren't you gonna open your door?"

"No."

"I swear, sometimes I think you don't like me."

"Sometimes?"

"I'm a nice guy."

I raised an eyebrow.

"Maybe 'nice' is a stretch," he said. "I'm definitely okay. Most of the time."

I raised the second eyebrow.

"Some of the time," Briggs said. "Anyway, you might as well let me in because I'm not leaving."

I unlocked my door, and Briggs followed me into the kitchen. I dumped my messenger bag on the counter and said hello to Rex.

"What's the problem?" I asked Briggs.

"I have this thing about heights. I get panic attacks. I get all sweaty and my heart goes nuts and I pass out."

"And?"

"And Lula's all set to do this bungee jumping show. I wasn't worried about it in the beginning because I figured we'd get the *Naked and Afraid* gig. Now *Naked and Afraid* fell through, and I'm looking at bungee jumping."

"Don't do it."

"She'll find someone else, and I won't get a television show. I'm not the only little person in town. Ronald Brickett would jump at the chance to do this. He's fearless. He used to get shot out of a cannon. He was making good money until those PC idiots told him it was demeaning and he had to quit."

"What's he do now?"

"He runs a meth lab. It's a small operation, but the money's tax free and he gets food stamps."

"So what is it that you want from me?"

"I have a dilemma. The naked bungee jumping isn't a bad idea. I'm motivated to do it. Problem is, I'm gonna need help getting myself up to wherever we're going to jump from."

"Not going to be me."

"You owe me."

"I owe you nothing."

"It was worth a try," Briggs said. "What'll it take? I'm desperate. I don't want to do this, but I don't want to miss out on it. This could be my big chance. Think about it . . . if you help me do this and we get a show I'll be out of Trenton. I'll be all over the place. You might never see me again except on television. And some of those places we go to could be dangerous. I could get shot or blown up or eaten by a crocodile."

So helping Briggs had some appeal.

"I got a call from Lula about an hour ago," Briggs said. "She's got a location for the filming, and it's set up for tonight." His upper lip was sweating, and he was doubled over, holding his stomach. "I might have to use your bathroom."

"No way. Not going to happen."

His eyes rolled back into his head, and he crashed to the floor.

I soaked a kitchen towel in cold water and draped it across his forehead. His eyes opened, and he stared up at me.

"Are you okay?" I asked him.

"Yeah," he said. "I feel better now. Good thing I'm short, and I don't have far to fall."

"If you faint at the thought of bungee jumping, how are you going to get through a whole season of TV shows?"

"I'll be able to afford drugs. Right now all I have is you. You're free, right?"

"What do I have to do?"

"We're shooting this at the junkyard at the end of Stark

Street. Nine o'clock. I thought you could blindfold me and get me up to the catwalk. They'll get me hooked up, you can put me into position, and then they'll take the blindfold away, and I'll jump."

"And you think that will work?"

"Yeah. You can lie to me the whole time. You can tell me it's not real high."

"And if I do this you'll never ask me for another favor?"

"Swear to God."

• • •

I got to the junkyard a little before nine o'clock. The chain-link gate was open, so I drove in and parked in visitor parking next to the trailer that served as an office. A bunch of people were milling around a short distance away. Lula, Howie with his camera, the makeup 'ho, and a woman I didn't know who was holding the clacker. Briggs was off by himself, pacing. I joined the group, and two men came out of the trailer and walked over to us.

Both men were in their fifties. They were wearing hard hats and work boots. They looked like they ate a lot of pasta and didn't have a gym membership.

"Who's Lula?" one of the men asked.

"That's me," Lula said.

"And you're running this clusterfuck?"

"Yep. Me and Howie."

Howie raised his hand. "I'm Howie."

"I'm Joey," the guy said. "And the ugly guy next to me is Boomer. We're gonna help you get the job done, and then we're gonna expect a big tip."

The makeup 'ho and the clacker 'ho licked their lips.

"Not that kind of tip," Joey said. "Obamacare don't cover that kind of damage."

The chain link enclosed about five acres that were lit up like daylight from banks of overhead halogens. Not good for Lula's ass dimples, but it kept us from stepping on rats and assorted rusted junk. Most of the acreage was filled with cars waiting to go into the crusher. Two four-story elevators with a long connecting catwalk sat in the middle of the jumble of cars. A control room that looked like a freight container was attached to one of the elevator towers. The guy in the control room operated the electromagnet, the crusher, and the crane.

We followed Joey and Boomer to an elevator, and Lula, Howie, the makeup 'ho, and the clacker 'ho went up with Boomer. I waited with Briggs and Joey for the second trip.

Briggs was wearing a robe and sneakers. He pulled a scarf out of his pocket and handed it to me.

"Do it," he said.

He was in a cold sweat, and his face had no color to it.

"It's going to be great," I told him. "We're not going up very far. I'm going to hang on to you all the way."

"Yeah," he said. "Hang on to me. Promise you won't let go."

I wrapped the scarf around his head and made sure he couldn't see past it.

"Is he okay?" Joey asked. "He doesn't look good. And what's with the scarf?"

"He's fine," I said. "He's in the role. He's pretending to be scared. The scarf is part of the thing."

"That's good," Briggs said. "That's what I'm doing."

The elevator door opened, and I guided Briggs in. It started to rise and I felt his knees buckle.

"Steady," I said. "You don't want to get too much into the role too soon."

"Yeah," he said. "I gotta keep that in mind."

We reached the top, the door opened, and I looked out at the catwalk. It was about four feet wide. There were railings on the catwalk, but it looked like a piece had been removed from the middle. Everyone was in place on either side of the removed railing. A young guy with dreads motioned us forward.

"I'm the jump wrangler," he said. "Nothing to worry about. I've done hundreds of these jumps. Haven't lost anyone yet."

I shuffled Briggs along up to the jump wrangler.

The wrangler looked Briggs over. "Why's he blindfolded?"

"He likes to be surprised," I said. "As soon as you get him hooked up and ready we'll take the blindfold off."

"I'm not up very high, right?" Briggs said.

I looked down and wanted to throw up. We were at least forty feet above the crusher.

"We're practically still on the ground," I said.

We got Briggs out of his bathrobe, and the wrangler strapped him into an ankle harness.

"I'm getting cold," Briggs said. "Are we almost done?"

"We just have to raise you up a little more," the wrangler said.

He gave a signal to the control room and I saw the giant crane slowly swing around. There was a cage attached to the skyhook. The crane operator brought the cage to the opening in the railing, and the wrangler stepped in and pulled Briggs in with him.

"What's happening?" Briggs said. "Where's Stephanie? Are we going down?"

"We're going up," the wrangler said. "Ordinarily we'd start from the ground, but the salvage crane only lowers so far."

"And anyways this is a better angle for Howie," Lula said. "He'll get to film you coming and going."

The crane swung out a little, the cage rose, and the rest of us stood on the catwalk gobsmacked at the height of the jump.

"Holy frijoles!" Lula said, head tipped back, watching the cage swinging high above us. "You gotta be nuts to do this."

The scarf floated down, the cage door opened, and I could see Briggs look out. Next thing he was in the air.

"Eeeeeeeeeeeeee!"

Briggs fell like a rock past us, the cord stretched to its limit, and for a nanosecond Briggs stopped in midair. The cord recoiled, and Briggs shot up past us.

"Arrrrrrrrrrrrrrrrr!"

"Did he look like he was having fun?" Lula asked.

"He looked like he was peeing hisself," the clacker 'ho said.

He dropped past us again and bounced around for a while until he was just hanging there by his ankles.

"This here's not a complimentary angle for a naked man," Lula said, looking down at him.

Joey waved at the crane operator. "Swing it around here!" he yelled. He turned to Lula. "You're up next. As soon as we get him onto the catwalk we'll bring the basket down and you can get in."

"What are you, crazy? I'm not doing that," Lula said. "I'll rupture something. You'd have to be an idiot to do that. Out of my way. I'm going down. Which way's the elevator?"

The crane was slowly bringing Briggs up, and he was full-blown rabid dog. His eyes were bugged out, and he was clawing at the air with his hands. He was making wild animal sounds, and I think he might have been foaming at the mouth.

"I'll go down with you," I said to Lula.

We left Joey on the catwalk to reel Briggs in, and the rest of us crammed into the elevator. We got to ground level and looked up as Briggs was hauled off the platform.

"He looks okay," Lula said. "That had to be some experience. I bet it was exhilarating."

"He don't look exhilarated," the make-up 'ho said. "He's a ways up there, but he looks gonzo nuts."

We stepped a safe distance from the elevator and waited for Briggs to come down. We heard the car descend. The door opened. Briggs walked out. He didn't have the benefit of his robe, and his winkie was stiff as a stick. His eyes were totally dilated. He looked around at us and licked his lips. His attention focused on Howie.

"Did you get it?" he asked Howie, his voice unnaturally shrill. "Was it good?"

"It was epic," Howie said, "but it happened so fast I didn't catch it. Could you do it again?"

Briggs launched himself at Howie and took him down to the ground. It was like a wild animal attacking prey. We all rushed over and pried Briggs off Howie.

"He bit me," Howie said. "I need a shot or something."

"This was a dumb idea," Lula said. "Who's idea was this anyway?"

We all stared at her.

"Well, it looked good on the Travel Channel," Lula said. "Fortunately I still got my zip-lining idea."

Briggs's eyes got squinty, and he growled at Lula.

"He's unstable," Lula said. "Someone needs to take charge of him."

I supposed that would be me.

"Come on, Randy," I said. "Let's go home."

I walked him to his car and watched him get in.

"Do you have clothes?" I asked him.

"I had a bathrobe. I guess it's still on the catwalk. Maybe someone will mail it to me."

"You can't drive home like this."

He looked down at himself. "I've still got a stiffie."

"So it's not all bad," I said.

"I'd sort of like it to go away."

"Not my rodeo," I said.

"You want to go to a bar? Get a drink?"

"You're naked."

"There must be a bar where nobody would care," Briggs said.

"We could try Kranski's in north Trenton. I know the bartender."

• • •

Briggs followed me to Kranski's, and we walked in like there was nothing unusual and climbed onto barstools. A couple guys were watching Monday Night Football, and an older woman was nursing a drink at one of the high tops.

Bertie sauntered over and looked at Briggs.

"Short Stuff hasn't got any clothes on," Bertie said.

"He's had a hard day," I said. "He went bungee jumping and it sort of went downhill from there."

"I don't mind, but I'm going to have to Lysol that stool when he leaves," Bertie said.

"Vodka rocks with a bourbon chaser," Briggs said. He cut his eyes to me. "No pockets. No wallet."

"Run a tab," I told Bertie. "I'll have a beer. Surprise me. And we could use some nachos."

"I know this is one of those pity things, but it's still nice," Briggs said. "It's like we're friends."

"It's not a pity thing. You got dropped a hundred feet. You deserve a drink."

"It was sort of a rush."

"Really?"

"No," Briggs said. "It was heart attack scary. I thought I was going to die. For all I know I did die. Just not forever."

"Are you going to do the zip-lining film?"

"Maybe. I'm getting to like being naked."

Bertie brought our drinks and the nachos, and I asked him about Kenny Morris.

"I haven't seen him today," Bertie said. "He doesn't usually come in on Mondays."

"Do you still think he should be high on the list of suspects?" I asked.

"He has motivation and anger," Bertie said. "I don't know if he could pull the trigger."

I nodded agreement. That was my assessment too.

"Don't fool yourself," Briggs said. "Under the right circumstances anyone could pull the trigger."

We finished the nachos, and Briggs was looking more mellow. His stiffie had deflated, and his teeth had stopped chattering.

"You've had a lot to drink," I said. "Do you need a ride home?"

"Yeah, that would be great. I'm only about a mile away. I can walk back for my car tomorrow."

"I thought you lived by the DMV."

"That didn't work out. I live on Poplar Street now."

"Here's the thing—I really don't want you in my car naked."

"I feel your pain," Bertie said to me, handing over a big

black garbage bag and some scissors. "See if you can dress him up in this."

I cut holes in the bag for Briggs's head and arms and dropped the bag over him. It came to below his knees. It was perfect.

Bertie looked down at Briggs. "The dude's stylin'."

TWENTY-TWO

IT WASN'T A sleepover night for Morelli so I went to bed in my most comfy, washed-out, ratty sleep shirt. I fell asleep when my head hit the pillow, and I wasn't ready to wake up when the alarm went off. I fumbled for the clock, and as the fog of sleep cleared, I realized I wasn't hearing the alarm. The phone was ringing.

I found my phone in the dark room and saw that it was my parents' number. This jolted me wide awake because it had to be an emergency.

"What?" I said.

"Stephanie? It's your mother."

"I know! What's wrong?"

"It's your grandmother."

Omigod. Grandma was dead.

"What about Grandma?" I asked, barely breathing.

"I think she has a man in her bedroom."

"Excuse me?"

"I got up to go to the bathroom, and I heard talking. At first I thought she had her radio on, but then I realized it was your grandmother I was hearing. And a man."

"What were they saying?"

"He was calling her his little honey bunny. It sounded like Bertie."

I looked at my clock. It was two o'clock. Bertie was off work.

"What do you think I should do?" my mother asked. "I don't want to wake your father. I don't know what his reaction would be. It might not be good. How do you suppose a man even got into our house?"

"I imagine Grandma let him in."

"Should I knock on her door to see if she's okay?"

"Is she calling for help?"

"No."

"Then we can assume she's okay."

"It's not right," my mother said. "It's . . . icky. And we don't really even know this man. We don't know his intentions. He's a bartender with tattoos and a motorcycle."

"Where are you now?"

"I'm in the kitchen."

"Are you going to sit in the living room and wait for him to leave?"

"Yes."

I knew she would. When I was in high school and came

home from a date, my mom would be in the living room, waiting. Sometimes my dad would be there too.

"Don't you think it will be awkward to see Bertie leaving?" I asked her.

"Your grandmother should have thought of that before she decided to entertain a man in her bedroom."

"Maybe you should ground her."

"I've tried. It doesn't work. She does whatever she wants. She doesn't listen to me."

"I'm going back to sleep. You should too."

"Suppose they're doing things?"

"Eewwww!"

"Exactly," my mother said. And she hung up.

It was hard to fall asleep with the thought of Grandma doing things. I thrashed around for a half hour and finally got up and had some cereal. I went back to bed, and the next time I woke up Ranger was in my bedroom, looking down at me. He was hard to see in the dark room, with his dark skin and black clothes. I knew it was Ranger because he said "Babe." I glanced at my clock. It was four o'clock.

"I have a problem you are uniquely qualified to solve," Ranger said.

Last time he said that it turned out to be the best night of my life.

I propped myself up on one elbow. "Oh boy."

"Not that problem," Ranger said. "Someone broke into the Bogart plant, and I want you to take a look."

"Now?"

"We need to do this before the plant opens."

"I'm tired. It's too early."

"It's four o'clock."

"People are supposed to be asleep at four o'clock."

Ranger flipped the light on and went to my dresser. Panties, bra, T-shirt, jeans got thrown onto the bed.

"Get dressed, and I'll buy you breakfast."

"This is weird. Usually when you're in my bedroom you're telling me to take my clothes off."

"Yeah, I'm having a hard time with it too. Don't expect it to happen again."

I sat up and swung my legs over the side of the bed. "Give me five minutes. And it would be great if you could make coffee."

He took in my bare legs and the clingy washed-out sleep shirt. "Babe," he said so soft it was barely a whisper.

Ten minutes later I was settled into Ranger's Porsche 911 Turbo. I had a to-go cup of coffee and Ranger's iPad. I was watching a rerun of a video feed from the Bogart plant.

"We have the cameras up and running," Ranger said, "but we haven't got all the doors alarmed, and we haven't changed out all the locks. After today I expect Bogart will allow me to replace his security staff with my own people, at least temporarily. The locks are scheduled to get changed out tomorrow." He stopped for a light on Hamilton. "Tell me what you're seeing."

"The Jolly Bogart clown comes into the plant through the back door to the storeroom. He grabs a gallon jug of something and a bag of something else. He walks through the storeroom and heads for the offices that are on the opposite side of the building from the manufacturing area. I'm watching him from a different camera now. He stops at one of the doors and knocks. No one answers the door, so the clown opens the door and goes in. He's off camera."

"Fast-forward."

"Okay, here he is leaving the office. His hands are free. He hasn't got the jug or the bag. He goes back to the storeroom and leaves through the back door."

"What do you think?"

"I could see Ducker doing this. He went gonzo when he realized he was still stuck being the clown."

"Anything else?"

"Have you already been to the plant?" I asked Ranger.

"Yes."

"It was Bogart's office, wasn't it?"

"Yes."

"And it's now covered with chocolate syrup and nuts?"

"Yes."

This got a smile from me. "Fun." I replayed the video. "So we know the Jolly Bogart clown trashed Bogart's office. Does this relate to the other crimes?"

"It's not clear. It's also not clear who's in the clown suit. The clown hair is covering a lot of the face, and the video is being shot in the dark by infrared cameras that only show color when the clown's penlight sporadically goes on to help him find his way."

"Jeez," I said. "It could be me."

"Only if you were wearing size ten running shoes. The clown stepped in some chocolate and left prints in the hall."

I ran the video again. "If it's not Ducker it's someone with a similar build."

"Do you know anyone at the plant with a similar build?"

"No. That's not to say there isn't someone."

Ranger turned into the Bogart parking lot and parked by the loading dock. There were two Rangeman SUVs parked there as well. All lights were on in the plant and the office wing.

"There's a second video I want you to see," Ranger said.

He took the iPad from me, found the video, and handed it back. I saw the door to the loading dock swing open. Bogart appeared, and lights flashed on. He was wearing jeans and what looked like a pajama top, and he wasn't happy. I watched him walk through the plant to his office and go inside. I fast-forwarded and caught him bursting out of his office and charging down the hall. The video was in full color, and Bogart's face was practically purple. His fists were clenched. He left by the same door he entered.

"The clown break-in occurred at one in the morning," Ranger said. "At two o'clock Bogart showed up, entered through the loading dock, and went straight to his office. He spent five minutes in his office, and left the building. Before he left he called Rangeman to report the break-in. My man at the desk asked Bogart if he'd also called the police, and Bogart said he didn't want the police involved."

"Why didn't your monitoring station pick up the break-in?"

"Bogart didn't want his cameras monitored in real time."

"This still doesn't seem like anything serious enough for you to drag me out of bed in the middle of the night."

"We can't find Bogart," Ranger said. "He never returned home, and his car was found abandoned about a mile from here. We've notified the police, but there's no indication of foul play or of a struggle, and Bogart has only been missing for a couple hours. Right now the damage to his office is considered vandalism."

"But you think it's more serious."

"I think no matter how you spin it this isn't going to look good for Rangeman."

We entered the building through the loading dock door and walked straight through to Bogart's office. The door was open. Bogart hadn't bothered to close it when he stomped out. I peeked in and grimaced. The office was a mess. The chocolate and chopped nuts were everywhere. They were sprayed on walls, bookshelves, the desk, and the floor. Some of the chocolate had been smeared, and DIE had been written in it. Other messages were DEAD MAN, BURN BABY, and BE AFRAID.

"This is beyond vandalism," I said to Ranger. "This is ugly."

"Yeah," Ranger said. "We've got a bad clown."

"Have the police seen this?"

"We had a uniform here, but no plainclothes. You might want to mention to Morelli that this might be more than a prank. It's not his problem, but he can pass it along."

"Is that my purpose here?"

"Partly. Mostly I wanted you to walk through the two videos and see if anything was off. I've got a problem with the clown. I can't see Ducker getting into his clown suit and doing this."

"I can. He's totally postal. Too many years of listening to the Jolly jingle."

"Someone blew up his truck."

"He hated the truck. He could have blown it up. He was in the men's room when it went *boom!*"

"So he's your prime candidate?"

"He's in a tie with Butchy. And I guess I can't rule out Kenny Morris."

"Could either of those men have been in the clown suit tonight?"

Good question. I reran the video in my mind. "I don't think it's Butchy. Butchy is built like a scarecrow, and he sort of hunches forward when he walks."

"What about Kenny Morris?"

"I don't know. I only saw him on a barstool. He's average height and build. Closer to the clown than Butchy."

We exited through the loading dock and walked around the building until we came to the back door to the storeroom. It was locked.

"Can you open it?" I asked. I already knew the answer. Ranger could open anything.

"The real question is can *you* open it?"

The door had a numerical keypad like the keypad to the freezer. I punched in 0000 and opened the door.

"Either Bogart is very trusting or very stupid," I said.

"So far in my dealings with him I haven't seen evidence that he's either of those."

We stepped into the storeroom and followed the clown's path through the rows of shelves. We left the storeroom and walked the hall to Bogart's office. We turned and retraced our steps to the storeroom's back door.

"Do you have any words of wisdom for me?" Ranger asked.

"No, but I have some questions. Why did Bogart come to check on his office in his pajamas?"

"He didn't say. His phone message to the control room was terse. And after that initial message we couldn't reach him. I assume whoever trashed his office called him. It was late at night, and the call rattled him enough that he rushed over half dressed."

"Question number two. Actually it's an observation. The storeroom is a maze of shelves, but the clown had no trouble finding the chocolate and nuts in the dark. He walked right to them. And then there's number three. It's a retraction of what I said a couple minutes earlier. I don't think Ducker would dress up in his clown suit to do this . . . especially if he killed Arnold Zigler."

• • •

It was six o'clock when I fell into bed fully clothed and pulled the pillow over my head. I woke up a little after ten and shuffled into the kitchen. I opened the fridge door and let the cold air wash over me, hoping it would jump-start my brain. I didn't feel a surge of intelligence so I gave up on the fridge and pulled a box of Froot Loops out of the cupboard. I made coffee and ate a couple handfuls of cereal. The fog started to lift after the coffee.

I wasn't sure what to do following my bizarre night. Ranger hadn't said anything about returning to the ice cream factory. No more phone calls about my honey bunny grandmother. The one bright spot of the day so far was remembering Briggs hurling past me on the bungee cord and bouncing back up. More entertaining the morning after than it had been at the time.

I had just one open file to clear for Vinnie, and it was a low-bond shoplifter. Hardly worth the effort. Probably I should go to the office and see if anything else came in. I brushed my teeth and put concealer on my nose. I thought about taking a shower, but it seemed like it would take energy I didn't have.

I grabbed my messenger bag and opened my door to leave my apartment. DIE was written on the outside of the door in chocolate. At least I hoped it was chocolate, because it was brown and the alternative wasn't nice. A note card was taped to the door below the chocolate.

The note card message was written in block letters. STICK TO YOUR DAY JOB OR ELSE.

Terrific. I dropped the note into my bag, scrubbed the message off the door, and sprayed the door with Lysol, just in case.

I called Morelli on my way to the office. I told him about

Bogart's vandalized office, the Bogart disappearance, and the note card.

"Don't you have CSI people who analyze things like the note card?" I asked Morelli. "Can't they look for fingerprints? DNA? Personalized cooties?"

"It's expensive," Morelli said. "It takes time."

"Sherlock would have figured it out right away."

"Yeah, but I hear he was a dud in the sack. Get the card to me, and I'll see what I can do. We can at least fingerprint it."

"Are you playing poker tonight?"

"Yeah. The game's at my house. You can come if you want."

"Not even for a moment."

I parked in front of the bail bonds office and called Ranger. "Anything new?" I asked. "Did Bogart turn up?"

"He's still missing. No one has heard from him."

"Is this normal behavior?"

"No. He's a man of routine. Never misses work. And he wouldn't just walk away from his car."

"Where was it found?"

"About a mile from the plant, in a convenience store lot."

"Was the store open?"

"No. Shut its doors at midnight. No one in the area saw anything."

"Did you check the trunk?"

"No body in the trunk."

I told him about the message on my door and the note card.

"Have you talked to any of your neighbors? Are there security cameras in place?"

"No and maybe."

"I'll have someone ask around."

I said adios to Ranger and went into the office. Lula was asleep on the couch, and Connie was on the phone. She waved a file at me.

I took the file and flipped through it. Benjamin Kwan. Arrested for human trafficking. High bond. No-show for court date.

Connie had a second FTA file. Dottie Loosey, fifty-eight years old. Arrested for armed robbery and assault with a deadly weapon. The only photo in the file was her mug shot. Gray hair cut short. Uncombed. Fierce black eyebrows. Mean, squinty eyes. Lips pressed tight together. The woman looked like she ate nails for breakfast.

"She looks scary," I said to Connie.

"I hate giving these to you, but I haven't got anyone else," Connie said. "I've never been able to find a replacement for Ranger. When he stopped doing fugitive apprehension no one else with his skill level came forward for the job."

"Have you done any phone work on either of these FTAs?"

"The usual. It looks like they're both in the area, living at the addresses I gave you. Loosey has a history of alcoholism and of being a nasty drunk. You want to be careful with her. She's also got a PCP history. If she's popped a couple of those she'll be fearless."

"I'll see if I can get Ranger to help me with Loosey."

Lula opened her eyes. "Ranger? Where?"

"Nowhere," I said. "You know Benjamin Kwan, right?"

Lula sat up and adjusted the girls. She stood and tugged

her skirt into place. "Benjamin Kwan? Yeah, I know him. He's a real scumbag, but he got a excellent wardrobe. He traffics in street kids. Helps them get dope and then rents them out. And he brings some in from Honduras. And that's just the beginning. He's got his fingers in a lot of pies."

"He didn't show up for court yesterday," Connie said. "I just got the papers."

"This here's going to be fun," Lula said. "I don't like this man. Let's go get him."

I knew Kwan too, and I didn't expect a lot of trouble from him if we could catch him alone. He was a businessman, not a street thug. Problem was, he frequently surrounded himself with an entourage of spiffy street thugs. He lived in a fancy high-rise condo overlooking the river, and he used the second and third floor of a three-story row house on the third block of Stark for offices. The Kwan Travel Agency occupied the ground floor. I knew all this because I'd apprehended Kwan twice before. He'd had several arrests but no convictions. Witnesses disappeared or recanted. Evidence got tainted. Charges were dropped.

"He probably skipped his court date because he didn't have the fix in place for his trial," Lula said. "He probably still has to kill a couple witnesses."

I drove to Stark Street and found a parking place in front of Kwan's building.

"How are we going to do this?" Lula asked. "Are we going in like gangbusters?"

"No. We're going in like sane, polite fugitive-apprehension

agents. I'm not looking for a firefight. If Kwan is ready to go to court with us we'll be happy to escort him. If he isn't ready and he's surrounded by his entourage of gun-crazy idiots, I'll give him my card and he can call me when he wants a ride."

"You could have just got him a cab with that attitude. And what am I supposed to do? I got a reputation to uphold. People think I'm a hard-ass."

"I was hoping you would stay with my new car so no one steals it."

"Good thinking. If you need help just yell."

A woman in a tiny, skin-tight silver dress with a plunging neckline was at the desk in the travel office. She was wearing red patent leather five-inch spike heels, a massive faux diamond ring, and a small diamond-like stud in her right nostril.

"I'm a travel specialist," she said. "Would you like to go somewhere?"

"I'm an apprehension specialist," I said. "I'd like to go upstairs to talk to Mr. Kwan."

"Of course." She put her headset to her ear and tapped a speed-dial button. "I have an apprehension specialist here to see Mr. Kwan." She nodded, replaced the headset, and smiled at me. "He's expecting you. The stairs are to the right."

I took the stairs to the second floor and thought this had to be how Briggs felt when he was going up in the crane cage. Not completely sure what sort of shape you were going to be in on the trip down.

The second floor was Spartan. A large oak desk that had

seen better days. Some folding chairs around a collapsible card table. A brown leather couch. A dorm fridge against one wall. A large shrink-wrapped pack of Bogart Kidz Kups also against the wall by the little fridge.

Kwan was at the desk. He was wearing a shiny bright blue suit with a black dress shirt. He was about my height, slim, black hair slicked back, forty-two years old according to the file Connie gave me. Not married. Three men lounged to the side of the room. They were all slim, wearing black suits with tight trousers and obvious bulges. Some of the bulges were due to large guns. A massive man stood behind Kwan. At least six foot five. Barrel-chested. Couldn't see any bulges for the excess of flesh. I figured the skinny cubs were for amusement and the mountain man was security.

"So nice to see you again," Kwan said to me. "I would have been disappointed if Connie sent someone else out."

"Connie doesn't have anyone else."

Kwan smiled at me, flashing a gold tooth in the front of his mouth. "Lucky me."

"Would you like to come with me to get re-upped into the legal system?"

"Actually, it's inconvenient for me right now."

"No problem," I said. "I'll leave my card. You can call or text when you're ready."

"Thank you so much," Kwan said. "Is there anything I can get you? Would you like my travel associate to arrange a trip to the Bahamas?"

"No," I said. "I'm good, but thank you."

He nodded. "Chewy will see you to your car. I hope you took precautions. The neighborhood is aggressively entrepreneurial."

"Lula is waiting downstairs," I said. "I haven't heard any gunshots so I assume there wasn't an issue." I glanced over at the Kidz Kups. "Your Kidz Kups are going to melt if you don't get them into a freezer."

"A very good observation," Kwan said. "I'll have them moved immediately."

The three-hundred-pound gorilla behind Kwan stepped forward and motioned me to the stairs.

"Chewy?" I asked him.

"Short for 'Chewbacca.'"

That made sense. I could see the hair curling out of the top of his shirt collar. We made our way to the first floor and walked past the travel associate, all of us smiling pleasantly. I reached the sidewalk and saw that Lula was out of the car and standing guard.

She looked Chewbacca up and down. "Who's this?"

"Chewy," I told her.

Chewy swept his hand under his suit jacket to his pocket and Lula went bug-eyed.

"Gun! Gun!" she said. "He's got a gun!"

She jumped forward and head butted him in the midsection. They went off-balance and down to the ground. Chewy gave a grunt and flipped Lula off him. He got to his feet and brushed at his suit.

"I wasn't going for my gun," he said. "I was going for

my banana." He pulled a banana out of his pocket. "It's all smushed," he said to Lula. "You ruined my banana."

Lula was on her feet. "Banana? Are you shitting me? Who packs a banana?"

"I like bananas," Chewy said. "They're high in potassium."

I shoved Lula into the car.

"Sorry about the banana," I said to Chewy.

"It's okay," he said. "I like your friend. She gives a good head butt."

I didn't know how to respond to that, so I smiled and nodded, got behind the wheel, and drove off.

"I swear I thought he had a gun," Lula said.

"He did. It just wasn't in the same place as his banana."

"I guess Kwan didn't feel like going to jail today."

"He'll get back to me."

I dropped Lula off in front of the deli on the first block of Stark. No parking places, so I gave her my order and circled the block. I was stopped at a light when Ranger called.

"You have a single surveillance camera in the lobby of your apartment building," Ranger said. "At six thirty-five this morning the Jolly Bogart clown walked through the back door and got into the elevator. Three minutes later he got out of the elevator, crossed the lobby, and left the building."

"That's really creepy."

"We need to have a conversation with Mr. Ducker," Ranger said.

"When do you want to do this?"

"Now."

I looked in my rearview mirror. Ranger was behind me.

"Let Lula take your car back to the office," Ranger said.

I double-parked in front of the deli and waited for Lula. She hustled out with two bags of food and two sodas.

I got out of my car and held the door for her. "I need to go with Ranger. I'd appreciate it if you could get the car back to the office for me."

Lula looked back at Ranger and gave him a finger wave. "Are you gonna have a nooner with him?"

"No. This is work related."

Lula gave me my bag of food and my soda. "Hard to believe anything you could do with that man would be work."

Ranger was in his black Porsche Cayenne, and he was wearing perfectly pressed Rangeman black fatigues. He smelled great, and he didn't look tired. I suspected I looked like roadkill.

He glanced at me and grinned. "Did you sleep in those clothes?"

I buckled my seatbelt and narrowed my eyes at him. "Someone woke me up at four in the morning."

He looked at the bag. "Lunch?"

"Ham and Swiss. Would you like half?"

TWENTY-THREE

RANGER PARKED IN front of Ducker's apartment building, and we looked for the Kia. No Kia. We went to the door and rang the bell. No answer. Ranger knocked. Nothing. He took a slim pick from his pocket and opened the door.

It was a completely unmemorable apartment. Beige carpet, beige couch, beige drapes on the windows. Television in the living room. A maple table and six chairs in the dining room. Probably the dining room table had never been used. Not ever. Shoes under the coffee table, and an open bag of chips and an empty soda can on top of it. Dirty dishes in the kitchen sink. Not a lot in the refrigerator. Bogart Kidz Kups in the freezer.

I went room by room with Ranger. We looked in the medicine chest and the closet.

"No man-sized freezer," I said. "No Bogart locked in the bathroom."

Ranger went through Ducker's dresser drawers. "And no gun."

We returned to the living room, and Ranger looked at the shoes under the coffee table.

"No chocolate on the shoe," Ranger said. "And it's a size eleven. We measured the print on the floor in Bogart's office. It was a size ten."

There was the sound of a key being inserted in the lock on the front door, and I looked at Ranger.

"Our lucky day," Ranger said. "We don't have to go searching for Ducker."

Ducker opened the door, spotted Ranger and me, and went for the gun tucked into his jeans.

"Don't even think about it," Ranger said.

"You're the security guy, right?" Ducker said. "What's going on? And what's with the minimum wager with you?"

"Stephanie works with me," Ranger said. "Where were you at one o'clock last night?"

"I wasn't anywhere," Ducker said. "I was here. Like always."

"Someone broke into Bogart's office last night and left threatening messages. He was wearing the Jolly Bogart clown suit."

"Big deal," Ducker said. "Anyone can get that suit. They sell them at the party store at the mall. You can get the wig and everything. It's real cheap too."

"Do you have any idea who broke in last night?" I asked him.

"No, but I'd kiss him on the lips if I found out," Ducker said. "Bogart is a real asshole."

"So what do you think?" I asked Ranger when we were back in the Cayenne.

"This is why I'm in the security business and not investigation. I'm good at protecting people. I don't enjoy this. Unfortunately I've failed to protect a new client and I feel compelled to find him."

"And I'm along why?"

"I need some fun in my life."

"Jeez."

He grinned at me. "It's more than that. I was the point person in my unit when I was in the military. I can sense danger the way a dog can sniff out a rabbit, but I'm not a detail man. You notice things that don't show up on my radar."

"Do you think Ducker is a killer?"

"If he is a killer it's not because he's gone postal from the Jolly jingle. I think there's something more going on here."

"For instance?"

"I don't know. The crimes are all over the place. They start with industrial sabotage and progress to a bizarre murder, then a murder that's premeditated but not especially creative, an explosion, and vandalism. It's almost like they were all done by different people."

"Don't forget my door. Someone doesn't like me snooping around."

"Another threat like that and you might have to come live with me so I can protect you until the danger has passed."

"I expect there's an ulterior motive involved."

"Yeah," Ranger said. "There's that."

I pulled Dottie Loosey's file out of my bag.

"I have a favor to ask. I could use some help bringing this woman in."

Ranger flipped through the file. "Has Connie placed her at this address?"

"Yes."

. . .

Dottie Loosey lived in a row house by the button factory. There were several blocks of the small two-story houses. They were originally built as housing for button company workers, but over the years they all went to private ownership. At least half were now rental properties. They had started out all the same, and were now all fiercely different.

Dottie's stood out for its neglect. In fact, it looked a lot like Dottie. There was nothing to pretty it up and soften the years. It was raw and weathered, with peeling paint and window trim down to bare wood.

Ranger parked one house down, and we sat and watched Dottie's place for a while. It was early afternoon. No one was moving around. No car or pedestrian traffic. This wasn't a part of town sought after by young parents. The houses had no front yards, and minuscule backyards.

Ranger read through the file again. "She has a history of drug and alcohol abuse, and violent behavior. She's been in and out of jail for the past twenty years. Public drunkenness, possession, two armed robbery convictions. Her daughter

225

posted her bond. The daughter has a Massachusetts address. It looks like Dottie lives alone." He handed the paperwork back to me. "Let's do it."

We went to the door and rang the bell. No answer. No sounds from inside the house. No television or radio. Ranger knocked. Nothing. He tried the door. Locked. He picked the lock, opened the door, and yelled "Bond enforcement." No one responded.

We cleared the house, working our way through, room by room, looking for Dottie. Her furniture would have been discarded by a sober person. Stained and torn couch in the living room, stained bare mattress on the floor in the bedroom, a faded quilt on the mattress, an empty whiskey bottle on the floor. No pillow. Cigarette butts overflowing a cracked dish.

The smell wasn't great.

We ended in the kitchen. A couple food-encrusted dishes in the sink. Crumpled fast food bags everywhere. Empty refrigerator. A cracked and peeling Formica countertop littered with empty whiskey and beer bottles, a squeeze bottle of mustard, and a Bogart Kidz Kup.

"Look at this," I said to Ranger. "She can't be all bad. She likes ice cream."

I picked the cup up and it rattled. I peeled the lid off and looked inside.

"Not ice cream," I said to Ranger.

Ranger took the cup. "She's got some pharmaceutical grade meth, a small amount of crack, and I'm not sure about the pink pills."

"This is a new Kidz Kup container. It's never held ice cream. There's no chocolate stain on the bottom, and it doesn't have any markings from the machine that puts the lids on. I have firsthand experience with Kidz Kups lids."

Ranger put the lid back on and returned the Kidz Kup to the counter. "I haven't heard anything on the street about Bogart Kidz Kups, but it's hard to keep up with this stuff. It's more likely that some unused containers were discarded and Dottie got hold of one. I'd like to think that's the case, because the alternative is ugly."

"Packaging drugs in something designed for children?"

"When you were working at the plant did you run across anyone who might have a business on the side?"

"Butchy has a garage filled with microwaves, toaster ovens, and Nikes."

"Did you get into his house?"

"No."

Forty minutes later Ranger and I walked around the outside of Butchy's house, and Ranger let us in through the back door. The kitchen was as I remembered it, but the cardboard box was gone from the table. I couldn't help wondering if it had been filled with Bogart Kidz Kups. Four six-packs of beer and six packages of hot dogs in his fridge. No rolls anywhere to be seen. No Kidz Kups in his freezer. I went to check out his over-the-counter cabinets and found they were filled with pint ice cream containers still stacked together and wrapped in plastic.

"What do you make of this?" I asked Ranger.

Ranger stood looking at them, hands on hips. "Let's talk to Butchy."

"Now?"

"As soon as I finish the walk-through. I want to see if he has a clown suit in his closet, and I want to check his shoe size."

· · ·

Ranger called his office from the road and asked to have someone keep an eye on Butchy until we got to the plant.

"What about Bogart?" I asked Ranger. "Any word on him?"

"I have Tank taking point on that one. So far there's nothing. Bogart hasn't been home. He hasn't called in. His wife and daughter are supposedly at a family reunion at Disney World. They say they haven't heard from him, but they only seem mildly worried."

"'Supposedly' at a family reunion?"

"We've checked and there was a family reunion, but it was a one-day affair last week. The wife and daughter are still at Disney. If someone went missing in my family under suspicious circumstances I'd be home and I'd be frantic."

"Are the police involved yet?"

"Yes. And the FBI. They've impounded his car."

"Who's running the plant?"

"Jeff Soon. He's the vice president and in charge of plant operations. He has an office two doors down from Bogart. Word is that Bogart owns the company, but lately Soon's

been running it. If you remember there was an empty file on
J. T. Soon in Zigler's office, and a note on his desk to run a
background check on Soon."

"Have you been working with Soon?"

"No. My dealings have been with Bogart. Soon is a shadow
in the hall."

When we arrived, Butchy had an eighteen-wheeler pulled
up to the loading dock. Two men were helping him load it.

"Hey," Butchy said when he saw me. "Looks like they got
you working security with the black shirts now."

I smiled and nodded. Friendly. "Is there someplace we can
talk?"

"I don't have an office or anything, but we can go to my
truck and I can get a smoke if that's okay with you."

We followed him to his truck, and he got a joint out of a
cooler on his front seat.

"You want one?" Butchy asked. "I got plenty."

"That's illegal," Ranger said. "It's a controlled substance."

"No way," Butchy said. "It's marijuana. And, besides, we're
on private property so it's okay."

"It's not legal on private property in New Jersey," Ranger
said.

"Okay, but it's medicinal. I'm even thinking about getting a
service dog to help with my medicinal issues. I might get one
of those little Chihuahuas. I hear they're feisty."

"Ranger and I happened to be in your neighborhood, and
when we walked past your house your garage door happened
to open," I said.

"Shoot," Butchy said. "That's no good. It shouldn't do that. I got a load of shit in that garage. Did it close again?"

I cut my eyes to Ranger. Ranger looked like he was contemplating smashing Butchy's head into his truck to see if any brains fell out.

"About the stuff in your garage," I said.

"If you want a toaster oven I can't sell it to you," Butchy said. "It belongs to someone else. I'm just storing it."

"Tell me about this storing," Ranger said.

"It started small," Butchy said. "Like, I started just keeping a couple boxes for one of my neighbors, and now I got three off-site storage units. I just keep the overflow in my garage these days. You got something you want stored?"

"It looks to me like you might be storing hijacked property," Ranger said.

"I don't ask questions," Butchy said. "I just rent storage."

I saw a small smile twitch at the corners of Ranger's mouth. "Have you ever stored anything for Larry Virgil?"

"Sure. He was a good customer. It put a real dent in my business when he got run over."

"How about ice cream?"

"I can't store ice cream," Butchy said. "I haven't got a freezer unit."

"So where was Virgil going to store the ice cream that was in the Bogart truck he hijacked?" I asked Butchy.

Butchy grinned and shook his head. "Larry Virgil was the dumbest guy I ever met. I guess he thought *I* was going to store it."

Ranger and I exchanged glances. If Butchy thought someone was dumb they had to be *really* dumb.

"I'm home watching TV and I get a call from Virgil saying he's got an eighteen-wheeler full of stuff he wants to store," Butchy said. "So I meet him at one of my empty units, and he pulls in with a freezer truck. It turns out he was on Stark Street, and he came across the truck double-parked with the keys in the ignition. So he couldn't resist taking the truck."

"Where on Stark Street?" Ranger asked.

"I don't know," Butchy said. "Just Stark Street. Anyway, I look at the truck, and the condenser's running, and I recognize the truck. I tell Virgil that I loaded the truck, and it's full of ice cream, and I can't store ice cream. He looks at me like I got corn growing out of my ears, so I have to explain to him that just because I got climate-controlled units don't mean I can freeze shit. So we both went home after that. I guess Virgil was taking the truck to his garage until he could figure something out."

"Have you told any of this to the police?" Ranger asked.

"Naw," Butchy said. "They never asked me."

Ranger had the hint of a smile again. "Didn't it occur to you that Zigler fell out of that truck?"

"Sure, but I didn't put him in there. So it's not like I got something to contribute."

"What about the pint containers in your kitchen?" I asked Butchy.

"What about them?"

"Why do you have so many?"

"Well, they're free and they're perfect. A bag of high-quality shit fits in them just right. And it's all disguised. You put it in your freezer and it's like money in the bank."

"Where do you get the containers?"

"The storeroom, of course."

"That's stealing."

"Everybody steals from the storeroom. It's one of the perks of working for Bogart. He don't give you free ice cream, but he lets you steal. It's like a company policy."

"I'm curious," Ranger said. "Do you steal during the day? Just walk out with whatever you want?"

"If it's small, but mostly you use the back door to the storeroom. We all try not to abuse the privilege and be too obvious. Only problem is there's no light at the back door so you have to be careful where you're walking if you forget your flashlight."

"Did you kill Zigler?" Ranger asked Butchy.

"No, sir," Butchy said. "I haven't killed anybody lately."

TWENTY-FOUR

RANGER AND I walked back to the building and left Butchy to finish his joint.

"Do you think he's really that dumb?" I asked Ranger.

"I think he's conveniently dumb."

"I forgot to ask when we were at his house. What size were his shoes?"

"Twelve."

We went to the front reception desk and asked to see Soon. After fifteen minutes we were told he would speak with us.

His office was devoid of anything personal. A desk. A couple chairs. A bookcase. It was as if he didn't intend to stay long. He was a slim little man wearing rimless glasses. His hair was shoe-polish black and thinning. I placed him in his fifties. Partially Asian.

"Very nice to finally meet you," he said to Ranger.

Ranger nodded. "Mutual. And this is my associate, Miss Plum."

"Of course," Soon said. "She's already spent some time here at the plant. What would you like to discuss?"

"Tomorrow we'll have completed all installations and will be moving into a maintenance and monitoring mode. Since Mr. Bogart isn't on-site I wanted to make sure you were comfortable with the new system."

"Absolutely," Soon said. "I appreciate that you've taken the time to introduce yourself. This is an awkward time for Bogart Ice Cream. And it's especially difficult since Mr. Bogart has taken a leave of absence."

"I wasn't aware that he was on leave," Ranger said. "Have you heard from him?"

"No," Soon said. "I was trying to make it sound better than I fear it is." He passed a paper to Ranger. "I intended to take care of this business tomorrow, but since you've stopped by this is an excellent opportunity. Now that we have the system installed I think we would be better served to manage it in-house. I'm going to bring in my own security specialists and techs. I've done this in past positions, and I find it to be more economical and sometimes more efficient."

"Was this discussed with Mr. Bogart?"

"Most certainly. We were finalizing our hires when he suddenly disappeared."

"He'd made it clear to me that I was to keep my men in place."

"Unfortunately he isn't here to substantiate that. We will

make final payment to you when you present your itemized bill for installation plus consulting fees."

Ranger smiled. "I wish you the best of luck. I'm sure Mr. Bogart will make a speedy return from his leave of absence."

"We can only hope," Soon said.

We were silent walking through the building. We buckled into Ranger's Cayenne, and he called his office. "I want a full report on Jeff Soon. I want it stat. Get me the name of the primary on the Bogart investigation and get me permission to walk through Bogart's house."

He put the Cayenne in gear and drove out of the lot.

"You didn't see that one coming," I said.

"No, but it's beginning to pull together. I have to spend some time at my desk. I'm going to drop you at your car and we'll pick this up later tonight. I'll send you a text when I'm leaving the building."

It was a little after five o'clock when we got to the office, and the lights were out. My car was parked at the curb. Its doors were locked, but Lula had placed the keys in our usual hiding spot on top of the left rear wheel. I had no plans to see Morelli, so I drove to my parents' house to mooch dinner.

My grandmother opened the door for me. Her hair was red and she was wearing black Pilates pants and a Harley-Davidson T-shirt.

"What do you think?" she asked me.

"I like the red. It's pretty."

And it was pretty, but it was going to take some time for me to get used to seeing it on Grandma.

"I wanted a new look," Grandma said. "Bertie gave me the T-shirt."

"How's it going with Bertie?"

"It's going real good, but I'm not sure how long it's going to last. There's a lot of maintenance you gotta do to keep up with a relationship. There's tweezing and shaving and moisturizing. Plus you gotta pretend you haven't already heard his jokes. And I think I might be getting a rash down there from riding on his motorcycle. I don't know if I'm cut out to be a biker chick."

"Is that Stephanie?" my mother yelled from the kitchen. "Is she staying for dinner? Tell her we're having meatloaf and mashed potatoes."

"I'm staying!" I yelled back.

My father was in his chair, watching television. I passed him on my way to the kitchen, and he grunted at me. "The news is terrible," he said. "Every day it gets worse. I don't know why I watch."

"Is Bertie coming to dinner?" I asked Grandma.

"No. I'm meeting him later at the funeral home. They finally released the body of the Bogart Bar guy, and his viewing is tonight. It's going to be big. I bet the TV people will be there. Bertie and I are going out after. We might go to the movies. There's a horror flick at the multiplex that Bertie wants to see. I think it's got zombies in it."

My mother was mashing the potatoes. "You can't go to the

viewing dressed like that," she said to my grandmother. "And I don't want to hear that you tried to get the lid up if it's a closed casket."

"I'm hoping it won't be closed casket," Grandma said. "I wouldn't mind seeing what a Bogart Bar man looks like."

"I'm sure he doesn't look like a Bogart Bar man," my mother said. "He's had an autopsy!"

"And I guess he would have melted by now anyway," Grandma said. "Still, it would be interesting to see what's left."

"Stephanie," my mother said. "Stir the gravy."

My grandmother took the meatloaf to the table, and I leaned toward my mother.

"Whatever happened last night with Bertie and Grandma?"

"I don't know. I fell asleep on the couch, and when I woke up it was morning. I guess he tiptoed past me."

"Did you talk to Grandma?"

"No. I don't know what to say."

"I wouldn't worry about it. I think it'll resolve itself."

"Where's the potatoes?" Grandma said. "We gotta keep on schedule. I don't want to be late or I won't get a good seat. Marion Wurtzer is picking me up at six-thirty sharp."

We all took our places and filled our plates.

"You should go to this viewing," Grandma said to me. "The killer might be there. That's the way it is in the movies. The killer always makes a showing."

"Why on earth would she want to see the killer?" my mother said.

"Gravy," my father said.

Grandma passed the gravy to him. "Everybody wants to see the killer. And besides, Stephanie is working with Ranger to get to the bottom of this."

"I'd think you were switched at birth," my mother said, slanting a look at me, "but you have the Mazur nose."

"It's a good one, too," Grandma said. "It's one of our best features."

Grandma might be right about the killer showing up at the viewing, but how was I supposed to recognize him? He wasn't going to have "Killer" tattooed on his forehead. Plus, I don't share Grandma's enthusiasm for viewings. The flower smell makes me nauseous. I don't like looking at dead people. And I'm not all that excited about talking to the live people.

"I wonder if the Bogart people will be there," Grandma said. "I'm hearing that the big Bogart guy, Harry Bogart, has taken off for parts unknown. It wouldn't be right if no one from the company showed up. I mean, the deceased was made into a Bogart Bar. Seems like the least they could do is honor that memory."

I didn't think there would be much representation from the Bogart family. Possibly some co-workers, but even that seemed unlikely.

"When is the funeral?" I asked Grandma.

"Tomorrow morning. It's going to be a traffic stopper. Bertie and me are going on his motorcycle."

My mother gave a gasp. "You are not!"

"Not what?" my father said. "Where's the dessert?"

Grandma hurried off to the kitchen and returned with cookies.

"These are store-bought cookies," my father said. "What's this world coming to?"

"You always eat store-bought cookies," my mother said.

"Not for dinner. I eat store-bought cookies for television."

Grandma went upstairs to change clothes, and I helped my mom clear the table.

"She's going to a funeral on a motorcycle," my mother said. "She's going to wear a motorcycle helmet to the church, and when she takes it off she's going to have red hair."

"She's enjoying herself. I think it's okay. It's not like she's robbing banks."

"Your Aunt Marge and Uncle Tub moved to Scottsdale. They make it sound nice. I might like it there."

"I don't think it's that easy. Grandma would go with you."

"I could put her into Senior Living," my mother said. "They have bingo every night. Her friend Alice Besty is there. They could have dinner together."

"Really?"

"No, but I like to think about it sometimes."

Grandma came into the kitchen to tell us she was leaving with Marion. She was dressed in skinny black slacks, a black-and-white-checked jacket, a white shirt, and black flats. And she was topped off by her red hair.

My mother stared at her for a moment.

"You look nice," my mother said.

"Thank you," Grandma said. "Don't wait up."

TWENTY-FIVE

I TOOK THE elevator because I didn't have the energy to walk up the stairs to my apartment. I let myself in, locked my door with three locks, and gave Rex a green bean. Ranger was going to call to do who-knows-what, and I was exhausted. It had been a long day. I stripped and stood in the shower until I felt a little revived. I might not be totally energetic, but at least I was clean. I dressed in a navy short-sleeved T-shirt and jeans and I crawled into bed.

The text message came in a little after nine. He would pick me up in ten minutes. I dragged myself out of bed, laced up my running shoes, and went downstairs to wait for Ranger.

I'm in and out of the building at all hours and don't usually feel vulnerable, but I had a hollow feeling in my chest tonight. The building seemed unusually quiet. The parking lot looked unusually dark. I had my messenger bag with a small canister of pepper spray, some plasti-cuffs, and a stun gun that probably needed charging. Beyond that I was unarmed.

I was relieved when I saw Ranger's headlights swing in. He was still driving the Porsche Cayenne and wearing the black Rangeman fatigues. I relaxed when I got in beside him.

"What's the plan?" I asked.

"I have unauthorized permission to go into Bogart's house."

"What exactly does 'unauthorized permission' mean?"

"It means the Trenton PD primary on the case, Gary Marble, will look the other way while I'm in the house but will charge me with breaking and entering if I get caught."

"And me?"

"You too."

Yeesh.

Ranger drove across town and into an affluent neighborhood. Large yards. Large houses. Lots of neatly trimmed shrubs and flower beds. Landscape lighting.

"Have you been here before?" I asked him.

"Yes. I talked to Bogart about a security system for his house. It wasn't a complicated job, but he was distracted by his problems at the plant and never moved forward on the house system. I think he felt he was capable of protecting his family. He has an extensive gun collection. I got the impression he'd be happy to find justification to use it."

"Did he carry?"

"Yes. Always."

"Isn't that odd for a guy who makes ice cream and dresses his minions in yellow so everything looks happy?"

"Looking isn't being. Bogart was a businessman. And he wasn't happy. His business was going south."

A Rangeman SUV was parked in front of Bogart's house. Ranger pulled into the driveway.

"Lookout?" I asked him.

"Yes. And if someone stops to ask he can say we're running routine checks on the house for Bogart."

We got out of the Porsche, and Ranger strapped on a sidearm. He unlocked the front door, we stepped inside, and he switched a penlight on.

"I want to do a quick walk through the entire house," he said, "but I'm really only interested in his home office."

"What are you looking for on the walk-through?"

"Bodies. And evidence that someone has been in the house in the last couple days."

We covered the downstairs first and didn't find any bodies. The milk in the fridge was expired. The loaf of bread on the kitchen counter had some mold. The upstairs bedrooms were also body free. Closets and dressers were full of clothes. Medicine cabinets were filled with the usual. The Bogarts obviously expected to return to their house.

Bogart's home office was on the first floor. Ranger drew the drapes, turned the light on, and looked around.

"No computer," he said. "He worked on a laptop, and it wasn't in his office."

"The cameras should have been working when Bogart left the factory on Monday. Did he have his laptop?"

Ranger called his control room and told them to have Tank

run the Monday video and get back to him. He went through the desk drawers and file cabinet, briefly looking through one file before returning it.

"I was hoping to find some financial information," Ranger said. "Everything is digital now, but most people still keep paper copies of loan agreements and tax forms. Bogart didn't have any in his office at the plant, and he doesn't have any here."

"Safety-deposit box? Home safe?"

"His home safe is small. Just enough for some cash and a little jewelry. I'd proposed a larger safe installation. If he has a safety-deposit box it's not available to me."

"Can't do your magical lock-opening thing on a safety-deposit box?"

"I could, but I'd have to have a better reason than this."

"Are you able to talk to his wife or daughter?"

"We had some initial contact, but they're no longer picking up calls. They'll sometimes answer a text message."

"Are they really at Disney?"

"Yes. We can trace the location."

"And Harry Bogart?"

"He used his cellphone to call the office to report the break-in, and an hour later the phone didn't exist."

Tank called and told Ranger they had Bogart on video, leaving his office. He had a computer case hung from his shoulder and he was carrying a paper grocery bag. No way to tell what was in the bag.

"We've been around the outside of this house," Ranger said

to me. "There's no sign of forced entry. So Bogart either had his computer case in his car when he went to the office in the middle of the night, or else someone drove him back here to get it."

"He was wearing his pajama top when he got to the plant. Hard to believe he would have taken the time or had the presence of mind to take his computer," I said.

Ranger flipped the light off and opened the drapes, and we left the office and the house. He stopped briefly to talk to his man in the Rangeman SUV before getting behind the wheel of the Porsche.

"Let's see if Dottie is home," he said. "Are you feeling lucky?"

I thought about it for a moment and decided the answer was *no*.

• • •

The neighborhood surrounding the button factory was asleep. No lights on in any of the houses. No car traffic. Dottie's house was dark. We parked on the street, went to the front door, and listened. All was quiet. Ranger was still wearing his Glock strapped to his leg. He had cuffs stuck into his gun belt, and he had a big-boy Maglite in his hand. I'd helped him clear a house before, and I knew the drill. He opened the door, stepped in, and I followed. Something went *spronnng* over my head, an alarm gave three blasts of noise, and I was instantly covered in gunk.

Ranger and I froze for a nanosecond.

"Booby trap," Ranger said.

Dottie thundered down the stairs. Ranger caught her in a beam of light, and she fired off a shot. The shot went wide, Ranger shoved me to the ground, and Dottie ran for the back door. Ranger threw the Maglite at her. It hit her square in the back. She said *"Unh!"* and went down to the floor. Ranger had her cuffed in seconds, and he came back to me.

"Are you okay?" he asked.

"I've been slimed."

He flipped the light switch and looked me over. He swiped at the slime with his finger. "It looks like cooking oil, and it smells like bacon and fried chicken. Hang on until I come back with something to clean your face."

My face and hair were soaked with oil. My T-shirt was soaked and my jeans were splattered with the stuff. I stood perfectly still until Ranger returned and wiped me down.

"Why me?" I asked. "You went through the door first, but you haven't got a drop of oil on you."

"I'm special," Ranger said.

No doubt about that.

He looked up at the top of the door. "She had a bucket rigged from a pulley attached to the ceiling. Pretty ingenious. When the bucket fell it set off the alarm. It might have done her some good if she'd been sober."

"It obviously wasn't rigged up when we were here last time."

"I remember seeing the hook in the ceiling, but it didn't compute to be a booby trap."

Dottie was lying flat on her back, looking like a beached whale in a faded multicolored floral muumuu.

"How drunk is she?" I asked.

"Totally wasted. If I hadn't hit her with the flashlight she probably would have fallen over anyway."

Ranger hoisted her up, dragged her to the Cayenne, and strapped her in. I was standing by the side of the SUV, and I didn't know what to do.

"I'm going to ruin your car," I said to Ranger.

"No problem. It'll clean up."

. . .

Ranger carted Dottie into the police station and returned with my body receipt. He drove me home and walked me to my door. We knew Morelli was in my apartment because his car was in the lot.

Ranger opened the door for me and helped me in. I was trying to be careful not to get slime everywhere.

Morelli got up from the couch and walked over. He didn't look all that surprised. He leaned forward and sniffed. "Bacon? Fried chicken?"

"Booby trap," Ranger said. "You might want to try tomato juice to cut the grease." He hung my messenger bag on a coat hook next to my door, and he left.

"Did he tie you to the roof rack, or did he actually let you in his car?" Morelli asked.

"What are you doing here? I thought this was poker night."

"The game broke up early so I decided to surprise you."

"Get me a garbage bag for my clothes. I need to take a shower."

"I could help you in the shower."

"No! Just get me the garbage bag."

Morelli came into the bathroom and stuffed my clothes into the garbage bag. "Explain the booby trap."

I told him about Dottie while I soaped up. "I'll get a big recovery fee," I said. "She was a high bond." I rinsed the soap out of my hair and stuck my head out from behind the shower curtain. "Take a look at my hair and tell me if it's clean."

Morelli got up and sniffed at my hair. "It still smells a little like bacon, but it's not bad. Especially if you like bacon."

I went back behind the shower curtain and shampooed my hair again. I stuck my head out. "How is it now?"

"It's fine," Morelli said. "If you scrub it any more it's all going to fall out." He pushed the shower curtain aside and did a slow appraisal. "Anything else smell like bacon? I'm getting hungry."

TWENTY-SIX

IT WAS DARK when Morelli left my bed at five o'clock. I opened my eyes, thanked him for his help with the bacon problem, and went back to sleep. When I woke up again the room was still dark, but there was something off. The fog of sleep cleared, and I realized someone was moving in the living room. I heard the rustle of clothing and the soft scuff of a shoe. I called out to Morelli, but there was no answer.

I was wide awake now, trying to steady my heartbeat. I lay absolutely still, straining to hear another footfall. The red LED on the light switch by my bedroom door suddenly disappeared, and I knew someone was in my room, blocking the LED with his body. I was paralyzed with terror. Completely scrambled brain. I think my mouth was open, but I didn't hear any screams coming out of it.

I heard him move toward me, saw the glint of a knife as it

reflected the light from my bedside clock. I rolled to the other side of the bed and grabbed the table lamp on the nightstand. He lunged at me and I swung the lamp, smashing it against his face. I saw the knife fly out of his hand, heard it clatter against my dresser. He was very close, and I could see that it was the clown. I could smell the greasepaint on his nose and feel his breath hot against my face. He grabbed my throat, and I kicked out and must have caught him in a strategic spot because he doubled over on a gush of expelled air. I jumped away, and ran out of the room, through my apartment, and into the hall. I took the stairs two at a time to the third floor and rapped on Mrs. Delgado's door. She lived directly above me and was an early riser. I knew she'd be up watching the morning news on television.

She came to the door, all smiles, lipstick on, dressed for the day.

"How nice," she said. "Would you like some breakfast? Some tea?"

I was wearing bed hair, an oversized T-shirt, and panties, but Mrs. Delgado took it all in stride. She'd been through an apartment bombing, a kitchen fire, and an explosion with me, and I suppose nothing surprised her. Still, I didn't want to start her day with a description of my near-death experience. And I especially didn't want it to get back to my mother, who saw Mrs. Delgado in church every Sunday.

"I was h-h-hoping I could use your phone," I said. "I have . . . a m-m-mouse in my apartment. I need to call an exterminator."

"Of course," she said. "There's a phone in the kitchen. Let me make some fresh coffee."

I called Ranger and asked if he could come clear my apartment of rodents.

There was a beat of silence. "Do these rodents have names?"

"Clowny."

The line went dead, and I knew he was on his way.

I kept my eye on the parking lot while Mrs. Delgado made coffee. A Rangeman SUV drove into the lot four minutes later. Not Ranger's car. The SUV pulled up to the back door, and two men in Rangeman black fatigues got out and entered my building.

"My exterminator is here," I said to Mrs. Delgado. "I should go downstairs to let them in."

"Would you like a robe?"

"Yes. Thank you. That would be great. I got so excited about the mouse that I just ran out of my apartment."

"Understandable," she said.

She went to her bedroom and returned with a pink robe. "This should do," she said. "You wouldn't want the exterminator to get the wrong idea."

I shrugged into the robe and padded barefoot down the stairs to the second floor. Ranger's men were standing at my open door. I knew one of them. His name was Calvin, and he was fairly new. I didn't know the other.

"Ranger is on his way," Calvin said. "Would you like us to clear your apartment of the . . . clown?"

I peeked into my apartment. No clown in sight.

"The clown has probably left," I said, "but it would be great if you'd take a look around."

They both drew their sidearms and moved into my apartment. I followed them in and checked to make sure Rex was unharmed. I didn't care what else happened to my apartment as long as Rex was okay.

They moved through the dining area, the living room, the bedroom, and the bath. It didn't take long.

"We didn't see any clowns," Calvin said, coming back to the kitchen. "Your bedroom window was open, and I noticed you have a fire escape balcony and ladder. The clown might have left through the window."

"As long as it's gone," I said. "I appreciate that you got here so quickly. The clown was scary."

"We'll wait outside your door until Ranger gets here," Calvin said. "If the clown returns just yell. And for what it's worth, I'm not crazy about clowns either."

I left the door open and started coffee brewing. The panic was beginning to leave me, but I was shaky from adrenaline letdown. I put my hands to the counter and told myself to breathe. You're good, I thought. You're not dead or hurt or anything. Ranger will be here soon, and he'll take you out to breakfast. Think about that. Pancakes and bacon. Hash browns. Scrambled eggs. Real maple syrup on the pancakes. I was still shaking. Adrenaline, I told myself. It'll burn off. Hang on.

Rex came out of his can and looked at me, whiskers twitching.

251

"I'm okay," I said. "I'm fine."

Rex thought about it and went back into his can.

Animals have instincts, I thought. They know when people are okay. Rex decided I was okay, so I must be okay.

I heard the guys in the hall shuffle around, and I knew Ranger was there. Not that I needed him, because I was okay, but still it would be nice to see him.

He came into the apartment and closed the door behind him, and I burst into tears.

"Babe," he said.

He wrapped me in his arms, put his face against mine, and kissed my neck. I was sobbing and sniffling and felt like an idiot.

"It's the adrenaline," I said. "I'm sorry."

"Just breathe. It's okay now. You aren't hurt, right?"

"Right."

"My men tell me your apartment is clean."

"Right."

His hand was on my wrist, and I realized he was taking my pulse.

"How am I doing?" I asked him.

"You'll live. I wish I could get your heartbeat up this high."

I relaxed into him. "Morelli left at five, and I fell back to sleep. I'm not sure why I woke up. I guess I sensed something was wrong. I heard the rustle of cloth and a footstep, and I knew someone was in my room and it wasn't you or Morelli. He came at me and it's all a jumble after that. He had a knife. I hit him in the face with the lamp on the nightstand. He was close. He had his hands on my neck, and I could see that it was the clown. I could smell him. I could feel his breath on my face. I kicked out and was able to get away and run. I ran up to Mrs. Delgado."

"She's the one with the cat," Ranger said.

"Yes. I can't believe you remember that."

He had me cuddled close, and he felt warm and strong and safe.

"I'm okay," I said. "I was scared, but I feel better now."

"Too bad. I like this."

"Me too, but my nose is running. I need a tissue."

I got a tissue and followed Ranger into the bedroom.

"I don't see a knife," Ranger said. "What kind of knife did he have?"

"It was big. The sort of knife you'd use to stab someone."

He went to the window and looked out. "I assume this is how he left."

"I wasn't here at the time, but that makes sense. The window was closed and locked when I went to bed."

Ranger closed and locked the window again. "Do you have any idea who was in the clown suit?"

"No. It was dark, and everything happened fast. He didn't say anything."

Ranger picked my lamp up from the floor, set it on my nightstand, and plugged it in. It had a smear of blood on it. I soaked a paper towel with rubbing alcohol and wiped the blood off.

"New bathrobe?" Ranger asked.

I looked down at myself. "It belongs to Mrs. Delgado. I left my apartment in a rush."

"We need to talk."

"Can we talk over breakfast? When I was scared I thought about breakfast."

"That's what you think about when you're scared?"

"It was a distraction. Pancakes, eggs, hash browns."

Ranger smiled. I'd amused him again.

He dismissed his men, and I took a fast shower. I got dressed in my usual uniform of jeans and a stretchy, girly T-shirt. I was at my front door, ready to leave my apartment, and Ranger stopped me.

"What have you forgotten?" he asked.

I looked at myself. Shoes, check. Jeans, check. Shirt, check. Underwear, check. Messenger bag on my shoulder, check. Keys, cuffs, pepper spray, hairbrush, hairspray, gum, mints, extra hair scrunchy, lipstick, lip balm, mascara in my messenger bag, check.

"I don't know," I said. "What have I forgotten?"

"Your gun. Someone just broke into your apartment and tried to kill you. It might be a good idea to carry a gun."

"I don't like guns."

"Do you like dead?"

"No, I don't like that either."

Ranger went to my brown bear cookie jar and retrieved the small semiautomatic he'd given me.

"Do you have anything to put in this?"

"You mean like bullets? No. I keep meaning to buy some."

He dropped the gun into my messenger bag, we stepped out of my apartment, and he watched me lock my door.

"Here's a problem," he said. "You have three locks plus a slide bolt on the inside of your door. It keeps you relatively secure. From this side of the door you have just one lock. It's a good bump-proof lock, but it's still only one lock, and someone skilled can open it. I'm guessing that when Morelli left you didn't follow him to the door to secure all your locks."

I nodded. "You're right. I didn't do that."

"When you enter your apartment you need to clear it the same way you would clear a house when you're looking for an FTA. When you're inside you need to use all the locks on your door. And you need to be vigilant when you're out. You also have the option of moving into Rangeman until we get this sorted out."

Moving in with Ranger was by far the safest way to go. Unfortunately it was also the most dangerous, because it was impossible not to fall in love with Ranger's silky smooth 1,000-thread-count freshly ironed sheets, his perfectly made, delicious organic breakfast delivered to his kitchen by the breakfast fairy, his Bulgari shower gel and fluffy white towels. And then there was Ranger. I almost had an orgasm thinking about it. The problem with all that falling in love was that eventually it had to come to an end, and the end would be painful.

TWENTY-SEVEN

WE WENT TO the diner in Hamilton Township for breakfast. I ordered pancakes, bacon, sausage, hash browns, scrambled eggs, rice pudding, and coffee. Ranger had black coffee.

I drenched my pancakes in butter and syrup and took some for a test-drive. "Yum!"

"It looks like you've recovered from your fright."

"I've recovered, but I haven't forgotten. I'll be more careful."

"There has to be a reason why you're being targeted. Initially you were warned to go back to being a bounty hunter, and now someone has tried to kill you. Think about it. Someone feels threatened enough to want you eliminated. You must have seen something or heard something incriminating."

"I can't imagine what it might be. It would have to be something really serious to warrant killing me."

"Killing comes easy to some people. It's seen as a fast way to solve a problem."

"Did you get the report on Soon?"

"He was born here but grew up and spent most of his early adult years in Hong Kong and Singapore. His parents were minor diplomats. Since returning to the States he's been employed by several companies that ultimately failed. He was brought into these companies as a time management consultant."

"Were any of them ice cream plants?"

"No, but they were all in New Jersey, eastern Pennsylvania, and Delaware. They all made products that were shipped locally and nationally."

I ate my last piece of bacon and spooned into the rice pudding. "Are you thinking he might be mob?"

It was a classic mob maneuver to get their hooks into a company and then bleed it dry. Typically money is borrowed with interest compounding so quickly there's no hope of repaying the loan. If the investment is big enough and the company can be used for mob purposes, they bring one of their own in to supervise on-site.

"It feels like mob, but we haven't been able to tie him to anyone," Ranger said.

"So maybe Bogart brought you in as a last resort to protect himself."

"Most likely he wanted the cameras to collect evidence. Extricate himself by blackmailing the bad guys."

"I'm thinking it didn't work."

"I'm thinking we need to talk to Mrs. Bogart."

"Is she still at Disney?"

"Yes. The daughter's cellphone moved to Miami, but

Mrs. Bogart is still at Disney. If I can get a plane we can be there by noon."

Ranger flies privately because everything he owns has residues of gunpowder, and he can't get past security.

• • •

Tank drove us to the small business jet at Trenton-Mercer Airport. It's not a big airport, but it's convenient, especially if you have your own plane. I've flown once before with Ranger and, much like sleeping with him, it pretty much ruins you for the ordinary.

Tank had exchanged my gun for one with ammo, and that was the extent of my flight preparation. No time to pack mouse ears.

The plane seated eight and had two pilots. There was a small hospitality area with drinks and snacks and sandwiches for lunch. And there was a pleasant little bathroom. No TSA agents. No unhappy children. Cushy leather seats and lots of leg room. Just Ranger and me. I buckled myself in and felt like a movie star.

Tank had given Ranger a messenger bag with a MacBook Air and a stack of papers. No downtime for the man of mystery. I had plenty of downtime, and I spent it thinking about the clown and why I was a threat to someone.

Dressing as the Jolly Bogart clown would serve a couple purposes. It was a disguise. He'd be unrecognizable on camera, though if the right people looked at the video someone could probably recognize him. Someone would notice the way he walked, his height, his body build, his skin tone, his shoe size and style. I realized that I hadn't looked at his shoes when I'd looked at the factory video. I didn't know if he was wearing dress shoes or running shoes. I didn't know if he was wearing gloves so he wouldn't leave fingerprints.

The guy who tried to choke me wasn't wearing gloves. I could remember the feel of his fingers closing in on my neck. Probably he'd left prints on my door. Probably I shouldn't have wiped the blood off the lamp. Probably I shouldn't have sprayed Lysol on the message on my door. Damn! I was doing everything wrong.

So what was the other purpose for the clown? He was a big smudge on the Bogart brand. So far it hadn't gone public. I wondered if someone was disappointed at that. Who would benefit if Bogart Ice Cream tanked? Mo Morris. I didn't buy it. I thought Mo Morris was doing his own thing. And Mo Morris would have no reason to kill me. I'd worked in his plant for half a day. I'd spent a half hour at a bar with his son. Who else would benefit? Someone who was associated with Soon? Big question mark there, but Ranger would dig around and come up with a name.

I looked out the window and saw coastline below me. I was going to Disney World.

"Babe," Ranger said. "Are you okay? Your face is flushed."

"I'm going to Disney World."

"Have you never been there?"

"When I was nine and when I was fourteen. How about you?"

"I never went as a kid. I went as a teenager when I was living in Little Havana. It was local. We'd drive up to Orlando and get there when the park opened. We'd drive back to Miami after the fireworks. Four hours each way."

"Did you love it? Was it magical?"

"It was okay. Not entirely my thing."

"What was your thing?"

"I liked girls. I belonged to a gang. I was too cool for Disney."

"How about now?"

"Now is a lot more complicated."

"I know this is business, but can we go to the Magic Kingdom?"

"I'd rather set myself on fire."

• • •

We touched down in Orlando and left our messenger bags and guns on the plane. Disney World frowned on guns.

"How are we going to find Mrs. Bogart?" I asked Ranger.

"She's staying at the Contemporary Resort. I have photographs and her room number."

"How did you get her room number? This is Walt Disney World. It's like the Pentagon when it comes to security."

"We hacked into their computers."

Our driver dropped us at the entrance to the Contemporary and we walked into the lobby. Everyone was in shorts and colorful T-shirts and flip-flops. Ranger was in black fatigues and looked like he was doing recon for a SWAT raid.

"Now what?" I asked him.

"It's lunchtime. We check out the restaurants and the pool. These people have been here for over a week. They aren't going to be standing in line for the Haunted Mansion."

"Are you thinking Harry Bogart is here with his wife?"

"It's possible. This is a good place to hide."

"Hiding in plain sight."

"Exactly."

We wandered into a restaurant with a massive buffet. Everyone was having fun. Donald Duck was there, and I got a selfie with him.

"This is so great," I said to Ranger. "They have Mickey Mouse waffles."

He hooked an arm around me. "You like this?"

"I do! Can we stay to see the fireworks?"

"We'd have to spend the night."

"Yes! That would be awesome. Omigod, is that Minnie Mouse? Can we have lunch?"

"We had lunch on the plane."

"I know, but Donald and Minnie weren't on the plane. If we have lunch here I can get more pictures."

Ranger looked over at Donald. Donald was waving to everyone and making Donald Duck sounds.

"Babe," Ranger said. "You need to focus. We're here to talk to Mrs. Bogart."

"Sure. I know that. It's just that it's not every day you get to take a picture with Donald."

"I don't see Mrs. Bogart here," Ranger said. "Let's try the pool."

The pool was jammed with moms and kids and an occasional dad. Harry's wife, Susan, was poolside, reading a book. She was blond and tanned and toned. The perfect corporate wife. She answered a call on her cellphone and glanced over at the hotel. She checked her watch and finished the call.

"Are we going to talk to her?" I asked Ranger.

"No. We're going to talk to Harry. He's in the room."

"How do you know?"

"Instinct."

We went back to the lobby and took the elevator to the third floor. Ranger rapped on the door and looked at me.

"Housekeeping," I called.

After a moment the door opened and Harry Bogart stared out at us. The shock of seeing Ranger was obvious. He tried to close the door, but Ranger was already halfway in by then.

"What are you doing here?" Bogart asked. "What's going on?"

"Two people have been killed, the Jolly truck was blown up, and this morning someone tried to kill Stephanie," Ranger said.

"I don't know anything about any of that," Bogart said. "I swear."

"You went to the plant in the middle of the night in your pajama top. You walked into your office, and after a few minutes you left the building, abandoned your car, and disappeared."

"I felt like getting away. I can do that. I own the company. I can do whatever I want."

"I can do whatever I want too," Ranger said. "And I might feel like pitching you off the third-floor balcony."

Bogart narrowed his eyes. "Don't threaten me. The tough-guy act doesn't work."

I could see where Bogart might think this was an idle threat, but I've seen Ranger in action and he doesn't make threats he isn't capable of carrying out. I saw him throw a man out a second-floor window once. He was a really bad guy, and no one much cared what shape he was in when he hit the ground . . . but still.

"I need answers," Ranger said.

Bogart blew out a sigh. "I'm in a mess. I thought I could handle it, but it keeps getting worse and worse."

He removed a piece of paper from a computer case on the small writing desk.

"This is what it's come to," he said, handing the paper to Ranger.

Ranger read it aloud. "'Your time is up.'"

"It was on my desk. Either I hand my company over to them or else I'm next in the freezer," Bogart said. "I got a phone call from some man. I didn't recognize the voice. He said he'd just visited my office and left me a message. He said he was sure that I knew now what they were capable of doing. He said a lawyer would present papers to me first thing in the morning, and I needed to sign them. I got off the phone and I was angry, and I guess I was scared. I don't even know what I felt. I wasn't thinking. I pulled on some pants and drove to the plant and went to my office." Bogart's face was flushed, and he was breathing heavy. "It was like that scene in the *Godfather* movie where he finds the horse head in his bed. Horror. Panic. I was sick with it." Bogart took a beat to get it together. "I ran. I didn't know what else to do. I knew if I signed the plant over to them it wouldn't end there. They'd have to kill me. I'd disappear like Jimmy Hoffa. So I left the car in a parking lot and called a friend I trusted to pick me up. I went back to the house, got some clothes and my computer, and had my friend drive me to the airport. I just wanted to get far away from them. I thought I needed to go someplace where I could figure it out. My wife was already here, and I thought it was a good place to hide. I mean, who would think to look for me at Disney, right?"

"Who's 'them'?" Ranger asked.

"I don't know. I needed money, and Soon appeared. He represents a businessman who invests in growth companies. That's what I was trying to do. I wanted to expand. It seemed like a sure thing. Short-term loan. Almost immediately bad things started to happen. Tainted ice cream. Freezer malfunctions. Jeff Soon moved in to help get things back on track. I was so stupid. Naïve. I couldn't make my loan payments, so I gave them a piece of the company. Now they're making impossible demands. And people are dying. First Zigler. I have no proof, but I think they made an example of him because he was suspicious of Soon. And then Gus. I don't know why Gus was killed, but he worked the loading dock and maybe he saw something. Or maybe he was just convenient because he was usually the last man in the freezer. Soon wasn't happy when I hired Rangeman. I suppose Gus was another warning to me."

"Why *did* you hire Rangeman?" Ranger asked.

"You have a reputation for being the best and for taking on special security issues. I hoped you might scare them off. That they would decide it wasn't worth the risk with you on board. I thought by bringing you in I might get some control back. Maybe they wouldn't want to deal with you, and they would move on and ruin someone else. And if that wasn't enough, I was hoping to get something on them with the security cameras."

"Why didn't you go to the police?" I asked.

"I can't. I'm in the middle of it. I'll go to jail. I'll lose my company. My God, I'm practically an accomplice to two murders. How do you explain something like this?"

"I want to see whatever documents you signed," Ranger said to Bogart. "Do you have them with you?"

"No. They're in a safety-deposit box in Trenton."

"You're going back with me," Ranger said. "And you're going to get the documents for me."

"They'll find me and kill me," Bogart said.

"I can keep you safe."

"And the rest of my family. My wife and daughter."

"I can put you all in a safe house. I'll straighten this out as best as I can, but eventually you're going to have to deal with the police."

"I don't see where I have much choice," Bogart said. "I need a little time to explain this to my wife and my daughter. They know something is wrong, but they don't know the extent of it."

"You don't want to tell them everything," Ranger said. "Tell them only enough to make them cooperate. We'll fly out at nine o'clock tomorrow morning. I'll make the arrangements."

We left Bogart and went back to the lobby.

"Do you think he'll still be here in the morning?" I asked Ranger. "Or do you think he'll run?"

"If he runs I can find him. We can find his wife's and his daughter's phones, and I dropped a GPS locator into his computer case when I returned the note."

TWENTY-EIGHT

WE GOT A room, and we went to the Magic Kingdom.

"You owe me big," Ranger said. "This is worth a lot more than one night of fun at the Contemporary Resort."

"This is the happiest place on earth," I said. "I heard it on television, so it has to be true."

We were on Main Street with shops on either side of us.

"I need a T-shirt," I said, going into a store. "I don't have any clothes with me."

"Babe, everything has the mouse on it."

"Not true. There are Disney Princess T-shirts and Tinker Bell T-shirts. And I need some undies. Don't you need undies?"

"I'll go commando."

"I think it might be illegal to go commando at Disney." I pulled some boxers off a shelf. "Buzz Lightyear."

"I don't think so."

"I could take you to infinity and beyond if you were wearing these briefs."

"You're going to take me there anyway."

I got a hot flash. "I'm a little flustered," I said.

"Maybe this *is* the happiest place on earth," Ranger said. "I'm starting to feel happy."

I bought Tinker Bell panties and a pink Tinker Bell T-shirt with glitter on it.

"We should go back to the hotel so you can put the panties on," Ranger said.

"Not now."

"When?"

"You have to wait for it."

He wrapped an arm around me. "Tinker Bell brings out the best in you."

I wasn't sure if that was true, but the physical distance currently between me and my life in Jersey gave me a sense of freedom. Jersey seemed very far away, in more than just miles.

"Instead of going back to the hotel, I think we should have ice cream and go on rides."

"Don't even think about the tea cups," Ranger said.

We watched the fireworks from Main Street and took the water taxi back to our hotel. Ranger called his control room to check on Bogart.

"He's still here," Ranger said to me. "I'll get a text if either of them moves."

I've spent some time in the bedroom with Ranger, but not

lately. We have incompatible goals in life. It's hard for me to have goals beyond the end of the week right now. Things like marriage and children dangle in front of me but I see them in the distance, as if I'm looking through Bernie's cataract. Ranger has big long-term goals. Life everlasting and saving the world from evil. His short-term goal is to get me into his bed. I'm sure he has other short-term goals but this is the goal of the moment. It's a decent goal but it puts me between a rock and a hard spot.

The Tinkerbell part of me was in a mental shouting match with the Wendy part of me. Tinkerbell was dying to sleep with Ranger and she was telling me to go for it. Wendy was saying it wouldn't be the responsible, adult thing to do. And it certainly wouldn't be a nice thing to do to Morelli.

Ranger was watching me from across the room. "Is there a problem?"

"It's our goals. They're different."

"Not at the moment."

"Long term. I'm drifting through life without direction. The only thing I see in my future is a hazy picture of marriage. You have a clear direction and marriage isn't a part of it."

"This is true."

"So I need a man who shares my goal of getting married and starting a family."

"Do you have someone in mind?"

"Morelli."

Ranger smiled at that.

I narrowed my eyes. "What?"

"Babe, he's been stringing you along since you were five years old. You're no closer to marriage with him than you were in kindergarten."

"We might be engaged to be engaged."

"You're not sure?"

"Of course I'm sure." Sort of. "We just don't talk about it a lot."

In fact, we didn't talk about it *ever*. He avoided dinner with my parents so he didn't have to talk about it. The subject never came up between us. Not even during intimate moments. Plus, there was the billiard table. Initially I thought he was saving his money to buy me a ring, but he bought the table with the money. Face facts, Stephanie, when a man is thinking about marriage and starting a family he doesn't replace his dining-room table with a billiard table. Besides, I don't even like billiards.

"Sonovabitch!" I said.

Ranger gave me a slightly raised eyebrow. "You've had an epiphany?"

Ordinarily an unpleasant piece of news would send me to 7-Eleven to load up on Reese's Peanut Butter Cups and pints of Häagen-Dazs. 7-Eleven wasn't immediately available to me but I had Ranger. And Ranger was the mother of all delicious, self-indulgent treats. A peanut butter cup was chump change compared to the possibility of sinking my teeth into Ranger. Not that I would do any real damage, but the temptation was getting stronger by the minute. I mean, what the hell, I was at Disney. I was one step away from the magic kingdom. This wasn't the time to hold back on what might turn out to be the happiest experience of the day. In the interest of mental health, I needed to do this.

"Babe," Ranger said. "Your eyes are dilated. Are you all right?"

I was better than all right. I was Tinkerbell, and I was about to uncork the bottle and release the Ranger genie. Ranger is an alpha male. Leader of the pack. Always. In the bedroom he sets the pace. There's never an awkward moment because he's focused on the prize, the pleasure, the human experience. He knows where to touch. He knows when to ask the question. He's strong and hard where it counts. He's smart. He's patient. He's magic. In short, he assumes the decision burden that I was currently very relieved to give up. Again, in the interest of mental health.

"Bring it on," I said to him. "Let's see what you've got."

• • •

I showered and got dressed in my new Tinker Bell T-shirt and panties. They were fun but anticlimactic after the night with Ranger.

"Are you coming to breakfast with me?" I asked him. "Goofy might be there."

"Going to pass. I'll have something sent up."

"You'll be sorry. You're going to miss the Mickey Mouse waffles."

He stopped scrolling through emails on his phone and looked over at me. "I like the shirt."

"That's nothing," I said. "Look at this."

I unzipped my jeans and flashed him a look at the panties.

He stood and slipped his phone into his pocket. "The car is picking us up at eight o'clock."

I looked at him in his black fatigues. "Are you really commando?"

"Only one way to find out, babe. How bad do you want those waffles?"

. . .

It was early afternoon when I rolled into the bonds office.

"Good shirt," Connie said, looking up from her computer. "I've always admired Tinker Bell."

"I like the way she leaves a trail of fairy dust when she flits around," Lula said, "but I think she's self-absorbed. And she needs to control that jealous streak."

"Vinnie is making noise about Kwan," Connie said. "He's a high bond, and Vinnie is worried he's going to jump."

I didn't want to ask Ranger to help again. He had his own business to run, and he was busy with Bogart. The only way I could capture Kwan before he was ready to get caught was to get him alone, without his posse. That meant surveillance.

"No problem," I said. "Easy-peasy." Tinker Bell was in the hood.

Lula was on her feet. "I'll go with you. We might run into the banana man again. I've been thinking about him."

Running into the banana man wasn't in my plan, but I'd be happy to have Lula riding shotgun. Surveillance was boring at best. It was deadly when you did it alone. As soon as you went to find a ladies' room the mark took off and you didn't even know it.

"Where are we going?" Lula asked, settling into my car. "Are we going to sit and watch his travel office?"

"It's a place to start."

I drove to Stark Street and parked half a block away and across the street from Kwan's office. Four windows ran across the front of the building on the second floor. Occasionally a shadowy figure would cross behind a window. Occasionally someone would look out. Not Kwan.

At five-thirty a black Mercedes sedan drove up to the travel office and parked. Kwan and three minions came out of the building and got into the car. The car drove them to Sadie's Steak House on Liberty Street. Everyone went in and the car drove away.

"They're having dinner and we're sitting out here like hungry idiots," Lula said.

"We're less than a mile from my parents' house," I said. "We can hop over and get something to eat and be back here before they leave the restaurant."

I called ahead to warn my mother that Lula and I were coming to dinner.

"I have a ham," she said. "And macaroni and cheese. There's plenty to go around. We're already at the table, but I'll put out two more settings."

Grandma was at the door when we stepped onto the porch. "Your mother's heating things up," she said. "Good thing you came, or we would have been eating ham for a week."

"Whoa, Granny," Lula said. "Badass hair!"

"I did it for my honey," Grandma said, "but I'm thinking of kicking him to the curb. I might not want to be tied down to just one man at my age."

"I hear you," Lula said.

"I don't know if I want any man," Grandma said.

"I'd rather have a dog," Lula said, "but my landlady said it wasn't allowed."

We took our seats at the table, and my mother brought in reheated macaroni and cheese and green beans.

"This is a feast," Lula said, forking into the ham. "This is all my favorite food. I'm all about macaroni and cheese."

"How did the Zigler viewing and the funeral go?" I asked Grandma. "Did anything interesting happen?"

"First off, it was closed casket. A lot of people were real disappointed at that. You get dressed up and you make an effort to pay your respects, you should at least get something to look at."

"I hear there was an overflow crowd," Lula said. "Marjorie Bend said they were handing out numbered wristbands just to get in."

"I was lucky. I went early. Even going early I didn't get the best seat, but I still did pretty good. From what I saw there weren't any Bogarts there. I think there might have been a couple people the Bogart Bar man worked with, but I didn't know any of them. I heard the clown was there, but I didn't see him personally."

"Was he dressed in his clown suit?" Lula asked.

"No, but you always know the clown by his red nose. The

greasepaint doesn't come off," Grandma said. "Everybody was talking about it. You see the clown going around in his Jolly truck, and you never think of the hardships of the job."

So if I want to find the guy who tried to kill me, all I have to do is find a guy with a red nose. I know Stan Ducker's shoe size was wrong, but until I find a second red nose he isn't off my list.

We left my parents' house a little before seven o'clock. Sadie's Steak House had a small parking lot, but there was on-the-street parking for the overflow. I drove up and down Liberty and through the lot but didn't see the black Mercedes. I dropped Lula off, and I circled the block while she went inside. I picked her up minutes later, and she said Kwan and his boyfriends were about to leave. I double-parked in the lot and watched the black Mercedes glide down the street, pick the men up, and glide away.

"I bet he's going home," Lula said. "He lives in one of them fancy high-rises. How are you going to get him once he gets in there?"

"According to his profile he lives alone. I'll knock on his door, and if he doesn't cooperate you can tackle him and sit on him, and I'll cuff him."

"That sounds like a plan."

I followed the Mercedes to a complex of high-rises by the river. I held back and cut my lights when the Mercedes stopped at one of the buildings. Kwan got out. The three young men got out. The Mercedes drove off, and the four men went into the building.

"Oops," Lula said. "He might live alone, but he don't party alone. I bet these dudes are getting a bonus in their paycheck this week."

"They could all live in the building."

"You gonna go knock on his door to find out?"

"No. I'm going home."

. . .

I had my gun in my hand when I got out of my car. I walked to the back door to my apartment building, practicing vigilance. I took the stairs, careful to listen for other footsteps. I walked down my hall, unlocked my door, and pushed it open, pausing for a moment before going inside. I stepped in, locked my door with all my locks, and cleared my apartment. I returned to the kitchen to say hello to Rex and give him a walnut. I put the gun on the counter in plain sight. I got a beer out of the fridge and rolled it across my forehead. I had the beginnings of a headache. Didn't get a lot of sleep at Disney, and it was catching up to me.

I called Ranger to see if he'd made any progress.

"I have Harry Bogart and his wife and daughter locked away in a safe house," he said. "I have the documents I wanted from him, but they haven't told me much. I have someone working on it, tracing through offshore holding companies. I have someone watching Soon. And I spoke to Bogart about drugs in his Kidz Kups. He swears he knows nothing about the drugs, but he knows there's theft from the storeroom. It was one of the reasons he wanted the locks changed and the cameras installed. He went pale when I suggested they might be shipping drugs on his trucks, packaged up like ice cream."

"Do you think that's happening?"

"I don't know, but I wanted to throw it out to see his reaction. I think it's possible. It would make the company valuable to a big-time dealer."

I ended the call with Ranger and dialed Morelli. He was on a night-shift rotation, and I was sent straight to voicemail. I told him I was simply checking in. Just as well. I needed some time to come to terms with my Disney epiphany. Truth is, my relationship with Morelli was probably okay. It didn't really matter that we weren't engaged to be engaged right now. We cared about each other. We enjoyed being together. And maybe sometime in the future we'd move forward with the marriage and family thing. End of discussion.

I went to bed early with my gun on my nightstand. It seemed like the sensible thing to do, but I wasn't entirely comfortable. My fear was that the clown would break in, I wouldn't wake up, and the clown would shoot me with my own gun.

I woke up relieved that I'd gotten through the night and was still alive without any additional holes. I rushed through my morning routine and was out of my apartment by seven-thirty. By eight o'clock I was in the parking lot at Kwan's condo building, waiting for him to appear.

The black Mercedes drove up at eight forty-five. Kwan and his three buddies stepped out of the building at nine o'clock and got into the Mercedes. I followed the car to Stark Street and watched everyone file into the travel office building.

I could have slept later. This was a bust.

• • •

Connie was on the floor of the bail bonds office when I walked in.

"What's with this?" I asked.

"She threw her back out," Lula said. "She was in her chair, bent over, touching up her toenail polish, and her back went out. So here she is on the floor, and she can't get up. You think I should call someone?"

"I just need a moment," Connie said.

"You wanted a moment a half hour ago," Lula told her. "How long are you gonna lay there?"

"I'm going to lay here until my back feels better," Connie said.

Lula looked down at her. "What if that takes years?"

"It's not going to take years," Connie said. "Get me a donut or something."

"You can't eat a donut like that," Lula said. "You'll choke to death."

"Has this happened before?" I asked Connie.

"Years ago. I was in a step class at the gym."

"I don't get the whole exercise thing," Lula said. "Look at me. I don't get any exercise and I'm never hurt. That's because I pace myself when it comes to activity. It's my observation that there's nothing worse for a person's health than a gym. It's all designed to get you to strain something."

"Can you move?" I asked Connie. "You aren't paralyzed, are you?"

"No. I'm just in pain."

"Do you want an aspirin? Should I put a pillow under your head? Would you like a blanket?"

"Ignore me. I'll be fine. Pretend I'm not here."

"You better not be down on the floor like that when Vinnie comes in," Lula said, "or he'll hump you like a dog."

"Get me my gun," Connie said. "It's in the bottom right-hand drawer."

"I'm calling EMS," I said. "You need help."

"Hold on," Lula said. "I got some meds from a trusted source. One of these might help you." She pulled a small plastic Baggie from her purse. "I had a killer headache from the head-butt so I went to my pharmaceutical connection and picked up a couple things. These are all top of the line but they come from Canada and they might be a little expired. I got Vicodin and Oxy, and I don't know what the pink one is but it makes you think you don't got any thumbs, so I don't recommend that one."

"I'll take the Vicodin," Connie said. "How many do you have?"

I looked over at Connie's desk. "Do you have anything new for me?"

"No FTAs," Connie said, "but I ran a more complete real estate report on Kwan. He owns a lot of property in Trenton.

If you can't find him at his travel office he could be in one of his other buildings."

I took the folder from Connie's desk. "This is helpful. Thanks. I'm going back to Stark Street. I'm keeping an eye on Kwan, but I haven't much hope. He's never alone."

"I'll go with you," Lula said.

"No. Stay with Connie. Don't let her take too many Vicodin."

"How many's that?" Lula asked.

"Give her one."

I shoved the report into my messenger bag, took a donut from the box on Connie's desk, and drove to Stark Street. I parked across from Kwan's building and settled in. I had my gun, my pepper spray, my stun gun, my cuffs, my doors locked. If I saw an opportunity to capture Kwan I'd call for backup.

Connie's report itemized Kwan's properties. He owned an office building on State Street, a parking lot on Mulberry, two blocks of warehouses on upper Stark and Eighteenth Street, the building with the travel agency, almost an entire block of semi-slum housing by the train station, and a mortuary on the fourth block of Stark. It occurred to me that the mortuary was a nice convenience for a guy who routinely made witnesses to his crimes disappear.

I read through the Kwan report four times. I checked my email on my cellphone. I called the office to see if Connie was still on the floor.

"I gave her one Vicodin like you said, but it didn't do nothing," Lula said. "So I gave her two more and a Ativan and

280

she's back at her desk. She's kind of dopey, but I'm keeping my eye on her. If she falls out of her chair one more time I'm taking her home."

I looked up at the second-floor windows and saw Kwan come to the window and look down at the street.

"I think I've just been spotted," I said to Lula. "Kwan is looking down at me."

"You could try showing him some booby to get him to come say hello, but after last night I don't know how he hangs."

There was a knock on my side window. I turned and looked into the eyes of a man with a red nose.

"Mr. Kwan would like to talk to you," he said through the window. "Please come with me."

"Oh shit!" I said to Lula. "It's the killer."

I dropped my phone and grabbed my gun. I opened the door, pointed the gun at the red-nosed guy, and he took off running. He ran across the street, and I ran after him. A car came out of nowhere and pitched me over the hood and onto the side of the road. I wasn't knocked out, but I wasn't smart either. I was stunned. The world was a blur. Words made no sense. I could feel my heart beating, and I wanted to get up and find safe ground, but my arms and legs weren't taking me anywhere.

I was being lifted and there was some pain, but the pain was far away. I was in a car or a truck. I was going somewhere. People were talking. I was being moved again. A chunk of time suddenly went missing. My next memory was of lying on something hard and cool. My mind was clear, and I realized I was strapped down, and I was under the glare of bright lights.

I looked around. The room was small and sterile. The smell was specific. Bleach, formaldehyde, stale cold air. I was in a meat locker. A holding room for the dead. And I was on a tray that could slide into a drawer for storage.

A door opened and I could hear people talking. They were walking closer. They entered the room, and my heart jumped in my chest. Kwan, Soon, the man with the red nose, and two others.

"Miss Plum," Kwan said. "We meet again. So sad that this will be the last time, but your death will serve a good purpose."

"Such as what?" I asked.

"It will be one more warning to Mr. Bogart. More important than that, it will allow me to continue my operation. It was unfortunate that you happened into my office when we were preparing to package happiness."

"I don't know what you're talking about."

"It was only a matter of time before you figured it out. You saw the Bogart Kidz Kups in my office. You mentioned that I should get them into my freezer, but you knew they didn't contain ice cream, didn't you?"

"No."

Kwan narrowed his eyes at that. Probably was looking forward to killing someone smart but now realizing I wasn't all that clever. Big disappointment. He pushed on anyway.

"Do you know why I'm so successful?" he said. "It's because I eliminate risk. You've been poking around, making an obnoxious annoyance of yourself."

I was having a hard time concentrating, because I was aching all over and my leg was killing me.

"I never thought of a mortuary," I said. "I was looking for people with freezers."

"We can't flash freeze like the ice cream plant," Kwan said, "but if we have a little time we can get someone rock solid."

"You froze Arnold Zigler."

"Yes."

"Why did you coat him with chocolate and nuts?"

"We needed to send a message. I thought it was brilliant. It made a mess that took forever to clean up, but it was worth it. I thought blowing up the Jolly truck was also clever. It was unfortunate timing that no one was killed."

"I think my leg is broken."

"No problem," Kwan said. "We're going to slide you into your cozy little drawer, and you'll drift off to sleep. All pain will be gone. I'm told there's a little chattering and shivering, but it's brief. Then we'll think of something appropriate for you. We've already done the Bogart Bar. Maybe we'll coat you in cherry syrup and make you into a Popsicle. We'll have to find a large stick."

I was incapable of saying anything more. I was overtaken with panic. I'd been doing my best to show some bravado, but I was losing the fight. The thought of being impaled with a Popsicle stick, whether alive or dead, filled me with horror.

"Close the drawer," Kwan said. "I have an appointment for a pedicure."

The drawer slid closed, and the light went away. There was just the beating of my heart. It was pounding so hard I thought it had to be shaking the drawer. I felt the temperature drop. I closed my eyes. Tears leaked out, but I couldn't wipe them away because my arms were strapped down. So many things I'd wanted to do. Places I'd wanted to see. I hadn't said "I love you" enough. I was very cold. There was no sound in the drawer. A soft whirring of air. I was shivering uncontrollably, telling myself it was a good thing. When my body temperature dropped low enough I would stop shivering and I would fall asleep. And then I would be gone forever.

And then there was light. It was the light at the end of the tunnel. I knew all about it because I'd read the book about the little boy and heaven. I opened my eyes and saw . . . Lula.

"Holy fucking shit," Lula said. And then she crashed over into a faint.

I was back to the teeth-chattering stage. "W-w-w-wha . . ." I said.

Morelli was working at the straps. He released them and lifted me off the metal tray. The room was filled with people. EMTs, cops, a bunch of Rangeman guys, Morelli, and Ranger. Lula was back on her feet.

Morelli carried me out to the ambulance. I was covered with blankets and hooked up to an IV. My jeans were cut off above the knee and my right leg was put in a temporary air cast. Morelli stayed with me on the ride to the hospital and walked me through to the emergency room.

"I think you have a broken bone," Morelli said, "but I don't think it's a compound fracture. You've got some scrapes and abrasions."

"How did you find me?"

"Lula heard you go after the killer. She knew you were

staking out Kwan and might need help, so she took off for Stark Street. She called me, and I called Ranger. I thought Ranger could get a man there faster than I could. He's always got someone patrolling.

"Ranger's guy found your car with the driver's door still open. He asked around and someone saw you get hit by a car, scooped up, and driven away."

"He had a red nose," I said. "That's how I knew it was the killer. I ran after him. I had a gun with bullets in it and everything. I swear I was ready to shoot him. And then *bam.* Hit by a car."

"A witness said the car was a big black Mercedes, and one of Ranger's men found it parked in front of the funeral home. It had some front quarter-panel damage where you made impact. We had an army here by then."

TWENTY-NINE

I WAS IN my apartment with my leg propped up on the coffee table. The break was midway between my knee and my ankle, and the leg was encased in a plaster cast. Morelli sauntered in with a roll of paper towels and a couple cold bottles of beer to go with the pizza he'd brought for dinner.

"How's the leg?" he asked.

"It's fine. No pain. Just inconvenience. Anything new on Kwan and his henchmen?"

"They're going away for a long, long time. Like forever. You'll need to testify."

"There's something I never understood. Why did they put Zigler in the ice cream truck? Why not just put him in the Bogart freezer? And who stole the truck in the first place?"

"One of Kwan's guys stole the truck. It was easy. It was sitting at the loading dock, and it was taken when the security guy was in the building doing rounds. The plan was to load Zigler into the truck and then leave the truck at the Super Shopper loading dock on Route 130. They were supposed to get a big ice cream delivery for a street fair event that was going to be held in the parking lot. Kwan figured someone from Super Shopper would open the truck, Zigler would fall out, and Bogart would get a lot of negative press on it."

"They must have been nuts when the truck got stolen."

"Yeah, that's an understatement."

"And all this so they could take over his ice cream plant?"

"The ice cream plant was a convenience. They were packaging drugs in Bogart Kidz Kups and transporting them all over the northeast."

I helped myself to a second piece of pizza. "How about Harry Bogart?"

"He's plea-bargained. He might get a little time, but I doubt it'll be anything major. He was an accessory after the fact, and he's been completely cooperative. Mostly he's guilty of being stupid."

"Who's going to run the factory if he goes to jail?"

"His daughter will take over, and Mo Morris is going to help. When all this went down the family pulled together."

"Do you know why these two guys disliked each other so much when all this started?"

"Apparently they never got along. Not even as kids. Just oil and water personalities."

"And yet these two personalities both went into the ice cream business."

"It was originally one company. Universal Ice Cream. It was owned by a common relative who died and left half of the company to Harry and half to Mo. People tell me they almost killed each other as partners and finally divided everything up and went off on their own."

"So maybe something good will come of all this and they'll get along," I said. "Maybe Kenny Morris and the Bogart girl will get together again too."

"Not likely. I think Harry and Mo will get along just fine while Harry's in jail. After that I'm not sure. And it turns out Kenny was a lot more enamored with the Bogart girl than she was with him. Plus she was freaked out with the whole dating-a-cousin thing. She was using her father as an excuse."

"Too bad. Kenny seemed like an okay guy."

"Yeah, he's in rehab," Morelli said. "He'll be even more okay when he dries out."

"Franklin Delano Roosevelt married his cousin Eleanor."

"Go figure." Morelli looked down at my cast. "I remember when I had a cast on my leg, it was a real pain to take a shower. You might need some help."

"Are you volunteering?"

"I'm insisting. What until you see what I can do with a loofah."

Am I a lucky woman, or what?

ABOUT THE AUTHOR

JANET EVANOVICH is the #1 *New York Times* best-selling author of the Stephanie Plum series, the Fox and O'Hare series, the Lizzy and Diesel series, the Alexandra Barnaby novels and *Troublemaker* graphic novel, and *How I Write: Secrets of a Best-selling Author.*

Evanovich.com

Facebook.com/JanetEvanovich

@JanetEvanovich

ABOUT THE TYPE

This book was set in Minion, a 1990 Adobe Originals typeface by Robert Slimbach (b. 1956). Minion is inspired by classical, old-style typefaces of the late Renaissance, a period of elegant, beautiful, and highly readable type designs. Created primarily for text setting, Minion combines the aesthetic and functional qualities that make text type highly readable with the versatility of digital technology.

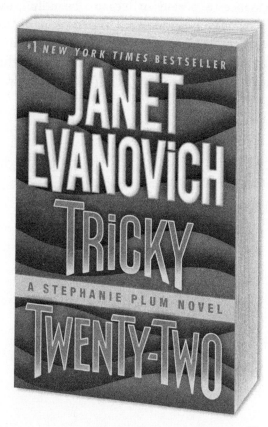

Join JANET EVANOVICH
on social media!

f

Facebook.com/JanetEvanovich

@janetevanovich

Pinterest.com/JanetEvanovich

g+

Google+JanetEvanovichOfficial

Instagram.com/janetevanovich

Visit **Evanovich.com**
and sign up for Janet's e-newsletter!